Stanley Waterloo

The Launching of a Man

Stanley Waterloo

The Launching of a Man

ISBN/EAN: 9783337164041

Printed in Europe, USA, Canada, Australia, Japan

Cover: Foto ©Andreas Hilbeck / pixelio.de

More available books at **www.hansebooks.com**

THE
LAUNCHING
OF A MAN

BY

STANLEY
WATERLOO

AUTHOR OF

"ARMAGEDDON"
"STORY OF AB"
"A MAN AND A WOMAN"
ETC.

CHICAGO AND NEW YORK:
RAND, McNALLY & COMPANY, PUBLISHERS
MDCCCXCIX.

CONTENTS.

THE LAUNCHING OF A MAN.

CHAPTER I.

AT THE UNIVERSITY.

"J'ai un grand besoin d'un cheval."

The professor sat before a desk upon a raised platform in the recitation room in which the sophomores were assembled to have trouble with conic sections. Upon the wall behind the professor was a huge blackboard; between him and the blackboard stood a young man holding in one hand a slip of paper upon which a problem was indicated and in the other a chalk pencil. The professor, as he was situated, could not see the blackboard without turning in his seat, as he did occasionally, to note the progress of the student with the problem. So it was that he did not see the sentence in moderately bad French which the student had written with a grin and then swiftly obliterated after it had been seen by the laughing class. The sentence conveyed to sympathizing friends the idea:

"I am in great need of a 'horse'."

At once half a dozen of the more mathematically gifted became interested in writing upon bits of paper and, in a few seconds, "pat, pat, pat,"

5

little wads, deftly flipped and unnoticed by the grim questioner in front, fell at the feet of the man at the board. He picked one of them up, opened it, concealed it in the book in his hand, turned again, smiled affably at the class and calmly began his work again upon the problem. A "horse" or "pony" meant a demonstration already in hand, and he was now prepared for the emergency.

The two men, old and young, professor and sophomore, were such as would attract a degree of attention anywhere, though as different in appearance as in age. Each was striking in his way, the professor markedly so. He was a man perhaps fifty years of age and, when a boy, he must have been the most distinctly tow-headed youth of all his region. Now, he was cleanly bald save for a fringe of sandy hair which made more prominent and striking the dome-like forehead. The eyebrows, though light in color, were heavy, and imparted a certain saturnine dignity to his countenance, but the mouth of the professor was his most striking feature. It was large, very large, and two immense white teeth in the front of the upper jaw projected outward and, despite the fact that they were close together, suggested an old white boar who had wandered into the open and was about selecting a victim for those same tusks. It was a stern face, but there was an amelioration to its ruggedness. The close observer could now and then detect a twinkle in the eyes, deep set beneath the looming eyebrows, and the older men in the University, those whose feet were near the mountain

tops, gave patronizing information to the under-
lings to the effect that "Old Syllabus" was very
fine indeed. He was loved more than feared,
but, even to sophomores, any sort of liking for him
seemed, necessarily, an acquired taste.

Famous upon two continents as a mathematician was the professor, and his text-books were
among the standards. He tolerated the Greek and
Latin professors, and others in the strictly literary
field, some even more widely known than he, but
he was not of them. How could anything in litera-
ure compare with the beauties of an intricate equation? How came it that many in his class, fine-
looking fellows, too, cared more for the Iliad than
for dalliance with the "Witch of Agnesi," that problem where X and Y disport themselves so gaudily?
He was a wonderful man, just the man for the place,
and even those who feared but had not yet learned
to love were very proud of him as one of the giants
of a great university faculty.

The young man behind the professor, he of the
flagrant performance at the blackboard, was a
creditable animal. Twenty years of age, dark
haired, about six feet in height, deep-chested and
big-legged, he was decidedly an athlete and, as his
clear face and supple motions showed, one in the
best of training. There was no better man
physically in all the sophomore class. Mentally,
though the features were strong and the head well-
shaped, there was a shade less apparent develop-
ment than appeared of the body. The lacking thing
was to come. There was a laugh in the dark eyes

and a certain careless air which spoke of the day rather than of the morrow. It was evident that Robert Sargent, for such his name chanced to be, was still, despite his thews and sinews, much of a boy. He was a wholesome object, certainly, as he stood at the board working rapidly, strong of jaw but flush in the appreciation of life, enjoying even his own half-humiliation in calling for the assistance of his grinning but sympathizing classmates.

He was a Wolverine, this student at the blackboard, and to be a Wolverine is what no man nor woman need feel ashamed for. When white men first trod the forests of the lake-surrounded state named Michigan they found there a creature such as interested them while it created something of a dread. Not "little wolf," as the ignorant think, is the signification of "wolverine," but something of greater dignity, an embodiment of the terrible spirit of the wild life of prehistoric forests. Wonderful in its strength and courage, a tree-climber on occasion, not immense of size but with limbs nearly as heavy and claws as great as those of a bear, with a muzzle almost hog-like but with great white fangs, the beast had still an element of the grotesque in its make-up, with its sweeping bushy tail and the broad bands of yellow-white upon its back and shoulders. Woe to the smaller beast or the deer upon which it dropped from some great low-hanging branch or before whom it suddenly appeared in the dense windfalls. And no lion of the Orient, no grizzly of the Occident has such a pedigree, for the wolverine has hardly changed his form with the passing ages, and is as he was before all history began. The geologists respect him as deeply as does, to-day, the hunter of the far Northwest, where he is still the "Indian Devil" of the trapper and an enemy not to be encountered carelessly, so bloodthirsty and knowing and ferocious is he. Of all the continent the Michigan Peninsula was the chosen habitat of the wolverine and he struggled long before back-woodsmen drove him from his heritage. So endur-ing was he, so desperately courageous, that his name became a synonym for pluck and prowess, and proudly the people of Michigan accept the nickname which has been given them. It may be because the state lies all between blue water that its air has such a vigor to it, but, as the wolverine had, so the people there have brawn and energy. Therefore, to say truly of this young student at the University that he was a Wolverine does him some credit.

The questioning of the class came to an end at last and the professor turned to Sargent for an elucidation of the bewildering problem now pre-sented on the board by numerous glaring and caba-listic designs.

"Go on; make your explanation."

There was, as the young man began talking, a decided lack of that fire which appertains to the orator dealing with a subject which he loves. There was nothing impassioned in his manner. Far from it. He, metaphorically, walked in strange ways and as if on eggs, but somehow he emerged from the labyrinth, and, the explanation ended, looked ques-

tioningly at the professor, who was smiling, more or
less sarcastically.

"Are you quite sure you comprehend it all, Mr.
Sargent?" he asked blandly.

The young man, to whom in mathematics Scylla
was as Charybdis, and whose galley had been ever
perilously near the rocks, spoke somewhat placat-
ingly:

"It was bungling, I know—my explanation."

"I cannot find it in my heart to disagree with you.
That will do, young gentlemen;" and the class filed
from the room.

Not a jot abashed by the rebuff administered was
the young man who had not done well at recitation.
There was a laugh as he joined the out-pouring, but
such an incident was too common with too many of
them to be of much importance. In other branches
of study Sargent could hold his own, and the demi-
gods in students' eyes are never dependent upon
their places in class for their loyal following.

As the class issued from the building out upon the
graveled walk, there emerged from another struc-
ture another class, larger in number, but, though
noisy, apparently less at home. It was the freshman
class of the year. Sargent looked toward it critically
and turned as the man beside him spoke:

"Those new things are lacking in all deportment.
When shall we begin our kindly duties in the reform-
atory way?"

"To-morrow, I imagine," was the careless
rejoinder.

"How do you think it will come out?"

"I don't know," said Sargent, surveying closely the long line of young men whom they were passing and who looked upon the sophomores much as a herd of buffaloes might look upon encircling wolves. "They're a well put-up lot. How, for instance, do you like the look of the fellow in the brown hat? Would you like a grapple with him?"

"Not I," answered the other. "You're the man for him, if matters get too personal. He's the best man in the class, they say. He's bound to be in the football eleven, for he's reported to have been a whale that way in high school. You're in trim, but, if you two meet, I think you'll have your hands full."

"Well, we'll rely upon luck and the law that new troops get panicky. Were you with the crowd that smoked out one of them last night?"

"No."

"I'm glad of it; I don't like that smoking out. I believe in kindness to children. A rush is different, because the odds are different. Holy Moses! There's a little duffer with a cane!"

Sargent stepped from his own column and deftly twitched from the hands of a natty young freshman a light rattan which he was twirling in all innocence. "Don't you know that you are impious and immodest?" the sophomore roared in the ears of the late cane-bearer. "A freshman with a cane! It's a wonder the lightnings don't fall from heaven and lick you up! Young man, I've saved your life!"

There was a rallying of other freshmen around the plundered one and sophomores ahead came back, but there was no encounter. It was not the time for

that. There was much jeering, though, and ponderous announcements by the sophomores as to what
the morrow would bring forth, to which the freshmen responded valiantly, though without the glib-
ness born of practice.

CHAPTER II.

THE RELATIONS OF THINGS.

In autumn, when the sky is clear, the scene about one of the largest and greatest universities in the world is assuredly a fine one. The huge buildings give a dignity to the campus and the sun glorifies a thousand windows, as it does the reddening leaves of the trees along the broad thoroughfares and upon the distant hills. Nature and man have in their work combined to make a splendid picture—even the freshman should be glad in his new and unaccustomed home—but, of all there is to be seen, nothing may compare with the young men. They come from the mountains of the far Northwest and from the distant land of grapes and oranges on the western slopes of the Sierras, from Florida and Oregon, from every state in the Union, and from Canada; youth of varying tradition, training and appearance, but all led by the same ambition and destined to attain, by companionship, a schooling perhaps as broadening as that gained from the learned professors to whom they listen daily.

Different in gait, in dress, and in pronunciation, are these knowledge-seeking youths. It requires no keen eye to distinguish the Texan from the Pennsylvanian, or the Californian from the Tennesseean, but, as the four years of study and association slip

away, the members of the great mass conform more
and more in garb and walk and manner, and there
goes forth, finally, into the world, a group of resolute, clean-cut Americans who think little of state
lines and are as lacking in dialects as in prejudices.
The influences about them have been such as to
make strong men.   The breeze across the hills is not
more wholesome.

It was October and the flurry of the opening of
the collegiate year was over. The returning
students had become domiciled and the new ones
who had passed examinations were settled down to
the life which was to them a novelty, a life the varied
experiences of which were all before them and
entered upon with mixed delight and doubtfulness.
Already the freshmen had decided among themselves
that their class contained material to make it famous
in future annals of the University, and lacked no confidence that the year of their graduation would be
one of importance to the country. Their very
existence was, it is true, unnoticed by the seniors,
but the juniors were most friendly, and as for the
sophomores, they were, at best, but as the dingoes
of Australia or the dogs of the Deccan, creatures
whose friendship was impossible and who were to be
looked upon, at best, with apprehension.   In college
the adversaries of each class are the classes immediately before and behind it, the oppressors or
the oppressed.

Sufficient time had not yet passed for completion
of the curt pour-parlers in open air preceding the
usual merely surface class vendetta which comes up

like a mushroom between sophomores and freshmen, but the soil was tilled and waiting and the harvest promised to be plenteous. ·The crisis was imminent, but affairs among the interests outside of study required attention. There were class elections and Greek letter fraternity matters, and, particularly pressing, the necessity for work by the base-ball, foot-ball, and cricket teams. In the first of these young Sargent was deeply interested. He had distinguished himself the year before and had now been elected captain.

Foot-ball was growing in favor in the University. There is no better discipline of body and of temper than that gained in foot-ball, and even those who were not enthusiastic over the game often became members of the two half-trained teams who made great clamor in their contests. There existed then no such strict rules as have come to regulate the game of late, and, though accidents were rare, there were many noble contests. Asked what the rules were by a Rugby man who had entered the University, the captain of one team responded blithely: "There are none to speak of, save that no man is allowed to use an axe." The ball was sometimes of rubber, and its existence was always brief.

To cricket pertained more dignity, because of a group of opponents existing outside, and of most admirable metal. These were, almost without exception, middle-aged Englishmen living in towns along the principal railroad line passing through the University town. They had been cricketers in the old country, and their hands had not forgotten their

2

cunning, their legs their sturdiness, nor their heads
their wisdom in the field.   They would come, these
graybeards; and the University eleven, reinforced
by picked men from the base-ball team, would meet
them manfully, but too often with most inglorious
results to the rash youngsters.   In vain the best
bowlers would send the ball whizzing fiercely at those
craftily-guarded wickets, in vain the best catchers
would hover about the field; slowly but surely those
old farmers and shopkeepers would add to their
score, and the showing made was always good.

But it was when the University men had come to
bat and the veteran bowlers were arrayed against
them that the youngsters learned what fine work
appertains to the game so popular across the water.
Those toughened and still keen-eyed old men would
deliver balls which conducted themselves in a most
sinister and mysterious way.   They would come
hurtling like cannon shot, they would roll lazily
along the ground in a manner most deceptive, or
they would start apparently far aside from the wicket
and then turn like a serpent and find it surrepti-
tiously and suddenly.   Most improving to a vaunting
spirit were these games with the old British experts,
who usually, though not on all occasions, gained the
victory.

And what suppers followed the contests, when the
graybeards, flushed with conquest and ale and made
affable by much eating and smoking, told such tales
of wonderful feats in youth as would have suited an
Indian chief about to give his personal history just
before a scalp dance!

These things were all well, but it was the "national game" which commanded the real attention of those students who were training body and mind together at the old University, which placed the captain of the first nine upon a pedestal, the captains of other and minor nines great men, and gave to every member of those organizations a standing which was most enviable. Sargent had won his position fairly and bore his weight of honor with more or less modesty and meekness. He had been a ball-player from his childhood. Born in the country, he had played "two old cat" with other farmer boys, and later, in the bustling town of the Saginaw Valley, where he had prepared for college, he had become captain of the high school nine and developed an executive genius which even surpassed his value in the field. He gained a place in the University nine almost immediately after his entrance to college and had done such work in many a hard-fought game as had marked and elected him for the place he held. He was an enthusiast and a hard trainer. "The Czar" they called him. He had clever and brawny youths to handle, among them his room-mate and crony, Sam Lathrop.

There were daily contests now, between the first nine and the others; for the season of matches was at hand, and to the sophomores who were among the players even the noble and necessary work of disciplining freshmen lost much of its importance.

"Bob," said Lathrop one night after an hour of silence between the two while they had been engaged in studies, "a scandalous thing occurred

to-day, something—I say it mildly—which was a dis-
grace to the University and the times! I was
coming down town and had reached a place on the
walk where repairs were going on, and where only
a single plank led over the dust to where the walk
was good again.   Three large freshmen reached one
end of the plank as I reached the other.   They
glared at me in a most offensive manner, and when
I started out across the walk they started as well,
one behind the other.   We met, and, when I
ordered the menials off the plank to make room for
me, they laughed in my face!"

"What!" said Sargent. "What are you telling
me?"

"They were three to one," said Lathrop, "and big
fellows, and they finally made me walk in the dust
while they occupied the plank!   Me! a member of
the base-ball nine and a passed sophomore, the first
by deserts, the last, I admit, by the skin of my teeth,
but still a sophomore!   Are the heavens going to
fall?"

Sargent gave a yell of indignation: "It's the
outrage of the century!   A sophomore walking in the
dust while freshmen keep their boots clean!   What
did you do?"

"Do?   I walked in the dust!   They were each as
big as I and three to one, I tell you.   True, I did
address the one who seemed to be the leader of the
savages, and expressed my intention of eating his
heart broiled, within a day or two, but he didn't
seem to get into any ague of fright on that account.
I tell you they're going to the dogs—those freshmen

—their minds haven't been improved, nor their morals! We have been neglecting the solemn duty imposed upon us by natural laws. We're morally responsible for the welfare of those creatures, and we've got to teach 'em the great lesson of humility and obedience right away. How about rushing them to-morrow as a preliminary?"

"There's no question about our responsibility," said Sargent, "and I suppose," he sighed, "that we might as well begin at once the performance of our more or less painful duty. I tell you, though, my brother missionary, that they have a big class, and have, I greatly fear, some most pagan and obdurate spirits among them."

"But they've never been in a rush!"

"True, my ardent co-laborer in the vineyard, but they are many, and, as I have noted, mostly heavy beings. It is possible that among the scraps of mathematical wisdom that have chanced to adhere to your memory from much sitting at the feet of Old Syllabus is something to the effect that momentum is a product of the mass and velocity of a body? Momentum is what tells in a rush. Now, we are great on velocity, but are we not, relatively, deficient in mass? They have nearly twice as many men as we."

"What of that? Don't shake any momentum at me! We've got it. A mass is where the particles move together, and the freshmen havn't got in the way of that yet. We'll pass the word in the class-room and later appear with the resistless force of a stampede of bisons. We will scatter the freshmen as the wind scatters the leaves, and they'll learn how good and pleasant a thing it is to obey superiors. They ought to be grateful, but I'm afraid they won't be.''

And the two sophomores arranged the details as to the manner in which the "rush" should be engaged in by all the class next day, and then slept the sleep of good digestion. The sky darkened and the rain came down in sheets, and continuous thunder affected the dreams of the warlike Lathrop and made him fancy himself already in the midst of the fray.

CHAPTER III.

A BATTLE ROYAL.

The sentiment that freshmen should be allowed to live, if properly subject to the sophomore class, was held by a majority of the sophomores. Warm personal friendships existed between members of the two classes—some sophomores had brothers among the freshmen—but this had nothing to do with the relations of the forces as bodies. At the gathering instigated by Sargent and Lathrop a fluent sophomore, addressing his classmates, expressed something like the general opinion:

"The freshman, my brethren," he began, "is, as we all know, a most irresponsible, contumacious and ill-bred creature, normally, when he first makes his appearance in classic abodes. Even the milling of the examining professors fails to reduce sufficiently his obtuseness and unbecoming independence, or to inculcate that humility which, in time, will become his greatest merit, and make of him a being at least endurable. He is morally and mentally a sort of missing link, with the simian predominating, and whether he shall advance or retrograde depends almost entirely upon the noble missionary work of the sophomore, whose happy fortune it is his privilege to follow in the University. Of course there are gradations, there are freshman classes and freshman classes, and I think I may say on this occasion that it is a truth indisputable that the present freshman class in this University is the least docile, the most impertinent and offensive, the most nearly related to the 'beasts that perish' of any that have ever walked on hallowed ground, while, on the other hand, the present sophomore class is one possessed of the highest moral character, the loftiest aims, the most profound sense of responsibility, the finest kind of brawn, and the utmost nobility generally, of any sophomore class ever occupying the same oasis! It is the class best qualified for disciplining, redeeming and elevating the freshman class just now so carnestly but inadequately referred to.   Brethren, it has been decided that we must do our duty.   This morning, at about eleven o'clock, the freshman class will, between recitations, wend sou' by sou'east along the gravel and plank walk between certain of the buildings. At the same time the sophomore class will, between recitations, be wending nor' by nor'west along the same narrow campus thoroughfare.   Shall freshmen occupy a walk while Sophomores are passing?   Far from it!   We shall come as the wind comes when hay-stacks are rended, we shall come as the waves come when big whales are stranded, and we shall rip up the formation of those callow ones, and teach them wisdom and their rank and ranking!   Are ye ready, my buxom, blooming missionaries?''

There was a general shout of applause, and it was understood that an outdoor rush was close at hand. Somehow, the information reached the freshmen.

All night long the rain had fallen and the campus now presented a scene far different from that of the day before. Where had been wide stretches of green, were now two shining lakes which the autumn breeze was ruffling into wavelets. The walk between the University buildings was a gravel one, somewhat elevated, near the center of which were inset parallel walks, along which classes, if peaceably inclined, might pass each other without annoyance. The flooding of the grounds, caused by the temporary stoppage of some outlet at a distance, left the walk, practically, a long bridge across a lake, the waters of which were a foot or two in depth. It was at the center of this accidental bridge that the sophomore and freshman classes must necessarily meet.

Eleven o'clock came, and from the buildings near each end of the long walk emerged the two classes. The sophomores formed swiftly, not in single file as usual, but in double file, thus occupying the entire walk, and advanced slowly as a solid mass. At the other building there was a swarming and hustling and buzzing among the far more numerous freshmen, and some time passed before they were similarly ranged, evidently taking the cue from their opponents.

The sophomores, upon reaching the lake, paused with kindly consideration. They wanted to meet the freshmen where the water was deepest.

Slowly the forces advanced until each body was encompassed on either side by the water and but a few feet intervened between them. Then each paused and the sophomores gathered more closely, each leaning a shoulder against the man in front and straining forward ready for the charge. Heading the sophomores were two of the heaviest men of the class, one of them extremely tall, red-haired, wide-mouthed, and truculent of aspect. To him came a sudden inspiration.

The sophomore advanced some paces to the front, glared wildly at the freshmen, opened his mouth to its widest extent and growled fearfully, at the same time beating his breast with great violence, after the manner of the gorilla of the jungles. He seized a piece of drift wood, which the breeze had stranded by the walk, and broke it with a crash across his knees, then waved the pieces wildly and leaped up and down, gnashing his teeth and emitting howls still harsher and more lugubrious and threatening. It was picturesque, but, as a sophomore in the rear shouted, it was not war. The sophomores gathered themselves together, and charged forward at the yell of command, while the freshmen met them as best they could.

The onset was irresistible, and, for yards, the compact body swept ahead, while the freshmen were cast aside to watery graves—of a moment. There were too many freshmen, though, in the rear. The lines upon the walk were too long. There were, in their columns, too many pounds of healthy flesh and bone to be entirely carried away by the sophomore rush.

Rightly had Sargent declared to Lathrop that momentum was the product of the mass and velocity of a body, and while the sophomores had the velocity, the freshmen had the mass. The advancing column slackened its speed, wavered, wobbled, and finally, after maintaining its position for a moment or two, went slowly backward. Meanwhile had come a threatening diversion. Muddy mermen were assaulting the sophomores furiously in the flanks.

The freshmen, some of them giants, thrown into the water by the first onrush, were scrambling to their feet, leaping fiercely against the sophomore line and from it tearing men down into the water with them. Each such rough abstraction weakened the hitherto solid column, and it waved and swung. The strong men in front grappled with those opposing them and they swayed and surged and then toppled into the water by twos and twos, with mighty splashes.

More men rushed forward and went off in turn, and so this well-planned rush degenerated into a mighty aquatic hand-to-hand struggle, with freshmen nearly in the proportion of two to one. It was a battle to become famous in college annals. There were cries and shouts, and the waters, so peaceful and apparently pure, a few moments ago, were now a roily expanse in which men splashed and wallowed and which some of them swallowed in unseemly quantity.

In all battles, or almost all, there is some great central incident which fixes the attention of the beholders. It was at the moment just described that something individually notable occurred. No sophomore was more loved, or widely known in the

University than Billy Barnes, and none enjoyed
more the excitement of a struggle. He had a
peculiar war-cry, all his own, a squall of most pene-
trating and far-reaching quality, one which he
emitted in times of stress, but sometimes on the
slightest pretext, and which had been a stimulus to
his comrades in many a conflict. By some strange
chance he had not been with his class throughout
the morning and he emerged now upon the broad
landing at the top of the steps of the Library building, where he had been engaged, utterly unconscious that his own class was doing desperate
battle.   In a fraction of a second he comprehended
all. He gave one joyous whoop, followed by his
strident battle-cry, then leaped downward and
hurled himself into the conflict.   He was received,
even as he reached the water, in the hospitable arms
of a freshman son of Anak, who gathered him in his
bosom, leaned forward, and fell at length into the
muddy flood holding his prisoner there, lifting his
head at intervals of seconds until a gasping surrender was admitted. Then something limp and
coughing was thrown out upon the bank, and Billy's
battle of just one minute and a half was ended for
the day.

Meanwhile the freshening western blast hadn't
aside "the shroud of battle cast," chiefly because
there wasn't any shroud—but it had sufficed to fill
again the lungs of some scores of men half drowned
and released to land, upon parole. Many of the
athletes of either party were still upon their feet
and struggling, and many more stood dripping on

either shore, freshmen on one side, and sophomores on the other. Gradually those still engaged determined the issue between man and man, and the struggle came to an end. In such encounter, where the column could be assailed from all sides, it was evident that the freshmen had somewhat the better of it. Providence, as in other instances, in other parts of the world, had favored the heavier battalion. As Lathrop put it regretfully, "the sophomore bowed his haughty head, and tamed his heart of fire," but it was a gallant fray.

Billy Barnes, now somewhat recovered, came up with beaming face so far as his countenance could be discerned. "This," he remarked thickly, but enthusiastically, as he sought to remove a portion of the mud from his eyes and ears, "This is a red-letter day to be marked with a white stone!"

The two classes stood thus, glowering across the water, and there were numerous verbal passages at arms, when the argus-eyed Billy discovered among the sophomores some half dozen gentlemen whose garb was in perfect order, unwet and unstained. He walked about them as certain wild beasts are said to walk about their prey before its seizure, and asked of them sweetly how it came that they were in such prime condition. He waxed eloquent, though retaining his purring manner, and intimated softly that gentlemen so natty of appearance must necessarily have been recreant in the time of recent conflict. He intimated also that if anything in the world were desirable in a sophomore class it was what he termed "homogeneity of appearance," and sug-

gested that a result so desirable could be easily
secured.   His suggestion was received with wildest
shouts.   There was a rush upon the infamously dry
ones and they were hustled to the water and
plunged beneath its murky flood.   This punitive performance was observed instantly by the freshmen
upon the other side, and with a roar they encircled
their own recreants, who were in far greater number.
It was a fine and edifying performance, a carnival of
sanguinary baptism, and all were happy save the
unfortunates who had been laggard in the late
encounter.

Among all the dripping heroes who stood upon
the sophomore side the muddiest was easily one
Sargent, sophomore of might and dignity, captain of
the base-ball nine of the University, and, but
recently, of such lofty bearing as became his standing.   The mighty had fallen, and evidently fallen
far.   As he stood scraping himself with a convenient
piece of shingle, some one wanted to know when the
clay bank horse would be in condition for another
run, and some one else suggested that there were
occasions which called for the use of a hose.   Sargent's experiences in the battle had been swift and
various.   One freshman after another he had half
drowned and sent to shore in ignominy, when there
had suddenly loomed before him the admitted
champion of the freshman class, the identical young
man to whom he had referred as an exceedingly
doubtful subject to practice athletic exercises upon,
and who was evidently anxious to cultivate a more
intimate acquaintance.   They grappled at once and

swayed and struggled more than knee deep in water, each seeking the first advantage, which, under existing circumstances, meant almost certain victory. No amateur at wrestling, Sargent found engaged with him, but one as apt as himself at all the different feints and tricks, and it was but a matter of merest chance 'which went underneath. They strained and twisted and became panting and scant of breath, when, suddenly, as they swayed about, Sargent stepped on something slippery, his foot failed him, and a second later he was under a foot and a half of cold water with some one hundred and seventy pounds of well-knit humanity above him. He held his breath and heaved valiantly, but it was useless, and he loosened his grip in token of surrender, rising, laughingly, to shake hands with his conqueror and to wade ashore on his parole, for the time. In later days he had vengeance, with the gloves on, but the acquaintance formed thus roughly with the brawny Levi Maxon was destined to be a lasting and a good one. Just at present, though, Sargent did not place a definite estimate on the circumstance. He was too busy with his garb.

Not far away, Maxon, as the conqueror of such a man as Sargent, was receiving, with becoming modesty, the acclamations of his classmates, properly due to a champion so notable.

And the sun dried the combatants for a long half hour, until class time came to all again and they entered the recitation rooms, still steaming. The professors made no comment. Not theirs to regulate the bathing times of their pupils, and, as one of them commented:

"Who knoweth the way of the wild ass, his coming or his going? Lo, all the desert is his pathway!"

CHAPTER IV.

AS TO ANALYTICAL GEOMETRY.

A young gentleman with sandy hair, gray eyes and square forehead stood beside the wall of one of the University buildings, holding the end of a base-ball bat against it at an angle and making an explanation in ponderous colloquial terms. There was a twinkle in the eyes of the thick-set gentleman as he talked, for, though a student of more than average ability, he had never shone particularly resplendent in pure mathematics, and now, after long study, he had solved the problem of the "Shading of the Sphere" and was not merely confident that he could face recitation without a tremor, but that he understood the subject so thoroughly that he could make it comprehensible to those of his classmates to whom had come less light. In the course of his remarks he would occasionally assume a heavy air and imitate for the moment the voice of the professor, but the real object of the talk was serious, and, though there crept into the explanation a certain amount of slang, there was an absence of abstruse phrases and the lesson was possibly more comprehensible to the listeners than one from the lips of a wiser man.

"You hold the bat so," the amateur pedagogue explained, "and you see how the shadow strikes the

8

wall, (Eastwood, if you don't keep still, I'll swat you
with the bat) and you'll suppose a sphere in the prop-
er place, and suppose a lot of other things of which I
shall assure you." Then, taking a piece of chalk
from his pocket, Mayo made various straight lines
and curves upon the wall, and made also certain
figures and equations, pausing only to indulge in a
magnificent anathema against all things geometrical
and all things algebraical. Grotesque as was his
manner, he certainly understood his subject, and
there was a sigh of relief from more than one who
had worked during the long hours of evening and
early morning as they perceived the missing link in
what had been their chain of reasoning. Analytical
Geometry is certainly a terror to those whom Providence has not gifted with the art of following the
foggy track from conclusion back to premise.

Among the beneficiaries of Mayo's address were
Sargent and Lathrop, and each blessed himself that
he had chanced upon the scene. Neither had set
out for the class room prepared for recitation,
though there had been hard study the night before
and almost a feeling, when the two young men
sought their beds, that they had solved the mystery
of the equation upon which they would be ques-
tioned. The morning found them less confident,
and they had come from their rooms not joyously,
as to a banquet, but with much fear of disaster.
The explanation of Mayo's had opened their eyes,
and when recitation came they survived its trials
easily.

The case of the two young men was one by no

means unusual among collegians. They, both of them, were pursuing among their studies some which were uncongenial, and lack of interest in these had resulted in such perfunctory work as must, in the end, bring with it disaster to the student. Mathematics is the most jealous of all mistresses. Her angular face, corkscrew curls and unyielding moods are, in the opinion of that lady, of sufficient attractiveness to command the undivided affection of all wooers, and those who are not ardent soon find her not at home whenever they may call. They may linger round the portal long, but stern conditions must be fulfilled before they are again admitted to her circle. As for Sargent and Lathrop, they had for months discarded hope of obtaining any honorable standing in this study. They had so fallen behind that each felt that, to retain even his place in class, he must make thorough much past work that had been slurred over.

The popularity of the two men had made what Lathrop called their "decadence" easy. When first the waters had become too deep for them, when, because of laxity of effort, they found themselves behind the majority of their fellows in the studies they did not like, there had been ready and clever assistance from the well-informed, and for a time all had gone well, upon the surface. But no man can be carried more than about so far in college recitations upon the shoulders of others. He must have within himself some relative knowledge, at least, of the task to be performed. Sargent and

Lathrop had lagged so far behind that upon some occasions they had failed in making a good showing, even with the assistance of learned and good-natured classmates. The explanations became as Hebrew to them, and they were in a bad way. In his heart of hearts, each felt that he had been a laggard and each felt also some slight prickings of conscience, which, for a sophomore, is saying much.

Of Sargent there is one thing to be said in extenuation of his present attitude. · The classes in the literary department of the University were at that time divided arbitrarily into two sections, the Classical and the Scientific, and he, though he had prepared for the first, had become a student in the second. He had made the change, doubtless un-wisely, but there had come upon him, just before his admission to the University, a vanity or ambition, whichever it may be called, to shine in all studies alike, and he chose the course in which he felt him-self the weaker. Impelled by a somewhat boyish confidence and loftiness, he did not realize the magnitude of the work he had taken upon himself and now he was suffering the consequences. The change, though, was destined to affect decidedly his future, and not, in the end, to his disadvantage. On the night after the "Shading of the Sphere" demonstration the two men worked resolutely. The narrow escape had taught each the necessity for a spurt.

"What time is it?" said Sargent, pushing from him books and papers, and laying his head on his arms as he leaned upon the table.

"Two o'clock," answered Lathrop wearily. "The light is going out. We may as well try to get some sleep."

In the darkness the talk continued, for the nerves of neither man could be calmed to sleep now, after many hours of clutching, unavailing brain activity without any real success of comprehension, or even apprehension as a reward.

"It is inhuman, by Jove!" Sargent declared. "I have a mind to give up—only that would be cowardly —but I feel like a sneak, anyway, what with 'coaching' and 'ponying' and all that!"

"When I think of the folks at home," returned Lathrop moodily, "I get savage. What would they say if they knew of the straits I am in to pass this examination in mathematics? I can't bear to think of it!"

"Well," Sargent sighed as he spoke, "if it weren't for father—and—well, mother too—they have both worked hard to send me here—if it weren't for them, I would drop the whole thing this minute, fail to-morrow, and be miserably happy over it. As it is I am going on like a sneak for their sakes; but, once out of this scrape, you may be sure I'll never get into such another. Next year—that is if I go on next year—I am going to work as I haven't worked yet, and I'm not going to get into such a hole again."

"That's just it," groaned Lathrop. "Let me go home this time, and I'll never—"

But the sentence remained unfinished, for Sargent, eager to think and talk upon a more cheerful subject, or not talk at all, gave his chum a poke in the region of the ribs which created instant diversion. The two fell to the floor together and in a minute arose, refreshed and invigorated, after a hearty trial of muscular strength.

The poor fellows were tormented as by fiends over the end of the year's examinations. While they were sure of passing creditably in most branches of study they were both marked by themselves and their intimates for a slump in mathematics. They were making the last desperate struggle to "pass" somehow in this study, by the help of friendly counsel, instruction and labored explanation from Mayo, who was proving now a genius in this direction, and by frantic exertions to "make up" for past heedlessness and preoccupation in class and study room. There were two scared fellows up there in that little bare room where Sargent and Lathrop passed their hours of study or of leisure—few enough there were of either. They were both laughing now, but not untroubled. After their tiger-cat roll on the floor the two fellows tumbled into bed to try to sleep until daylight, but sleep was laggard in its coming.

"I wouldn't care if I could see any use in the whole confounded business," broke out Lathrop, after a few moments' silence. "What do I want—what do you want to know of the manner in which lights or shades fall as represented by some harrowing equation? What do I care where a light falls or a strain comes as related by 'X' and 'Y', or about the 'steenth 'power' of anything? I tell you the old Inquisition wasn't in it with 'X' and 'Y'. They could give Torquemada and all his 'Familiars' points. The only decent thing I know of about 'X' and 'Y' is that they have the grace to fall in down close to the tail end of the alphabet. There's where they belong. May witches fly away with them!"

"That's all right," said Sargent, "I'm with you in your noble emotion; but there's something to the blundering grind. There's something in getting one's brain under subjection, one's imagination harnessed to the indefinable and abstract, and all of a fellow's personal thoughts and feelings submerged. There's something in it, and I wish I had the benefit of it and had been less absorbed in the stiff life we've been living this last year."

"Just give me another chance," chimed in Lathrop, "and see if I don't get hold of things!"

"If I only knew which particular torture would be applied to me to-morrow"—Sargent was weakening again, as his voice showed—"I could have some hope. As it is, anything, or many things, may come, and of course the very worst of 'em all will come. Was that candle burned clear out?"

"Oh! lie still, we've no light, sleep until day-light."

The first streak of dawn found the two over their table again, and sunrise showed them there still, a harassed pair of young giants, not without hope, but distinctly faint-hearted.

There was ardent and hurried work in the morning, for the two students had omitted the night before those studies in which they were best grounded, but of these they had no apprehension. In them they were well under way and no little interested, and they were soon prepared. A resumption of work on the unpleasant feature convinced them that they were letter-perfect, so far as that went, if not fully comprehending. They made a vast resolve that day, after stumbling through the lesson in rather better style than usual, that they would not only work later at night—the afternoons, or at best the later portion of each afternoon they still reserved for out-of-door sport—but that they would also rise an hour earlier each morning and devote that hour to the subjugation of the monster. This was a glorious resolution, but one hard of fulfillment, for they slept well, these two, and the cool mornings made the bed a delicious place. But they were firmly resolved and made a Spartan contract together, one which had a tendency to make their design successful. They agreed solemnly that if either of the two were not out of bed by six a. m. the other, if outside that blissful haven, should have the privilege of emptying the water pitcher over his sleeping friend. That night each, after retiring, fixed his thoughts resolutely upon the hour of half-past five, for each had read much of and occasionally tried to practice this particular feat of making the bodily senses respond in time to the command of a fixed idea. They slept soundly until a little before five o'clock, when Sargent awoke with a start, and, as his reasoning powers returned, exulted with the sense of keen delight in the sound of heavy, even breathing, from the figure in the other bed.

"It's six o'clock, and I've got him!" he thought, joyously, and his eyes turned to the little clock ticking industriously upon the mantel. The hands showed the time to be five, exactly, and Sargent gave a sigh of disappointment. "I set myself an hour too early," he muttered, and lay back drowsily upon his pillow, resolved to keep awake. The bed was warm, though, the light was yet dim, and lazy nature asserted herself. Within ten minutes the plotter was asleep again, dreaming of his home and friends, of good times in town and finer enjoyment still in the deep woods and along the streams, with dog and rod and gun, and no professors. As he wandered through the forest he reached a stream much deeper than the rest, and, though it was early in the autumn, great cakes of ice were floating with its current. Suddenly the bank gave way beneath him and he was plunged into the icy waters.

Scientific students of the mind say that dreams come instantaneously, sometimes a series of incidents in a second, as the result of some outside agency.

Lathrop had slept calmly until nearly six, when he moved restlessly in his bed and seemed combating some impulse which assailed him. Finally, his eyes opened and he lay still, seeking dreamily to realize his own entity. Then, like a flash, came comprehension and memory of the agreement of the night before. He rose cautiously upon his elbow

and looked across at Sargent, who was sleeping like
a baby, with a smile upon his face. He looked at
the clock; the hands showed the time to be just one
minute after six.

Slowly and noiselessly, Lathrop slid from his bed
and tiptoed across the room to the table where the
water-pitcher stood. He noticed that the sharp
frost of the night before had formed upon the
water's surface feathery cone-shaped flakes of ice
reaching toward each other, and his heart was glad
within him. Silently he grasped the pitcher and
silently approached the bedside of his sleeping
friend. He stood there a moment, looking down
benignantly upon his unconscious victim, and then
began carefully the delicate task of turning down
the bed clothes. The work required time as well as
the exercise of utmost caution, but was at last
accomplished. Then, with cruel and deliberate
accuracy, the healthy wretch plumped the whole
contents of the huge pitcher upon the breast and
stomach of his chosen friend, at the same time
giving utterance to a whoop specially adapted for
the raising of the dead.

There was an answering yell, if possible more
piercing and far-reaching than the one preceding it,
and Sargent was uplifted clean over the bedside by
the unconscious springing of his shocked body. He
gasped, staggered to his feet and stood looking
wildly about. Never had human being been
awakened more ruthlessly. He recovered his wits,
dashed at the roaring Lathrop, who wisely eluded
him for the time, and then peace came and the two

men dressed and went sturdily at the work they had planned the night before.

In a few days the new rising hour became a habit with them and brought its good results. The cost of the dousing episode was two dollars, paid to the mistress of the house, accompanied by a lame story of an accident.

CHAPTER V.

THE GREAT BALL GAME.

The reddened leaves had turned to brown and were falling. The green had disappeared from the fields, and the base-ball season of the year was very near the end. It was before the time of college leagues, but the year had been one of triumph for the University nine. Many a gallant club had gone down before them, and the state championship seemed, to the more sanguine, a glory possibly attainable. But one club stood in their way, the great club of the leading city of the state; and in contest with this antagonist, one game of the series had, so far, been lost humiliatingly, while another had been won by the slightest of margins. The score of the clubs stood even, and it but remained to play the last game of the year to determine where the laurels for the state must go. The University nine had steadily improved—Sargent felt sure of that—but their opponents were a dangerous lot, athletic veterans and a city's pride, and the idea had existed that even the one game won from them by so slight an overlap was the result of accident rather than desert. But there was hopefulness in the nine, and daily the lithe young players practiced until they were, they believed, in such excellent condition as they had never been in before. There were men for an emergency among them.

The morning of the day of the great game opened in a manner declared by an enthusiast among the turbulent excursionists as "luridly promising." At least two hundred students were to accompany the ball players on the trip, and they gathered at the railroad station joyously. There was much clamor, which increased as the moment arrived for the advent of the players themselves, who were to appear just before train time, in full uniform and in · a band chariot rented from the chief liveryman of the town on all allowable occasions of student state. Much income accrued to that same liveryman from that same gaudy chariot, for there was a disposition among the students to utilize its splendors whenever the slightest excuse offered. As the nine were driven up to the station, broad-shouldered, brown-faced, all grinning amiably while grotesquely assuming a lofty demeanor, the air was shattered by a wild impact of applause, and the pets of the undergraduates were dragged from their conveyance and escorted to the parlor coach amid prolonged and blissful howlings. "We must keep their spirits up," declared Billy Barnes, "coz there's going to be Greeks meetin' Greeks, and they mustn't be shy on ginger! Oh, no."

The train rumbled from the station, the college yell ascended, and, with college songs and shouts and waving of flags, the country of little lakes and great apple orchards and far stretches of stubble-field was passed and the train drew near the City of

the Straits, where were awaiting them at the
grounds a trained and hardy nine and a multitude of
lovers of base-ball, the latter all earnest admirers of
the home nine and looking upon the invading collegians as foolhardy youth whose accidental late
success had made them vain, and to whom humilia-
tion at the end of the season would be wholesome
and beneficial.

Entrance to the city was accompanied by an incident most spirited and sanguinary. At this time
the hackmen of the town were noted far and wide
for their rapacity and impudence. They would sur-
round a traveler, take his baggage from him by main
strength, carry him captive to some hotel and inflict
an outrageous charge, which he paid under sheer
intimidation. As the advance guard of the students
issued upon the pavement from the city station a
burly Jehu rushed up to the quiet Mayo, who was
not in uniform, and who was carrying a handbag,
and, to the collegian's amazement, caught the bag
from his hand, and then, seizing him by the
shoulders, began hustling him toward a hack standing at the curb. In vain Mayo protested; the hackman was determined, but never hackman committed
a greater blunder! There was a swift wrench aside,
a terrific blow beneath the ear, and the hackman
went over under as clean a stroke as ever felled a
man. Never had such a thing occurred in all the
history of the drivers about the station. With a
shout, they hurled themselves upon the daring
Mayo, and in a moment he was lost to sight among
them. It was only for a moment, though. The

hackmen did not know what awful reinforcements were at hand.   There was a rallying cry, a rush of the students now pouring out by scores, and a moment later there were no hackmen to be seen near that railway station, except such as were in distress and gory in a nasal way.

> "Borne down, dispersed, in flight o'erta'en,
> They cumbered Bannock's bloody plain."

Pursuing their triumphant way, the students reached the ball-grounds and entered with such hilarious deportment as students manifest on such occasions.   From the already thronged benches went up mingled cries of applause and derision.   The players went to their dressing rooms, the remainder of the students gathered in a mass in the seating-space reserved for them, the nines finally appeared upon the field, the umpire gave his loud order and the game was on!

It is more or less difficult to describe, so that the layman may understand, the phases of a base-ball game, what the players do, and it is to be regretted that the story of this great game should not be told in detail and in the right way, because it was a battle of giants of the game and time.   There are, in the ordinary base-ball game, nine innings, and the one force or the other which is in the lead at the end of the nine innings, is the victor.   In this game, which, for the year, determined supremacy in the northern part of the Middle West, there were played eleven innings, before the issue was decided, so closely matched were the athletic forces.

The exploits of the individuals of the University nine cannot possibly be told within the space of a single chapter, nor can justice be done to their opponents. Base-ball in those days of only a few years ago was quite unlike the game of the professionals played to-day. Greater scores were made then and there was more of the spectacular. This is because the rules have changed. In any of all the base-ball clubs of all the country there are no keener eyes, no deeper lungs, no better judgment nor better muscle than were owned by the players in this strong game, though its score to-day reads oddly. At the end of the first inning it stood: University 7, City 0. In the second inning there was some clever work by the townsmen, and at its end the score stood University 7, City 1. In the third inning the playing was wild and brilliant on both sides, and then the score stood University 10, City 2, and in the next was scarcely changed, the University adding the single run.

In the next inning developed the strength of the urbanites; it was a hard fight well fought and there was brilliant playing all round, but the City added 4 to its tally, while the University did nothing, and in the sixth the scene was but repeated. The score stood now University 11, City 8. The next inning added 3 to the score of each; then came wild playing and brilliant individual work. Some faint idea of what happened, the University standing 19 and the City 17, at the beginning of the ninth and supposedly final inning, may be inferred from an account here faithfully reproduced from an edition, some weeks later, of the University paper, published by the students:

"The excitement was intense. Cheers and groans, yells of triumph and curses of despair were heard all over the grounds as the playing of the ninth innings went on. Now the City captain comes up to the scorer's table: 'How does the score stand?' 'Twenty to seventeen.' 'Three to tie and four to beat. We'll do it—we'll do it easy.'"

Then came another struggle, and the City men did well, for, at the end of the ninth inning the score stood: University 20, City 20, and there must be another inning. To quote again from the University publication: "Now the work is sharp and short—the friends of the contesting nines at one moment dancing, yelling, throwing their hats for joy, and at the next, with lugubrious faces, sitting in the depths of despair. . . . One tally beats the University, high into the air goes the ball, holding its course close to the foul line toward the left. What a cheer greets the successful batter as he strains every muscle for the home! But other eyes see the ball not at all, they are gazing at the white figure running with inconceivable rapidity across the field. At length the lines of vision of the City men and of the University men meet as the high fly drops into Mayo's hands. Full fifty yards he runs and then takes the ball almost at his feet. What a yell of triumph from the University men. Again it is a tie. Then came the struggle Titanic." And the Uni-

4

versity journal, even in its exuberance of spirits, did not much exaggerate. The inning to follow must be a test.

Then happened, for a longer time than is required for the ball games of to-day, what was excellent to see. The University nine was of the college athletic sort, which simply means clean, well-built young gentlemen who have practiced vigorously a certain sport, and who, in a straight-away manner, came into a strange land free as gladiators to do their best. What they did that day is part of the inside and outside records of a great University. The story of that contest has been told and re-told many a thousand times. It has been told in the University over and over again as one of its sagas. It has been told where the men live who were there that day, men who have since bred children, and have aided in making the greatest commonwealth of all history. It has been told from sea to sea.

It had been a tie in the ninth inning, a tie in the tenth inning, and in the eleventh all depended at the final stage, after none had been made by the City, upon what the captain of the University nine, who chanced to be then at the bat, did in the great emergency. It was worth while looking at him then. He was nervous and his hands shook until they picked up the ashen thing, the bat, fit thing for a strong man's hands to clasp. Then he seemed to forget his nervousness. He became another man. He stood poised, keen-eyed, virile, tense, an expectancy of muscle with mind in it, as the ball, a flashing mist, came. He struck once and missed.

He seemed dazed a little, but set his teeth. The shadow flitted again, and again he missed. Then his face whitened a little and the muscles and veins stood out well where the bat was clasped. The pitcher, big, steady of nerve, and fine, sent another twisting, invisible sphere toward the man at the bat, and the man, this thing of muscle and thought, seemed to spring all apart as he struck with the home-stroke.

There was a crack as when lightning has struck something. There was an upward-looking of all eyes. Upon a great green enclosed sward, men, out-fielders, were running like "whiteheads"— whatever a "whitehead" may be. Between the bases other men were running. The audience of thousands was composed no longer of anything in particular. It was a bawl! And, when the roar slackened for a moment, high above everything could be heard the ear-piercing squall of Billy Barnes, and his cry: "This is a red-letter day to be marked with a white stone!" No effort of the experts could save the city. The University had won!

At six o'clock, or later, that evening, among the surging crowd of hundreds of students who came down the main street of the city on their way to the train, was one, young, slender, dark-eyed, red-haired and with a wonderful keenness of perception in his look. In his hand he held a tiny bundle of straws. As he met some solid, middle-aged citizen of the town he would suddenly grasp that more or less venerable personage by the shoulder, thrust

the straws almost in his face and demand imperatively:

"What's them?"

The maltreated and astonished citizen could but
gasp and look bewildered, but relief came to him
at once:

"You don't know! You think they're straws!
Well, I'll tell you, them's runs!"

And so the jubilant young man with his hand
holding the straws corresponding exactly in number
to the runs the University had made swept down
with his comrades to the depot.

It was a great day for the collegians.

CHAPTER VI.

CLOSE TO A PROFESSOR.

The snow lay deep upon the ground one day in late winter as Robert Sargent took his way north-westward from the University buildings toward the chief entrance to the campus. His recitations for the day were done, and he was not dissatisfied with them. It was rather with himself that he was not content. The season of out-door sports long past, his attention had been more concentrated upon his studies and his prospects; though he may have worked with no more earnestness than before; and his thoughts had more reference to the future and to the reasons which led him to the University at all —for the opportunity had suddenly, and through his father's influence, been afforded him of entering an active business life with no more learning than had been gained at the high school. He had chosen the collegiate course, though it had involved something of a sacrifice on his father's part, and now he wondered if it were worth while. Had he chosen wisely? Would the finer education he was seeking bring return sufficient to repay him for all the travail of the present? Was he really gaining learn-ing of the sort which would give him an advantage in the coming struggle with the world? He dis-trusted himself. His course would fit him for some such work as engineering, but, save that it promised longer hours out-of-doors and a life of robust exercise, he did not greatly fancy the occupation. As an offset, he really enjoyed his French, and his English Literature. He enjoyed the studies, first, because his tastes ran naturally in such direction, and more because the professor of English Literature had that rare understanding which so many great scholars and teachers lack, an insight into human nature and a keen perception of and sympathy with the natural gifts and inclinations and ambitions of those so fortunate as to come under his tutelage. He was of such quality himself that he was loved as have been teachers more famous, for he did not live to attain his full fame. Even at this time, consumption had selected him as one of its victims, and, though he, seemingly, paid no attention to the disease, there was a flush upon his cheeks, made more apparent by the general paleness of his face, and sometimes a sudden, weary leaning of the head upon the hand as he sat at his desk during recitations.

Robert Sargent was walking slowly along the snowy path, deep in the puzzle of his own future, when he heard the sound of a step behind him, and then the salutation:

"It is as pleasant as it is cold to-day, Sargent."

The young man turned and recognized the professor of English Literature, and then the two walked side by side, the younger rather pleased at the attention paid him.

"How are you getting along? Are you satisfied

with what is coming to you at the University?" said Professor Curtin.

Sargent hesitated a little, and the professor noticed it. "I'm doing reasonably well, I suppose," was the answer which came, finally, "but I wish I were better in some things. I'm not—not quite satisfied with my selection of a course. To tell the truth, sir, I think sometimes that I've made a mistake."

"How is that?"

"Why, you see, I prepared for the Classical course and for the Scientific too. It was a good school which I attended. Then, when I entered the University, after thinking over the possible openings which there would be for me after leaving, I went into the Scientific section. I can get work at once if I become an engineer, but if I study with anything like literature or law in view, I shall find myself embarrassed when I graduate. The only thing I can do is to take a school and teach somewhere, and that would be purgatory to me; even such a short experience as would tide over preparatory work for one of the learned professions I should hate to endure. My real interest is all in the studies outside of mathematics. That is a burden to me."

The professor's face showed something more than a common interest. He had—he could hardly explain why himself—been attracted by the young fellow who, while intellectually one of the most promising of the students, had, at times, a certain boyishness of demeanor which was in sharp contrast with his usual air. Such a contrast, by the way, is not so uncommon as might be thought, and is certainly, in most cases, attributable to a good and gifted mother. Where a mother has the qualities which make her capable of becoming her son's confidante and friend, he, as he approaches manhood, is likely to retain the boyish way in his communication with her, and, unconsciously, sometimes drops into it with his closest friends outside. No indication, this, of weakness, either.

Professor Curtin had already become interested in Sargent, and he was a man whose friendship extended beyond the lines of official duty. The frank explanation of what was troubling the young man but drew him closer.

"Are your evenings all occupied?" he said. "Would you mind coming to see me? We'll talk over things."

Sargent was delighted. In the great University, where the number of students was such that everything like personal relations between the teachers and those taught, outside of recitations, was out of the question, it was somewhat unusual for a sophomore to be invited to a professor's rooms upon a social and familiar footing, and Sargent was the more appreciative because Professor Curtin was his ideal and because he felt the invitation to be more than one merely proceeding from good nature. He expressed his thanks and the next night made his call.

Professor Curtin was a bachelor and occupied a suite of apartments in a residence in the finer part of the town. As Sargent entered and was greeted as an equal, he noted the difference between the air of these rooms and those of other professors of which he had obtained an occasional view, chiefly toward the end of his freshman year, when he had undergone private examination in the attempt to lift a "condition." In those rooms the atmosphere had been distinctly bookish and pedagogical. Here it was merely that pertaining to a cultivated gentleman, a man of the world. Many volumes were scattered about, but they were not textbooks, and there were magazines on the tables and paintings and engravings on the walls. There was evidence of the little luxuries a man delights in who knows the fine art of living, though all was simple. It was a soft and enticing armchair in which Sargent was asked to seat himself, and the casual talk of the first half hour was of such a nature that the visitor was at ease and expressing himself earnestly regarding the athletic work of the next season. He was amazed at Curtin's intimate acquaintance with the year's progress in the different fields of college sport, and recognized the fact that this quiet man, whom no one supposed to be much interested in such things, had followed closely the fortunes of the different teams and was full of pride in their success.

"I wish I could have seen the closing base-ball game of the season, the one that gave you the championship," said the professor. "It must have been finely played and the triumph fairly deserved. I can imagine the trip homeward."

Here was a subject on which Sargent could grow

eloquent, and he told the tale of the great day enthusiastically and well. He forgot himself and talked as freely as if the listener had been his own room-mate and the professor, noting him carefully, was evidently pleased. He noted the speaker's lusty proportions and the unconscious grace of strength which characterized every movement, and commented, almost with a sigh:

"It was certainly well done. You gentlemen who played so well should be gratified that you had bodies equal to the need. That is what some of us are denied. But more than in your strength and skill I was pleased with the judgment which seems to have been exercised, the self-possession and the discretion in doing the best that was in you at a critical stage of the game. The gain is not all physical which comes in such contests. There is a mental training as well. You are fortunate that you are fitted for such sports. What made you so strong and supple? Can you tell that?"

Sargent told of his birth in the country, of the outdoor life with the creatures of field and forest he had led almost in childhood and as a boy, of the fishing and the hunting in later days, and, finally, of the sports while at school for which such life had so well adapted him. As he reached the present in his account, his enthusiasm dwindled. He had encountered his future now, and he paused somewhat abruptly.

With what tact the professor invited further confidence and secured with more detail than when the two had walked together the story of Sargent's present doubts and apprehension need not be told. It was but the kindly questioning and talk of a man of brain and heart. He spoke as Sargent paused:

"I can understand your feeling. I once underwent something like the same experience myself. Perhaps I should not advise you, but I can say some things without hesitation. Frankly, I do not think that inclination should alone determine the choice of a vocation. What is easiest for us is not always the best for us, and the mind, in youth at least, is flexible to many ends. Here, I understand, is your situation briefly outlined: You are taking a scientific course, though your tastes are rather literary; your future chances, because of certain relations in the outside world, are better in the engineering field than elsewhere, and you have fears lest you should fail to become a good engineer. That is about your case, is it not?"

"That is just how I am situated, Professor."

"Well, I should say this. I have noted pretty closely, I think, your apparent drift of thought and your capabilities. I've been glad of the interest you've shown in the studies pursued with me, and, I'll say freely, I've come to feel an exceptional interest in your welfare. I want you to count me as among your personal friends and let me help you as I can, if you will have it so."

Sargent flushed and did not speak at first. It is not a small thing for a college student to become the personal friend of a professor of such dignity and standing as Curtin. The reality of the liking, though, was what most touched him, for Curtin was one he had learned to love himself. He found words at last, very bungling ones, and contrived to tell how proud and glad he was.   -

"Then," said the professor, "since we are to work and advise together, I'll make a first suggestion. Stick to the preparation for engineering."

"You really think that best?"

"Yes; you are equal to it. Meanwhile we'll do what we can in literature. There will be enjoyment in it for both of us."

The evening was one always delightful in Sargent's memory. There was much more talk. He left the house hopeful and resolved, and in the days which followed worked steadily to a purpose. Difficulties gradually assumed smaller proportions. The great-hearted older man had made him practical.

Many evenings the two spent together, and the relationship, notwithstanding the difference in age, grew to be almost brotherly. Broader and better understanding of literary things the student gained and his courage was always fortified in his harder work. A "clear style" was one thing the professor insisted upon. A droll thing, somewhat humiliating to Sargent, occurred soon after his return to college at the beginning of the new college year. With pardonable pride, he showed to the professor a heavy manuscript book. In it were most of Macaulay's Essays, carefully transcribed. "I've got them almost by heart," he said; "I've had leisure, while helping my father in his office, and I copied them to improve my style."

The professor smiled; well he knew the fascination Macaulay's rolling sentences and finely culminating paragraphs, full of mellow Latin derivatives, have for young and ambitious students. How charming to the young man was the New Zealander, brooding curiously over the ruins of St. Paul's. But the professor was indulgent, and wise.

"All work of that sort is good," he said, "though strong Anglo-Saxon is the language we should seek, the language for the world-makers. Shall I tell you what is one of the best bits of writing I ever saw?"

"I would like to hear of it," said Sargent.

"There is a friend of mine, one of the faculty, in whose house a Norwegian servant is employed. She had a good education in her mother country, but does not yet grasp knowingly her English. Lately she was absent for a time, and, while away, had need to write a letter to her mistress. It was this letter the professor showed me. It was in English and was almost pure Anglo-Saxon. It was a striking letter, strong and clear and charming to a student. My friend asked the girl upon her return how it came that she had used the English language so well. The girl was surprised: 'I don't understand,' she said. 'I only wrote first as well as I could what I wanted to say; then I found in the dictionary the shortest words I could. I thought that would be simpler.'

"That," explained Professor Curtin, "accounted for the good work, the short Saxon words."

Sargent said nothing, but he did not forget the lesson. It required time to recover from the

Macaulay habit, but the recovery came. And all
such incidents as these were a delight to the two,
then, and in later years, to Sargent alone.

There came a time when Professor Curtin's cheeks
grew thinner and redder and when he was racked
by coughing. There came a time when Sargent,
sitting by the couch of the sick man and wiping the
perspiration from his forehead, suffered as one may
do for a friend. At last came the parting of the
two who had learned to care for each other, when
Professor Curtin made a journey to Southern France
in vain search for an atmosphere which would give
relief, and the end drew near. One day there
came to the University the not unexpected news
from Cannes of the death of a man who had helped
make other men. It was not into the eyes of
Sargent alone that the tears came then.

CHAPTER VII.

SURVEYING THE CAT HOLE.

As Sargent applied himself more and more thoroughly to his mathematics, the magnitude of his troubles dwindled but never quite disappeared. As a matter of fact there was really lacking in him the ability to become fully at home in what is known as "pure mathematics," however earnestly he might devote himself to study. There was in him, undoubtedly, as Professor Curtin had divined, the making, by effort, of an engineer, but not of an astronomer. With one professor of mathematics he was growing more and more at ease; with another he was still ever on the defensive. He was tolerably content, though. One day he was sent out in charge of a body of class-mates to survey the "Cat Hole."

In the region near the University were hills and hollows curiously formed. At one place was a little valley with a steep descent from all sides, in the midst of which rose a cone-shaped miniature mountain. This was known as the "Cup and Saucer." Not far distant was a similar deep hollow wherein was no elevation, but, instead, a broad, irregularly extending pond, which was never dry. To send a student out to survey this odd-shaped water surface and report its area in yards was a favorite device of one professor. It afforded a test which

was reliable of that particular student's real acquire-
ments, for, be it known, the pond, fed by invisible
springs, was a most erratic body and rose and fell at
regular intervals so that its superficial area remained
the same only for a day or two at a time. Had it
been otherwise the result of past surveyings would
have been easily at the student's command, and his
task a normal one. As it was, the result was
always uncertain, and the professor's occasional
verifications of the work left the student always at
his mercy. Surely that pond, the "Cat Hole," the
origin of which name was involved in mystery, must
have been placed there by thoughtful Nature purely
as a means for promoting the thorough education of
the young men of the land.

Sargent had never examined the "Cat Hole," but
he set out blithely, and his orders to his fellow
students, who were to act as chain men and rod
men and do other work under his austere direction,
were issued with a mock pompousness which did
him credit as a tyrant. The task was done carefully
and the notes taken were most voluminous, and,
when Sargent went home that night, he felt that he
had not been working blindly and that he was equal
to the computation still before him. He wanted that
particular survey of the "Cat Hole" to be the most
handsome and accurate ever made; he wanted his
conclusion put in plain figures, down to square yards
and feet and inches, and that night the lamp in his
room burned late. He worked carefully and with a
clear head, and, before morning came, he had his
deductions made and the result of his labor clearly

copied for presentation.   At recitation the next day
he had his reward.   The professor conned the
report closely and a smile appeared upon his face.
"You did that well, Mr. Sargent," he said; "I had
the survey made early yesterday morning, but your
results are carried out more closely and your survey
is the better of the two."

Sargent was gratified.   The next day he failed in
recitation in astronomy.

The weeks passed rapidly and the date of examination day approached again only to find Sargent once
more apprehensive.   Still elusive was full comprehension of the branch of study which had so worried
him, and, as the test day came nearer, the conviction
forced itself upon him that ignominy was in store.
So close at hand, finally, was the end of the semester
that upon the next day examinations must be held.
All day Sargent labored hard with the problems
which it was supposed might be given to the
students, but with most unsatisfactory issue.   The
night coming was that of the Junior Exhibition, an
event of almost as great magnitude to the sophomores as to the juniors themselves, for here was
afforded opportunity to harass their natural en-
emies.

Sargent had been active in preparing the somewhat ferocious literature circulated on such occasions, and it was imperative that he should attend
the exhibition.   A lady was to accompany him and
he did not regret the engagement, for he felt that
anything to distract his mind from the whirling
problems would make him more calm and clear-

5

headed for the morrow. He must face the trial, do
his best, hope for the best and take the consequences!

He sat beside the fair young woman, and in the
midst of the exhibition had temporarily forgotten
himself and his troubles in watching the performance
upon the stage and exchanging comments with his
companion.

It was at a moment of greatest interest when
Sargent felt a hand upon his shoulder. He turned
in his seat and looked at the clean-cut face of the
tow-haired Lathrop, who, in mathematics, as has
been told, was only a little better than he. Upon
Lathrop's face was an expression of mingled
excitement and anxiety.

"Come with me at once," he whispered. "Make
any sort of an excuse, but come, and say you won't
be back, too. Miss Vanne has friends in the next
seat—they live next door to her—I know 'em; and
they'll take her home. Don't waste a moment."

Sargent knew that Lathrop could have come in
such manner and at such a time on no trifling
errand. He leaned toward the lady beside him,
explained and apologized and got permission to go
away upon his urgent affair. Hurried arrangements
were made to place her with her friends, and after
a quick good-night, Sargent left the hall, and, a
moment later, he and Lathrop were on the street
together. Lathrop seized Sargent by the arm and
hurried him along, saying, pantingly, as he did so:

"We can get the papers!"

Sargent could not believe his ears. So strict had

been the guard preserved over the "examination papers," that is, the prepared list of problems to be submitted to the class, that, for some years, no inkling of their contents had been secured until the class to be examined had been confined in its room and the papers then given out to each man separately, to do the best he could within a limited time. Sargent was startled.

"How?" he asked.

"They are in the professor's desk in his study in his house. I saw him have a package when he left the college this evening and I followed him. The study is on the ground floor, you know. I kept close behind him until he opened his own gate and went into the house, then I jumped the fence into the garden, went up and looked in between the slats of the blinds of one of the study windows. Old Syllabus came in, after taking off his overcoat in the hall. He opened the package he carried, and I could see that it contained the examination papers. He sat looking over them for a while and then went to his desk and put them in. He didn't lock the desk. He's on the stage with the rest of the faculty at the Junior Exhibition now and he surely can't get out, unless something happens, before eleven o'clock. But we've got to hustle!"

"What's the program?"

"That's all simple. The house is about deserted. I don't believe the window is fastened down, but, if it is, I've got something to pry it up with. We can get in there in no time, get the papers, go over to Grindlock's and copy them and then return them to the desk before Old Syllabus gets back; he'll never know of it, and, as for us, we shall be loaded for bear!"

A thrill went through Sargent; he saw an end to his troubles over the examination and was momentarily exultant. Then came reflection as to the act he was to engage in—burglary, larceny, deceit. He was impelled to refuse, and began, hesitatingly, to express his views, when Lathrop cut him short with a "Pshaw, it's nothing of the sort! It's a fair fight with the professor and has always been so. We're going to steal nothing but some information. It's fair game and you're only splitting hairs. And, my boy, we need those papers badly, you and I!"

The salve thus applied to his conscience, Sargent admitted the idea of a mere student's trick, as he made himself call it, so pandering to his own desire. It accomplished its work and Sargent yielded. They were approaching the professor's house now. They climbed the fence and cautiously approached the study window. The shutters, left carelessly unlatched by the stern man who never dreamed of an invasion of his residence, opened easily, and the window followed. Lathrop, who had the exact location of the desk fixed in mind, claimed the right to enter and was assisted by his athletic companion. For a few moments Sargent waited anxiously and then Lathrop appeared again and was lifted noiselessly to the ground. "I've got 'em," he said. The window sash was lowered, the shutters closed, and the two fled noiselessly away and were soon in the rear room of a restaurant a few blocks distant.

Little was said between the two young men.   The work before them was merely mechanical and they assailed it eagerly.   For an hour the pencils flew over the paper, and then, with a long breath, each announced his portion of the task completed.   The papers had been copied in their entirety and now must be returned, or all had gone for naught or for worse then naught.

The two returned to the scene of their exploit and repeated it with but slight variation.   Again the blinds were opened, the window raised, and again Lathrop entered the room.   He was not gone long, and when the window was carefully closed again each of the two upon the ground breathed more freely, and freer still when they were upon the street.   As they emerged from the side street into the principal thoroughfare a gentleman, accompanied by two ladies, met and passed, but did not notice them.   It was "Old Syllabus."

"Thank heaven, we weren't any later!" said Lathrop fervently.   Long and arduous work was still before the abandoned sinners.   To have in their possession what problems they must solve the succeeding day was a great thing; but how about the solutions?   Assistance must be had, and there was but one resource for them.   They must make a confidant of Mayo, and demand his aid.   First they ate a bounteous supper together—for the weight of crime upon them did not affect their appetites—and then they invaded the rooms of their unfortunate friend and routed him from his bed. The conduct of Mr. Mayo under these circumstances was characteristic, and would have left to an observer a most hazy conception of his moral views. He listened in his night dress grinningly as the tale was told him, and, though above all need of the papers himself, being a natural mathematician, he was hilarious at its conclusion. He dressed hurriedly and talked jubilantly. He produced paper, arranged a couch near the lamp, seized upon the copied problems, and, with a pupil on either side of him, began his explanations. One by one, the problems and equations were gone over until each of the visitors had each problem fairly solved on paper and had obtained at least a glimmering of the meaning of his own figures and algebraic characters. By no means perfect were these solutions, for perfect papers from either Sargent or Lathrop would have excited prompt suspicion. Slight errors were purposely introduced, but a certain decent average was maintained. "We've got to make 'em about 80 per cent," said the astute Mayo. "That'll pass you, but won't look queer."

The darkness was turning to gray dawn when the work was done, and all three sought a little sleep before the coming day of trial. At ten o'clock Sargent and Lathrop were, together with a room full of other victims of the inquisition, working with apparent diligence upon the problems of which they already had such guilty knowledge. They made many computations and consumed much paper, but not a page of it ever reached the professor's hand. What did reach him were the papers prepared in the room of Mayo, and when they were handed in and all those examined separated to await the announcement of their fate upon the morrow, each of the two burglars wished Mayo had allowed them a somewhat higher percentage. "We're pretty low, but I don't believe Old Syllabus would have smelled anything at 85," said Lathrop.

About the bulletin boards next day were gathered anxious groups scanning closely the lists of the fortunate passed ones. In it appeared, "in shining letters," as one declared, the names of Sargent and Lathrop. And the chief conspirator rubbed his hands together and chanted gleefully: "We's ober de ribber, yah, yah, yah!"

"Yes," assented Sargent, "we's ober de ribber, but, somehow, I feel like a sneak thief!"

And he did. Lathrop said nothing. He looked grave, suddenly, and, without doubt, felt some qualms of conscience. Mathematics was a hard won victory, as both youngsters upon reflection decided. It was some years before Sargent's cheek ceased to burn whenever he thought of "Old Syllabus" and his desk, of the open window and the stealing away from it at night of two young desperadoes, one of whom had his own form and features, but with whom he could hardly identify himself, so unlike him, he hoped, was the whole adventure.

After all came good, as good often comes out of bad, for, in silent strength of feeling, Sargent resolved finally, that whatever he gained during the rest of his life, should be his by right, acquired in the face of day, and that to lose were better than to gain otherwise.

CHAPTER VIII.

A JUNIOR AND A YOUNG WOMAN.

Her hair is red as flame may be;
A glowing crown it seems to me;
    Warm, like her heart—O, heart of might!
    Her skin, like royal ermine, white—
Ermine goes with the crown, you see;
        Her hair is red!

The Queen's heart is a bubbling sea,
From scarlet geysers flowing free—
    Such blood is when the hair's so bright—
No lifeless, halting ruler she,
Tempestuous in each decree,
    Yet oft repentant, loving quite.
Who would not bend a rugged knee
    To rule so lofty yet so light?
        Her hair is red!

                            —The Red Rondeau.

A junior in college bears in some respects a striking resemblance to the Vice-President of the United
States. He has had, necessarily, something of a
career in his field; he has reached a point where
there is great dignity possibly awaiting him, for he
is likely to be a senior, but he is not prominent in
the active life of the present. His warfare and
trials as a sophomore over, he is no longer of the
turbulent element in the college, and there remains
for him only completion of the year of study before

he is one of the stateliest of all human beings, a senior. So it comes that the junior, being thus without great aims and duties outside his class work, becomes aware of the fact that there are in the world creatures fairer than men, and joys aside from those strictly related to the collegiate course. It is astonishing how swiftly his eyes are opened in this direction. Hardly has he become assured of his safe passage over the dangerous shoals in his examination before he begins to note the neat foot and expressive eye of the other sex and has opinions of profundity thereon. This fact in natural history has been noted and admitted in all colleges, without exception. It is not often, though, that juniors fall so suddenly into a new condition as did Sargent.

There had been many things to attend to after the examinations, and especially did those with athletic affairs on their minds have their hands full. There were many meetings having regard to the work of the coming year. Sargent bolted from one place to another like a politician at a convention. He was trotting, almost running heedlessly, but with the momentum of a man weighing well up toward one hundred and seventy-five pounds, and he was trotting like a fool, for his head was down, and he had to turn a corner. He swerved and turned about the almost right-angle of the pathway, and then there was an impact, and something slight gave way before him and went groundward. There came to his nostrils a faint perfume and to his brain came suddenly a little sense. In turning the corner of the building he had run down a young woman and had done the running down most thoroughly. He swerved, caught himself against the side of the building, and looked upon the ruin he had wrought. Something slight and fair was upon the grass, and something slight and fair recovered itself with wondrous ease and stood before him. The something was a young lady, who, with extraordinary calmness, under the circumstances, and with a woman's instinct, was arranging her tumbled hair. Her hat lay on the ground beside her. Now, that hair was of a rare tint like the red, unburnished copper, and, as the girl twisted its heavy waving masses into a great rope and coiled and fastened it at the back of her well-shaped head, she looked at Sargent calmly and without a word.

Sargent stepped forward and picked up the marvelous straw hat, while he recited an abject apology, and stood waiting until the hair-dressing was at such a stage as to admit the putting on of the crown, and then he handed the delicate mass of straw, lace and ribbon to the girl of the glorious hair, but he had recovered himself now, the young brute, and he couldn't help saying, as he glanced at her shining tresses—

"It's too bad to cover your hair, even with such a hat."

Sargent had spoken the crystal clear truth as the thought entered his brain just as a ghost of a smile appeared on the lips of the red-haired girl, but the brim of the straw hat was now poised over a face flushed with rose color, and, without a smile, the girl said, as she turned to go in the opposite direction from Sargent's way, "It's not your fault, I know—all this—but your comment is like your racing gait."

"I was awkward. You must pardon me!" pleaded Sargent, but the red-gold head, after a slight bow to him, was held up very high, and the fair face was turned away as the girl walked from him.

The young man stood looking after her in a dazed way, quite out of keeping with his usual manner in an emergency, quite out of keeping, even, with his usual manner toward ladies, for he was not a person easily abashed, and had grown up among clever sisters. Now he stood looking at the disappearing girl with the air of one who has seen a vision. For that matter, he had really seen one, and one which it was a privilege to look upon. Fairer vision seldom comes to mortals than that which was just disappearing round the corner of a building. Only when the last skirt-flutter was lost to sight did the young man recover himself, and his face again assume an expression of more or less intelligence. Then he started impulsively to follow the girl, but checked himself at once. "I'll find her, though, somehow. I'll find her!" he said to himself.

It was noted that evening by his room-mate that Sargent appeared absent-minded and speculative. Comment to such effect elicited but a good-natured growl, but the fact of absent-mindedness was indisputable. Sargent was thinking, and thinking hard, and his thoughts were all toward the solution of a problem of finding a fair "X." The equation was rather a difficult one. He formed it in his mind:

X = Identity of one fair unknown.

Y = One angelic creature with the reddest hair and whitest skin in the world.

XY = One guest among five thousand visitors at Commencement exercises = Something to be found among that five thousand.

Then X+Y = Result of efforts of self and friends, particularly self.

More definite understanding of certain features of the second half of the equation were, he decided, to be arranged for the first thing in the morning, and work on the equation which had suddenly become a thing so near the heart of Sargent began very early indeed.

The first thing to do was to interest Lathrop, and interest him deeply, and Sargent introduced the subject at breakfast in what he considered an extremely far-off and crafty way.

"I ran into a woman yesterday.'

"Yes, young or old?"—This in an uninterested way from Lathrop, who, as he ate, was reading the morning paper's account of Commencement affairs.

"Young; and I bowled her over, and I've got to find her and square myself. I was coming around a corner of the middle building, and on a run, like a fool. I might have known I'd lift somebody. I did, and it was a young lady! I've been feeling small over it, ever since."

"Description?"

"About eighteen, I should think, slender; eyes—

I don't know what color—just eyes that saw you, a skin like what comes when you squeeze milk-weed, and hair, a cross between copper and the heart of a coal fire. Furthermore, she's proud and 'hotty'— was stately when I tried to apologize. But I've got to find her."

The interest at once exhibited by the gracious young man, Lathrop, was, to say the least, suspicious. He was ardent in a moment, but he had remarks to make.

"We'll find her! Oh! we'll find her!—but, I say it in all kindness, what did you eat yesterday, or have you risen silently and sneaked away from me to some hostelry as the dawn broke gradually? Of course their isn't any hostel near here, and you don't drink, but I had to round out the sentence. I had reason, too! Something has got you. I think it's the hair.

> "Let me tangle a hand in your hair, Jeanette,
>   And you won't get away, you'll be mine, you bet!"

hummed the young brute. "Your hand shall, allegorically, be there, my boy! Give us further details."

Now, under ordinary circumstances, such an outbreak on the part of one Lathrop would have been followed by an immediate and violent personal assault, but, to the astonishment of the chaffer, no such issue came. On the contrary, Sargent, assuming a casual air, only said conciliatingly:

"Well, how are we to do it?"

Lathrop stood astonished, for he had braced himself against an attack, and such extraordinary demeanor on the part of his stalwart room-mate was too much for him. It seemed unfair. He had been imposed upon by an unaggressive appeal to his finer feelings. But he rose, or, in his own estimation, fell to the occasion. He became, on the instant, a young college Moses leading a friend out of the wilderness, a Galahad with but vague ideas in mind, a Damon ready to prance about in the interest of a Pythias.

"Sargent," he said, "she's as good as found! Behold in me the old man with the witch-hazel rod having a forked end! Great am I, begobs! I find not only hidden water, but hidden fire! Hoopla!" and the young man executed an ungainly dance.

It was chaffing, but, nevertheless, Sargent felt relieved. He was in earnest; he knew his friend to be so, as to finding the girl, at least, and here was aid.

They talked together long and earnestly as to the best method of discovering a nameless but recognizable young woman in a visiting force of five thousand or more people, and, after all, the result of their discussion was practical, Lathrop affording most of the brains in the debate, because his point of view was necessarily most objective and unobscured. "She wouldn't have come to the University," he declared, "unless she were going to attend the Commencement exercises. She'll be in sight somewhere among five or six thousand people. That means only opera glasses and work, thanks to the infatuated perfection of your description. Oh! we'll get 'er!"

The day of the Commencement exercises came and the great hall of the University was packed by the glittering assemblage such an occasion demands. There were the faculty and the graduating class in all dignity on the wide platform, there was a blaze of color and flutter of fans throughout the auditorium, where fair women were as numerous as men, and there, situated at a vantage point for viewing the audience, were two newly-fledged juniors, each holding an opera glass, and each devoting himself as strictly to studying the scene through his glasses as though he were a field officer in battle.

Very elaborate had been the preparations for this "needle hunting," as Lathrop called it, referring to that housewifely implement lost in the haymow, and in these preparations Lathrop had shone resplendent. He had secured two diagrams of the hall, and each diagram he had marked off into carefully numbered squares. This enabled a division of labor between the two young men, and, at the same time, made practicable an absolutely thorough search. Sargent was delighted with the idea, though, when his buoyant friend declared that he ought to have a "share in the girl," if they found her, his face assumed a grave expression. This was no subject to jest upon. Then, too, the whole search might be fruitless. The fair unknown might not be in the great assemblage. But the chances were against that, and Sargent was hopeful.

So the young men began their study of the audience, Lathrop sitting just behind Sargent, and

neither paying the slightest attention to the exercises. Square by square, each carefully made his
search, and half an hour passed. Upon the platform some man of dignity was making an address
and the only sound heard save that of the sonorous
utterance was the whir of a thousand fans. All at
once, this pleasant blending of sounds was broken
by a suppressed gasp of agony followed by an
excitedly resonant whisper which was so loud that
it was on the margin of common speech:

"There's your bonfire!"

The gasp of pain came from Sargent, who had
been hit in the back with awful force. The roaring
whisper came from Lathrop, whose eyes were ablaze
with triumph. There was a ripple of laughter all
about, the speaker paused for a moment in his
address and then all went on again. The episode
had been looked upon only as some foolish student's
freak in disturbance of a fellow. A moment later
Lathrop leaned forward and whispered again, but
this time, though excitedly, in a lower voice,
"There she blows, my hearty! There's your con-
flagration; square eighty-three!"

Sargent controlled himself for a moment or two,
then, as all attention returned to the stage, slowly
raised his glass and brought it to bear on the spot
designated. Yes! It was ture! There was the
vision again!

He could study her calmly now, and his case got
worse. She might not be what appealed to others,
but there was the face for him! It was in new
environment now and seemed fairer than ever above

the white garb and thrown out in relief by its red crowning against a background of other faces. He was becoming more or less daft when aroused to practical life by the restlessness of his companion, who clasped his arm tightly and whispered in his ear:

"We've got the whole thing! I know her!"

Sargent became excited and alive: "Know her? Who is she?"

"Well, I don't really know her, but I know who she is. She's Milton's cousin. I saw the old lady who is with her when with Milton yesterday and was introduced. I forget the name. But he spoke of his cousin who was here and hoped I'd meet her. She's Miss Barbara something, and from northern Michigan. Her father is a retired judge or something. We'll lay for 'em when the show's over, and have Milton introduce us. Oh! my boy, I'm worth my weight in gold!"

The exercises seemed longer to Sargent than to the blithesome Lathrop, but they came to an end at last, and the two crowded their way swiftly to the main exit. There came down the main stairway a young man accompanying an old lady and a young one, the young one having red hair. Lathrop crowded forward effusively; he grasped Milton by the hand. He was most respectful to the old lady and most obsequious when presented to the young one, Miss Barbara Sloan. Then came in Sargent. It was all formal until his eyes met those of the girl. He was rather awkward than otherwise, and she, dignified as she was, blushed a little. She recognized him.

6

As for Lathrop, he stood by grinning patronizingly. Billy Barnes came along, and Lathrop strolled away with him, and Sargent knew well enough what the two were talking and laughing about, as he saw the little diagram of the hall in Lathrop's hand, with Barnes considering it.   But he held his peace.   He was content with the outcome of the day.

CHAPTER IX.

A NORTHWARD DRIFT.

If there be a feature of a landscape different from any other feature of any other landscape in the world, it is the pine stump fence region of the Saginaw Valley, of eastern Michigan. It is a strong thing all alone in the world. The pine stump, dragged from the earth by a derrick, oxen, men, and the effect of much loud language, lies upon the sward looking like a great fanged and tentacled thing uplifted edgewise, six feet high and as many across. It will last. It will lie there uninfluenced when the heat of summer works and cracks all other wood exposed, when the soaking rains of autumn bring their slow disintegration, when the fierce cold of winter makes the ice bulge and crack in all interstices anywhere, when spring brings alternate frost and sunshine; it will lie there unchanged while the hair turns gray about the temples of the men who pulled it from the earth. So, in the Saginaw Valley they make fences of the pine tree stumps, piling them along in a bristling row about a field, a fence to last and defy.

The men who owned farms when the pine tree stumps were to be had could—if they were wise enough in time—have avoided the brush fence, the rail fence and even, for a period, the hedge of the

future.   But those who availed themselves of the
pine tree stump, the everlasting devil-fish on edge,
were among the few and the wiser ones of the
pioneers.   So it is that, as you go on the railroad
beside what they call the "Thumb" in Michigan—
that is where there is something like the thumb of a
mitten outstanding northward into Lake Huron and
protecting Saginaw Bay—you see these strange
fences about the fields which lie close beside the
road.

Nowhere else in all the world will you see such
fences—at least at their best.   Your grandchildren
will not see them, for even the pine roots will rot in
time, and then will come whatever may be the fence
of the future.   But, so long as they exist, the stub-
born things bristling about the fields, they will be
banners of a race, a standard set up to tell how
certain Anglo-Saxons conquered certain soil.   About
them in spring grow liverwort and pink and white
areas of anemones.   And there are mandrakes, too,
growing along the sides of these dragon-like fences.
You can see them near Port Huron to-day, and
near Seymour; they linger, hoary and strong, like
Methuselah.

To the village on the shores of the great Lake,
the village surrounded by farms fenced with pine
stumps, came Sargent on his vacation.   It was not,
to the uninitiated, a glorious region.   There to the
east, to be sure, was the vast blue lake, and the air
was purified by its drift over water, or scented in its
drift from the west over the wood, by the pines still
living,   because,   when   Attila   the   lumberman

passed, they were too slender for sawing into
boards. It was a land of vigor, but there was
bareness, and the dead pine here and there was a
skeleton, as the dead pine ever must be. But dead
trees respond heartily to the tap of the red-headed
woodpecker, the soil had produced its clover, the
bobolinks were everywhere, the bluebirds had nest-
ing places in holes of the pine stump fences, and
the song sparrow was all about. The sun fell hotly
on the sandy reaches of the roadways, and there
was too much glare, but the air one breathed was
like champagne in its effect, and the new growth of
things was making greenness where the lumbermen
had been.

To Sargent the place was home, and what we
have been born to is a standard all our lives. To
the forest-born the forest is perfection; to the child
of the desert, no doubt a stretch of yellow,
unrelieved to the horizon, is the perfect landscape.

He had seen more, this young collegian, he of the
blundering work and triumphant athletics, of the
red-haired girl, and the result was that she more
and more fascinated him. He had been earnest and
adroit, had been most deferential to the aunt, had
been much about the two during the brief day or so
of Commencement exercises, and had been invited,
if it should chance that he visited the Northern
Peninsula, to become a guest at the Sloan household. He had learned much about that household.

He was with his sisters now, and there were good
times in town and country, and a proud father and
mother made much of him, but he was mooning

over the girl with the red hair. He thought foolish thoughts. There were old pine tree trunks along the roadside where he drove. There were worms in the shallow depths of the decaying tall white trunks, and how to find these worms the red-headed woodpeckers well knew. They knew how to get at the heart of things. He'd ride along, this Sargent, sitting dreaming in a buck-board, and see the red-headed woodpeckers get what they wanted through the decaying shell. "I'm a worm," he said to himself, "and she's the red-headed woodpecker. They're not slender enough, though. The worm must turn!" he would sometimes say, half aloud— "I must get after the red-head!"

He had learned that Barbara Sloan was the sole child of Lysander Sloan, who had been an associate justice of the Supreme Court of the state; who had not, like others of his party, been re-elected when his term expired, and who, in half disgust, had invested the small money in his possession in a woodland area of northern Michigan, had built a house and improved its surroundings, and was trying to live on something very nearly resembling nothing, aside from what the cleared area of his tract produced. In time, the tract, as a whole, would be valuable. Meanwhile the small cleared space with intelligently directed work upon its acres did not yield much save food. There was no surplus of ready money. The daughter had graduated at a famous Eastern school, then had come to the place in the woods and had been brave with her somewhat broken father. Once in a while, as finances allowed, she emerged into the world again. So Sargent had met her. He had talked with her often before he left the University, when the students and guests streamed away upon trains at almost the same time.

It is hard to describe a red-haired girl, even in a story, and, for that matter, hard to describe the moods and blood and force and thought and love of a junior in an American university. But the junior, if he be one of the leading men, is ordinarily a fine fellow, and the red-haired girl, with cultivated mind added to her temperament, is surely a telling and piquantly dangerous addition to some equations in this world of ours.

Sargent went to parties with his sisters, talked of grave affairs with his father and hung about his mother. He did some shooting and fishing, and was foolish with a small sailboat at times when a storm was coming on, but that, though dallying, he was going to spend a week or two in northern Michigan before he returned to the University was as sure as that the sun would shine again. He knew that. He had talked with Barbara Sloan about her home, about the log house with a wing at the end of the sloping cleared space. He wondered just how the hollyhocks, of which she had once casually spoken, grew along the rough fence's side. He had imaginings about the pinks, and wagered with himself as to whether or not they were northeast or southwest of the east window of the front room of the house? Above all, he wondered what she would say when, some day, he came up the pathway from the gate? Something kept pulling and pulling. He hadn't much money, but, one day, he said he was going north for most of what remained of the vacation, and he had a little talk with his father, to whom he explained nothing, but who was a real man, and who had faith in his blood; and then there was a railroad trip across land where apple trees grew and where barns were painted, and then across barrens, and then where sugar maples grew close enough and small enough for thickets, with brooks springing in their midst, seeking Lake Huron or Lake Michigan, as the mood of the brook might be, and then a ride in a steamboat across the Straits and a buck-board ride, a ride of many miles, ending in a drive beside a creek where the scrub oaks were small and the birches were prominent, and then a climbing entrance to a clearing where there was a log house worth seeing, though unpretentious, because all about it were the signs of soul and of culture within the rude wooden walls. The boy's heart—you must remember that he was not, at this time, much more than a boy, for what is one at twenty?—beat very fast. Here was Her Castle! He had come and didn't know what to say or do now that he was here! He had come because he couldn't help himself.

Sargent had hired the buck-board man at the little village of Conway, the County Seat, close by the railroad, and ten or eleven miles from the Sloan residence. He had reached Conway by a foot trip, with many directions. There was but one horse to the buck-board, but he clambered easily along up-hill, for the wild country road was good. The driver had learned his fare's name—very adroit are these drivers—and had learned in an undetermined way, that he, the fare, must be respected, else there might happen something unpleasant. The driver had found out much on the way, and guessed more, though there had been little talk. He, though, poor hanger-on of a country tavern stable that he was, in comparison with Sargent, was as a banker to a beggar when they reached the gateway to the paradise in the stiff region of the northern peninsula of Michigan. The man with the buck-board was told to wait. Sargent was what athletic experts call "a good man," but his knees had a funny feeling about them as he went up the sanded path between the grasses from the road toward the doorway of the house. The hollyhocks did him a little good, and so, in even a greater degree, did a bed of pansies. Their faces smiled encouragement at him. He was half-way to the door when a huge collie bolted out from somewhere, and leaped forward fiercely until within a yard of him. Then the collie stopped. It's queer how we've bred up so close to ourselves some breeds of dogs. The collie knows a gentleman.

There is an expression in our tongue comparing strong attraction to being "drawn by a single hair." Sargent had traveled miles, drawn, not by a single strand but by a wealth of red hair. Imagine his condition. He stalked up the pathway and rapped on the door, because there was no bell. And the red-haired girl appeared.

CHAPTER X.

AN OASIS IN THE FOREST.

Clever young women are more self-possessed than young men. And this particular young woman was no exception to the rule. There was a little start as her gaze met that of Sargent, then swift recovery, a smile, and extended hand.

"I am very glad to see you, Mr. Sargent. What good fortune to your friends has brought you so far into the wilderness?"

The young man, by far the more disturbed of the two, had by this time somewhat regained control of himself. As he looked at the creature before him, there came an almost overmastering desire to blurt out the whole truth, to tell what had brought him there, but common sense prevailed.

He had a somewhat reasonable explanation at hand. Twenty miles farther on, where the great copper mines were, he had a college friend who had often invited him to make a summer visit. This visit was the ostensible object of his journey, and he told Barbara of where he was going, and said that he was perhaps too venturesome in turning aside to visit her. But—he wanted to see her.

The girl was perfectly at ease. "But you cannot possibly reach Minkville to-day," she said, "at least until very late. Send away your man with the buck-board and do us a kindness. A visitor is too valuable a prize here to be allowed an easy escape. You must meet my father and the people about here, and the fishing is better here, too, than it is near Minkville. We can send you on at any time."

Sargent's face must have shown his delight. He accepted without excuse, went down the path to the buck-board man and settled with that person promptly. His heart beat fast. Here he was, a guest in the house of the Red and White goddess! It had paid to venture!

There was due attention paid the guest, and when Sargent met the father of his divinity, he found him generously hospitable and commonplace as to reception, and dignified and cultivated as to appearance and conversation. He was exceptionally fond of young people. In his leisurely talk the scholarly old judge was delightful. To him the visit of a young man fresh from college was a rare pleasure, and he showed it.

It would have been a study had there been some knowing one to see all that followed when the old man and the young one met, and, later, talked together; the one more absorbed in his theories than in his red-haired daughter, though almost living in her, and the other, young, vigorous and hopeful, absorbed in the girl entirely, and anxious to make a great friend of her father. That he did with no great difficulty.

An exceedingly learned and clever man was Judge Sloan, and his family had grown up in comfort with him until he had reached the bench of the Circuit Court. Then, later, and deservedly, because of his

marked fitness for the place he occupied, because of
the direct justice and soundness of his opinions, he
was nominated to the Supreme bench of the state.
It was almost understood that he would, in time, if
elected, be the head of that highest tribunal of the
commonwealth.   He made in the political race a
great showing while all other members of his party
who were candidates were defeated by a strong
majority.   He was almost elected, despite the
change in the attitude of the more or less weak-
minded and fluctuating force, which makes first one
party win and then the other.   He had a few thousand dollars in money and he knew northern
Michigan.   His wife had died after but a few years
of happy life with him.   He had in the world but
his daughter to live for.   He bought the land in the
forest in the North and made the buildings and
brought the girl there, and adopted a new mode of
life, depending more and more upon the society of
books as the world of cultivated men and women
slipped away from him.   He had felt his daughter's
absence while she was away at school, keenly, and
since her return had been exceptionally happy in a
new way, in her companionship.   All this Sargent
saw and felt and heard as the days of his brief visit
slipped away.

A tall, rather masculine looking woman, of
unmistakable Norse ancestry, was the mainstay of
the kitchen, in this house of logs.   She was a strong
character, and interesting to Sargent by reason of
the native simplicity, tinged with sadness, of her
talk and ways.   She was the widow of a Norwegian

farmer, who had been one of the early settlers in the wilderness, and her son Michael, a queer combination of wildness, mischief and music, was her assistant, and the general factotum of the household. The two made a study of themselves, and an interesting addition to what commanded attention in and about the household of the Sloans.

Upon the garden, and the garden means the enclosed space all around the house in northern Michigan, Sargent gazed with interest in the early morning, after his first night's rest, beholding in the little area reclaimed from the Michigan forest the intimate surroundings of the every-day life of Barbara. It reminded him of what he had seen in another dooryard in another place and with other surroundings fifteen or twenty years before, in the home of his infancy and early childhood. Again he saw the golden coreopsis and the phlox and the "bouncing betties," each in their places, from close beside the house where the clay had been banked up for winter, and beside the pathway, the coreopsis leaning flauntingly toward the late September sun and saying, "We'll die together gently, and the frosts will find us gone." And the asters and dahlias said, "The golden coreopsis knows things." Anyway, that is what Sargent's sisters had once declared these flowers said.

Flower gardens show ancestry. You can tell the Puritan from the Pagan. We, that is, we who know, can tell from the flower garden what kind of people are living in a house we may be passing. This flower garden in northern Michigan, where the

arbutus has most scent in spring, and where the
hoarfrost is deepest and whitest in autumn, where
the beechnuts are big and the walnuts are small,
this was a place with a southern slope and loamy
soil, and a woman—the conditions for a garden; a
garden which, beside the other flowers named, had
hollyhocks and old-fashioned pinks, the pinks you
smell and remember, and peonies and phlox, and
lady-slippers and all the rest. They were in the
southern slope from the house to the gate, and,
somehow, it seemed as if each flower had at last
been admitted to its heritage and was content and
glad, and had only now to pay its debt to the other
things, and be as glorious as it could. The flowers
which Barbara tended, the flowers upon which
Barbara looked, certainly responded to her with love
and reverence. She, the red-haired, was as glowing
with color as they. She was close to nature, which
is respondent. This may have been only lover's
nonsense, but how the flowers grew and blossomed!

From the gate extended a sanded path to the
house, a path with a succession of planks laid
along its middle in a line, oaken things two inches
thick. The sand was clean, of course, because
things could not grow in its non-nourishment; but
on either side was the broad grass area relieved by
the cultivated, flower-bearing, brilliant patches,
which made the place so beautiful. The old-
fashioned grass pinks, now out of blossom, had their
beds, which lay blue-green in their places. The
fence on either side of the gate was loved and
leaned to by the rows of hollyhocks, and still farther

away the sunflowers swung to greet the sun. And there were more flowers here in their season, larkspur, and sweet-williams, and sweet-briar; there was bergamot, which was fine to crush between your fingers, and johnny-jump-ups, most hardy of the violets and grandmother to the pansies, and marigolds, most luxurious and symmetrical. There were caraway patches over by the fence, here and there. Outside grew sumach and elderberry bushes, cousins of the house-bred things inside. About the log house, climbing up its sides, was the Michigan rose, one of the sweetest roses in all the world.

There was the back-yard, too, and what a back-yard it was! There was a buckwheat field, a little one, but wonderful when in bloom, for there must be buckwheat cakes in fall and winter; still, the buckwheat field was only a sort of aside thing. Here in the clearing, which reached up to the edge of the wood, were raised the vegetables and light fruit which furnished food for the family. Currant bushes, and the wild raspberry transplanted from the clearing rioted here. Great potatoes grew in the sandy soil of the field, which, drained and well-hoed, hung downward from the woodland toward the creek. There were lighter patches, too, where melons grew to only moderate size but which attained the flavor of their zone. Flavor goes with zone, increasing in richness toward the poles. As for the other things, well, the judge knew what good things were. He knew that young beets, just little things an inch or so long, made the best "greens" in the world; he knew asparagus, one of nature's greatest gifts to man; he knew the summer squash, which fascinates with its prodigal great blossoms and scalloped fruit, and the Hubbard squash, the northern sweet potato; he knew parsnips and carrots, and all things in their degree, and all of them were coaxed and tended in the yellow-gray kitchen garden stretching northward from the house till the background, with its green lines, was lost in the black gown of the woodland. There was a blackened stump here and there, which had not burned well, and, at greater distances, a stub or two, standing higher.

Of cabbages, the judge made almost a specialty. He marshaled them in long lines, like ranks of hard-headed soldiers, but it is hardly worth while to speak of cabbages in telling of this garden. The judge knew his vegetables. The little field was excellent to see. The judge had ideas of an orchard, and there were trees, some of them quite well grown, some puny as yet, which sprung up all over the sweep of land, and dotted it with green touches. In these were nests of birds that sang. They made an orchestra each bright morning or bright evening in the combined though unblending volume when was trilled and flourished out the story of how near God is to earth. It was an inspiring little piece of ground to look upon, this field, for a man with eyes and brain, but, above all, to one with perception of what on earth is related to heart and soul.

CHAPTER XI.

SWEET CROSS PURPOSES.

The facility with which Sargent adapted himself to the home life of the household was astonishing. The judge fancied him greatly, and their talks together were most edifying. Even the rather somber Tilda and the silent Michael appeared friendly to him, and, as for Barbara, she offered a somewhat queenly comradeship. The two were much together, most of the time along the creek or in the forest, for Sargent's instinct led him thither as a buck seeks his haunt, and Barbara was herself a lover of all nature. There was no love-making, but there was an undercurrent of something which made ever a hunger in the man and in the woman, an alertness against any exhibition of senti-mentality. He was but a great man-boy, and undeniably in love with this slender, red-haired maiden, who puzzled him so much. She was not in love with him, in the way a woman should love a man, if she loved him at all. Thus, with the relations as they were, she had all the vantage.

They went out together, these two, the graceful, thoughtful, youthful lady, and the bungling animal we call a very young man of education. They walked often down the path to the southward where the creek quarreled with the stones, knowing some-how that it would get free of them presently, and

7

lose its own entity in blending with the great lake, but would have no more stones to hurt, just as, some say, a soul goes out to mingle with and be lost in the Great Unknown.

But Barbara, being a woman, and furthermore being a woman with red hair, was, in a manner, what we call "interested." The hours the two passed together were enticing to her. The man showed the woman a host of things she had never known about the wood life. He would explain to her the story told by the spoor of all the creek's small creatures. He would show her where the raccoon, the tracks of which looked like those made by the feet of a little baby, had feasted with his mate on the fresh pink clams, and would tell of the happy family living far aloft in the hollowed heart of the big dead tree. He would make interesting to her the stories of the mink and the muskrat and the otter, and even of the tiny, undeveloped creatures crawling about and making criss-cross lines on the creek's sandy bed. And ever, throughout what he said, ran a strain of half-way love-making, venturesome but fearful, and sometimes reproachful, because of her irresponsiveness.

The man had a fancy for rising early and rejoicing in the inhalation of the champagne morning air, and, sometimes, he prevailed upon her to go out with him on these ante-breakfast excursions. He was boastful one morning.

"There are a hundred rhapsodies over sunset to one over sunrise," said he, "and the reason is obvious; the laziness of mankind."

The girl laughed. "Possibly that is true. This morning at least is delicious. Are the colors of sunrise more delicate and tender than those of sunset? It seems to me that at sunrise only pink and rose prevail—that the more gorgeous colors are always subdued by grays."

"Oh, that is because you have seen only half a dozen sunrises in your life, and the memory of them becomes clouded by your 'grays.' The sun rises in a riot of fiery splendor, I tell you, I who have watched it a thousand mornings."

"Oh, sage, live forever!" mockingly.

He paid no attention to her gibe. "Yes," he mused, "I have seen many a fair sunrise, but never any to equal this. You see there's a great deal in environment. Alone, one cannot get the whole of anything, even of a sunrise, and there is always—"

He stopped clumsily, realizing that he was ever wandering toward the danger line, for the face of the young woman had taken on its anti-sentimental expression.

"Oh, don't talk about that," said she. "Tell me about the time when you were in camp in mid-winter, and of the pine woods, when the snow was four feet deep, and all that."

"It was very cold," he began, "but I have had, since then, a greater experience in coldness."

" 'The owl for all his feathers was a-cold,' " she recited, in a shivery voice. "But go on and tell me about that pine-woods experience. What did you eat and what did you do?"

And so Sargent was compelled to tell the story of

a winter experience to which he had made some chance allusion. What man ever reached his goal in talking when opposed by feminine evasion? Yet ever he returned to the tentative love assault, advancing cautiously, only to find the bridge raised and the portcullis down. There were, however, fair parleyings from the battlements, that and nothing more.

Sometimes the woman would be the seeker, for she was very curious about the man. "Tell me about yourself," she said one day. "I know almost nothing of you yet. What are you in your domain? Are you going to be a brigand, or study for the ministry? Have you sisters, and what are they like? And have you a favorite among them? And what is she like?"

"I would like to be a brigand," was his reply, "but circumstances beyond me prevent, and so I am only going to be a civil engineer, with the accent on the 'civil,' if you please, Miss Sloan. I couldn't go into the ministry, even if I wished, because, if I did, I should want to be a missionary, for the sake of the varied experiences and adventures, and there are tenets connected with the present missionary system to which I could not possibly subscribe."

"That's strange," she commented. "Will you give me an illustration?"

"There are a number of things with which I cannot agree," he said, "but I am inclined to the belief that the chief fault of the missionaries relates to angels. They do not teach the right sort of angels. Now, I take it, an angel is about the most

picturesque thing in Christian tradition. I know
that, when I was a boy, I didn't care to go and live
with the saints, but the angels caught me. So, too,
they would catch black or yellow people, if their
angels were of the right sort—if they were not
white—but who wants to go to be a saved saint to
be bossed over by angels of another color? Preach
black angels or yellow angels and you'll make con-
verts from Zanzibar to Pekin. But my ideas would,
I fear, be considered revolutionary, if not
unorthodox!''

"What a theologian is being wasted!" said she.
''But what about your sisters?''

''Oh, well, I have three, and I am fond of them.
If there is one of whom I am more fond than of the
others, I think it's Bessie. She's little and has
brown hair, and is in love with her brother. I wish
other people would follow her example,'' he added
reflectively.

"Go on," she said, imperatively. "Tell me more
about her. What do you do together?''

''Oh, nothing in particular, we're just birds of a
feather. We take delight in caring for each other,
and in being impractical and having fancies. We
live in Vagueland, Bessie and I. Don't you know
Vagueland?''

Barbara replied that as to Vagueland her geo-
graphical knowledge was incomplete.

''Well, to tell the truth, I don't know just where it
is myself, but it lies somewhere between Kalamazoo
and Dreamville. Bessie and I never have any
trouble in finding it.''

"What do you two do when you are in Vague-land?"

"Well, our adventures are partly military and partly matrimonial. Bessie usually marries a prince of excellent moral character, and I lead a successful army, or accomplish great engineering feats, and the girl I want is always good to me. I wish this were Vagueland!"

Here again was occasion for diverting the conversation, but Barbara was insatiate. "Were you ever in love?" she demanded.

"Do you mean up to date, or just in the past?"

"Oh, just in the past," she said, impatiently. "Don't be foolish. Were you ever in love before you went to college?"

"Desperately."

"Were you rejected?"

"W—e—ll—not exactly. In fact, my sweetheart was very good to me. She made much of me until the day she was married to another fellow."

"Then she must have been a hard-hearted woman," and the girl's eyes flashed a little as she said it.

"It would almost seem so from the bare relation of the facts, yet the plea that I was only twelve while she was twenty-nine at the time of our affair, seemed to be accepted as a degree of palliation by our mutual friends. She belonged to what might be called the horse-hair sofa epoch, and she was a good girl, with her hair in a net. She has four children now, and they are fine."

"You are but trifling," declared the indignant

Barbara. "Have you been engaged in no love affair of comparatively modern date?"

"I don't think there has been anything fully deserving the title," he said, musingly. "There is a friend of my sisters who is, in many respects, the most beautiful creature upon whom human eyes have ever rested; everybody raves over her, and my sisters, except Bessie, think I should devote myself to her. She'd make what we call a 'model wife.'"

"Why don't you make love to her?"

"Because I couldn't do anything with her if I tried. She lacks the understanding, emotion. I don't suppose Cicero could have convinced a fish or a canary bird. Who can play without a musical instrument—a piano, fiddle, or harp?" he added, laughing. "There isn't a hypnotist in the world who could affect a dressed dummy in a shop window. I know I'm mixing my similes, but I can't help it. She has a class in the Sunday-school, an excellent education, a well-to-do father, a sort of dimpled dignity of face, big blue eyes and wavy flaxen hair. I think it's the hair that disagrees with me most. Do you know I think there is a great deal of character in hair?" And he gazed earnestly upon her crown.

"I wish you wouldn't look at me that way," she said.

"You do! Well, the expression you see upon my face just now is intended to represent undisguised admiration."

She said that it looked like illness, but that she

would take him at his word. Appearances were deceiving.

Once or twice Barbara was nearly lured into earnestness by the ever-seeking Sargent. One day he led her into what was almost a debate regarding the relative love-perceptiveness and faithfulness of men and women, he became almost eloquent in his declaration that men were truer and tenderer; and he felt what he said, for his sensibilities had been disturbed. He told of how a man beatifies the individual goddess, of the purity and lastingness of it; how men have led their squadrons, written books, controlled the councils of nations, or triumphed in mere money-making for it, and how the ideal and idolized "She" may be pretty and good and thoughtful, but be hard and calculating and not appreciative at all, not half understanding the devotion that is given her. Though some great women, like men, do understand, he argued. "And the worst of it is," he declared, "that the greater the man and the more forceful, the greater is his loving and his possible suffering. Ever and ever the giant among men comes back to the feminine soul, the maybe helpful mate, upon whom he rests and who gives him life and strength. It is for her he accomplishes, because she is a part of his life. It is good for him. Where did they find Alfred before his greatest battle with the Danes? He was in his tent, set far apart, and the woman he loved was washing his long hair. They had to call him away wet-headed from her lap. Who says he did not think the better and fight the better for it! Do men so inspirit women?"

Barbara was indignant. "Of course they do—when they are the right men," she added pointedly.

And Sargent's heart fell, but he continued, in boyish emotion. "It is the man who guards and fights, and the woman who forgets. There was no grass on the tomb of Pericles when Aspasia had another lover. The Angle hunted the she-wolf down for a cloak for the girl to wear. She fled with the Briton foeman. They were your ancestors and mine, and the women have been doing the same thing ever since—the lighter ones."

And so the days passed. When Sargent felt that he could stay no longer, he went away, making, before his return home, a short visit to his convenient friend of the copper region. The young fellow left the girl of his heart with unspoken, forcibly suppressed feelings. He was not a whit downcast, though, so strong was his youthful hope and faith. "She must love me in time," he said to himself. "It is true I don't deserve it, but just because I love her so, she must love me!"

And nothing could shake this belief.

CHAPTER XII.

"LOVE WILL FIND OUT THE WAY."

Not remarkable for its vigor was the first month's work of Sargent at the University in the junior year. Ever between him and the pages before him came visions of a fair face and of woodland stretches, but Time, the balm-bearer, is as kind to the young as to the old. And enforced work is a great sedative. With ends to attain, the youth became once more engrossed in the labor of learning, and could reason more objectively. Besides, there came occasional letters from Northern Michigan, piquant, interesting, not altogether satisfying, but still forming a link between two people.

Sargent's own letters in reply were, like his conduct on his visit, somewhat uncraftily concealed attempts at love-making, held within reasonable limits by prudential considerations.

And, as time passed, the young man began to feel that courage which follows success in effort; he became a student who was a credit to the University. Even the hobgoblin of mathematics he no longer feared, and he felt that he was becoming an engineer, an engineer who would know his business, a man who could wrestle with natural obstacles and overcome them scientifically, a maker of paths. Side by side with him struggled the buoyant Lathrop, and when the academic year had neared its close, each was prepared to face examination with a confidence which was justified. There was no marauding expedition this time. One had been enough to last each for a lifetime.

Ten days before the end of the term, there came to Sargent a letter. He had been dreaming of another trip to Northern Michigan, and his pulse had beaten faster as he thought of it. He felt himself more virile now, more qualified for the breaking of a butterfly, one who might perhaps command that which he wanted, but the letter arbitrarily changed his plans, and there was no recourse.

Sargent was summoned to spend his vacation in the great city of the West, there, in the office of the engineering department of a railroad, to acquire an outline knowledge of the duties which would be his upon his graduation; there was no alternative in the matter, he must perform this work while the influence behind him and supporting him existed, or sacrifice, perhaps, his prospect of entering active life with an advantage. To have refused would have been the sheerest folly, even considering the ultimate attainment of what he most desired. He wrote a regretful letter to Barbara, bewailing the fact that he could not visit the north that summer, and received one too placid in return, though its very placidity may have done him good, in that it somewhat piqued him. He plunged feverishly into his work amid his new surroundings, and the vacation seemed but a few days to him. The practical

experience in work was of great value to him; it
showed him wherein was his strength and where
were his weaknesses, and enabled him to concentrate
his efforts in the senior year upon the attainments
most required.   He graduated with honor, and with
half a thousand friends; then came again an
imperative call to Chicago and the beginning of his
career.   He chafed and fretted somewhat, and his
imagination treated him unfairly.   The northern
letters, which still came regularly, partook, it is
true, a little of the coldness of the winds chilled in
their sweep over Lake Superior, but his heart was
warm and his hands were outstretched.   The face
in the woods had become wonderfully idealized and
the red hair had become an aureole.   The long days
of fall and early winter passed, and with the first of
January came a six weeks' vacation from drudgery,
and he fled toward the Saginaw Valley as fast as
steam could carry him.   There were joyous and riot-
ous times at home, where, as the pride of his sisters,
much ado was made over him, and where he liked it
all, though he was restless.   At the end of two
weeks he announced his intention of visiting the
Northern Peninsula, and a train which forced its
way through snow-drifts carried him toward the
Straits.   He crossed upon the ice and found himself somewhat perplexed in the little town, where
old eastern fur-traders had laid the foundations of
vast fortunes, and where yet the Indian and the
half-breed were part of the population, where
strange legends of lake and forest were yet of firm
belief, where, upon the mainland, the wood-roads

were buried deeply, and where dog-sleds or snow-shoes were a necessity for him who would go afield. Miles to the north lay the place he sought, lost for the winter.

He talked with the old trappers, who were drinking strong waters and telling hunting stories in the shanty-like boarding houses, hibernating until spring should come. He told them where he wanted to go and they advised him not to undertake the trip unless it were a matter of life and death; they told him that he would inevitably be lost if he made the attempt, that the forest roadways and rough trails were invisible and could not be followed by one unfamiliar with the region. He could not induce one of them to act as guide, for they, one and all, said that the snow was not yet packed hard enough for travel, that if he went into the woods alone he would not come out again alive, and that if he persisted, they would find his body somewhere in the wilderness the coming May. He but laughed in their faces, and went to a store where equipments for the lumbermen were sold. He was warmly clad, but he bought a heavy woolen suit, which he put on over the one he already wore; he bought a compass and a surveyor's map of the region he was about to enter, a strong knife, a revolver and some cartridges, and a heavy blanket. He bought a knapsack, which he filled with provisions for four or five days. He had been upon snow-shoes before, and he purchased a pair of these. Then, with his blanket in a roll above the knapsack at his back, amid the pitying and contemptuous remarks of the trappers, who called him a fool, he plunged into the wilderness, going as blithely as if to the wedding which he hoped might come.

It was a cold, gray morning when Sargent entered the wood, following the roadway which was clearly enough defined for miles. The snow, as the trappers had said, was soft and feathery, and, despite his snow-shoes, he sank too deeply for comfort as he strode along. It was wearisome work, but he was strong, and as he walked he hummed to himself a more or less foolish song he had often heard, the burden of which was to the effect that "Love will find out the way," over all obstacles whatever. The turns of the roadway were such that all sight of the clearings was soon lost, and he was striding along where there was half darkness because of the dense overhanging of the forest growth on either side. An occasional opening or marshy lowland afforded greater light and cheerfulness, but the march was somber as a whole. By noon, he was ten miles from human life; at three o'clock in the afternoon he had traveled five miles farther and was very hungry, and beginning to be tired. He brushed the deep snow from a log by the pathway, sat down upon it, and ate heartily; he resumed his tiring walk somewhat refreshed, and again humming cheerily as he walked, the refrain exploiting Love's ability as a pathfinder. The roadway now led downward into a hemlock swamp extending for miles ahead; a swamp lying so low that he could look over the tops of the trees before and beneath him—a great dismal sea, which seemed more black than green. It was easy going down-hill, and he was soon where there was almost darkness, though it was only four o'clock in the afternoon. The trail was dim now, and all caution was required to keep it. He was miles in the swamp when there was presented to him a puzzle. He emerged into a little open space where the light was better and looked across it to see where the roadway resumed its course. He saw four snow-filled spaces, once wood roads, no doubt, almost alike in appearance and diverging like the spokes of a wheel.

Not all the mathematical knowledge acquired in the University, not all the engineering ability attained, not the assistance of the compass, could give a man one tota of knowledge as to which of the four paths to take. Three of them were roadways made in summer by the bark-gatherers, and must end somewhere in the swamp. Sargent knew the general direction he should take, but the entrances were so close together that the compass could not aid him; the right path might be the one that started seemingly in the wrong direction, for the regular trail had many turns. He could but venture. Even love could not certainly find a way. He chose the route which seemed to trend most nearly in the right direction, and entered it hopefully. He was soon in the half darkness again, which was now being intensified by the waning of the light of day. He was tired, too, for the snow-shoes were unaccustomed things and were bearing heavily upon his great toes. Snow-shoe wearers know where the strain comes, until one gets accustomed to the lift.

The pathway was relatively easy to follow, and Sargent struggled forward, hoping to emerge from the swamp upon the higher land before night should set in completely, but there were many windings, and, after an hour or two of fatiguing work, he felt that he was still far from the uplands. The gloom intensified, and he could follow the roadway with difficulty. It was just as night fairly settled down upon the forest that he stumbled forward into a small clearing, with felled trees lying upon all sides, and great stacks of hemlock bark piled here and there. He crossed the little opening and found no exit into the forest beyond; it was the end of the roadway. He had walked miles out of his course, only to find himself in an abandoned camping place of the bark-gatherers!

It was not a pleasant situation, and Sargent realized it; here he was, alone, in mid-winter, practically lost in a forest of Northern Michigan; he was miles from any human habitation or any human aid. For a moment he was somewhat dazed, but it was not in him to make much of a situation of the sort. He pulled a broad strip of the hemlock bark from one of the heaps, laid it on the snow, crowning a hemlock log, and sat down upon it to think a little and pull himself together. That was not a difficult task; he had spent midwinter nights in the woods before, and after a few minutes of rest he aroused himself and began the work before him.

Two great logs lay side by side, four or five feet apart. Using a piece of the stiff rectangular bark as a shovel, he cleared away the snow between them, for a distance of ten or twelve feet. One end of the bottom of the excavation he covered with bark from the heaps for two-thirds of its length, leaving an open space of some three feet. Here he made another little flooring of bark, and upon this pro-ceeded to build a fire. There were bark and dry limbs in abundance, and to build a fire was no feat at all; a merry blaze was soon leaping upward into the night, and enough dead wood was piled at hand for the fire's replenishment as need might come. Across the logs over the floored space more bark was laid, until it was fairly roofed, and more bark still was piled leaning against the end farthest from the fire. Here was now a little cabin, dry, open at one end, and with a blazing fire in front. Next, with the heavy knife he carried, Sargent cut a great armful of small hemlock branches, and with them made a soft and fragrant bed upon the hut's even floor. He was delighted with and interested in his work. All perplexity had gone.

Seated in the door of his cabin the man ate heartily, smoked his briar-wood pipe, and from placidity grew buoyant of mood again. He even sang his foolish song aloud, and, unaffected by "Love's" failure of the late afternoon, announced buoyantly to the forest that Love would find a way. Toward night it had become warmer and a soft snow was falling. At last a drowsiness came upon the singer; he heaped more wood upon the

8

fire, wrapped his blanket about him, and lay back among the soft hemlock boughs, with his feet toward the warming flames.

He slept dreamlessly for an hour or two, then awoke with a start, aroused by some sound from the forest. The fire had waned, but the blaze still uplifting made queer dancing shadows among the hemlocks, as if the black wood spirits were holding a carnival about him. He could hear the patter of soft feet, as the great white rabbits frolicked about among the bark heaps. Then from the wood came a sudden hoarse-prolonged shriek, so strident and threatening that Sargent started to a sitting posture, but settled back upon his couch again, for he recognized the sound. He had a neighbor in the great snowy owl of the north, that terror of all small four-footed things. Then something waveringly big and white swept silently and swiftly by, there was a struggle in the snow, the agonized squeaking of a hare, and silence again. The great owl had found its prey. A little later, from a distance, came the long moaning howl of a wolf, but that mattered little to Sargent, for the big gray wolf of the Peninsula has long since learned to fear man above all living things, while fire is to him a terror. There came the snort of a startled deer, but Sargent was becoming oblivious to what was about him. His eyes were heavy and he slept again.

There came dreams, wonderful dreams, there were a thousand fair happenings, and the red-crowned girl flitted through a world strange and beautiful with him. He reveled in a land of summer;

flowers blossomed about him, and birds were filling
the air with their untaught music.

It was all queer, but everything seems natural in
a dream. He wanted to find Barbara, and it seemed
to him that Barbara was anxious to be with him,
but there were difficulties in the way. There were
high walls and there was something about a sheriff
and a bear. He couldn't understand very much
about the sheriff and the bear and didn't care much
about them, but the high walls were real and there
was nothing to clamber up by, and so he couldn't get
to Barbara, who was somewhere on the other side.
Then suddenly he was happily surprised to hear
her call to him that she was coming over herself,
and that he needn't bother about the climbing.
She came over at once in the form of a beautiful
brown quail, but instead of alighting beside him she
sailed down in the sunlight across a meadow, then
settled beside two maple trees where the clover was
thick and heavy. It seemed all right that Barbara
should come in such form, but it seemed a little
unfair that he should have to walk so far to get to
her and he said to himself, quite naturally: "The
girl hasn't learned how to fly well yet." Then he
stalked across the meadow to where he had seen
her alight beyond the maple trees, just where the
ground dipped up into a little hill, and began parting
carefully the tops of the red blossoms that he might
find her. It was quite a search, but he succeeded at
last and found her crouching cozily in the midst of
all the bloom and fragrance. He asked her why she
had flown so far. She said she didn't know, that

the air had carried her, and that she couldn't help floating down upon it. She had dropped into the clover as soon as she could. He said that was all right, and then they walked away together, for somehow Barbara seemed a young woman again, and there was nothing out of the way about the transformation. He began to tell her of the hawks that were once accustomed to alight upon certain dead limbs of the two maple trees, for it seemed to him, now, that this was one of the meadows of his childhood. Then both of them became so interested in the singing of the birds about them that they forgot the subject of their conversation, and could talk only of the singing. Sargent awoke.

Morning had come. The man lay quiet in his blanket, and as he began to realize where he was, he thought he must yet be half asleep and dreaming, for the song of birds was still ringing in his ears. They were calling to each other all around, and there was music everywhere. He could hear distinctly among them all what seemed the notes of the phoebe-bird, the bird of the summer, which builds its nest in the bridges over creeks, or in pleasant places about the barns and meadow sides. Through the open doorway came to the man's eyes the flash of a million crystals, as the bright sun smote the frosted hemlocks; it was all wonderful, and Sargent leaped to his feet to look upon the morning scenes.

It was all real enough, the sun was shining brightly, and the birds were singing, but it was not the phoebe-bird which had so puzzled Sargent; it

was the wood pee-wee of the far North, the note of
which is so similar to that of the phoebe; and it
was accompanied by a host of its northern friends.
This was their summer time and they were in a
joyous mood. The crisp air and the glorious scene
were enough to inspirit any man with health and
courage in him. Sargent laughed aloud. He ate
heartily and then sat down to ponder.

Should he retrace his steps and seek another trail
in the swamp at the point where the ways had
diverged? He would not waste the time. Could
not he, a born woodsman, find a way of his own?
What to him were trails? He took out his
surveyor's map of the region and studied it carefully. With his compass he laid a course for where
lay the Sloan homestead and coming happiness;
then he girded himself and strode into the forest
depths full of strength and hope. Within an hour
he had emerged from the swamp and was among the
birch and oak and maple, holding his course
steadfastly, and his progress was fairly satisfactory,
though the snow was softer still because of the
slight fall the night before, and the walking required
much strength of leg and depth of lung.

In his present mood, Sargent could rejoice in all
he saw, and he saw much. Not a journal in all the
country gave more news that morning than did the
sheet of fresh new-fallen snow. The squirrels had
left bulletins everywhere upon the snow-clad tree
trunks, and upon the ground were page after page
of added information. In some bank a crumbling
breakage in the snow showed where the ruffed

grouse had buried itself for protection against the cold, and beneath the birches the brown fleckings gave proof that the same bird had taken its bud-breakfast in the tree-tops. There were the tracks of the fox, but, somehow, he had missed the grouse in its bedroom. Along beside the logs, the queer twin pads of the weasel or the mink showed what hunting had been done, and beside the creeks, where the air-holes in the ice were, the otter had left his mark. Here and there seemingly a great dog had passed in the night, but this was the trail of the old gray wolf; and here and there were the bunched hoof marks of the running deer. Snow buntings had scattered seeds from the reed clumps, and wood mice, their light bodies barely sinking in the snow, had made lace work all about. It was a great morning for a tramp, even though one were alone with no companionship save that of the wild creatures.

Noon came, and with it hunger, which was appeased again from the knapsack. Valleys were descended, and hills climbed, and dense woods and thickets threaded, with slight turning aside, for the course must be held firmly, or there might come disaster. At last, at four o'clock in the afternoon, a hill was climbed, a slope partly descended, the wood came to an end, and there, fair and white before him, Sargent saw lying the Sloan farm. From the house the smoke curled high and white, and there came to the mind of the grateful and happy youth a thought of the pillar of cloud by day which led the Children from the Wilderness into Canaan.

He walked on again, until he reached the clearing's edge, then climbed the fence and sat there resting. There was his heart's desire, but a sudden timidity came upon him; he overcame it at last, though, plunged through the snow across the fields and creek, and up the slope and the well-remembered pathway, and knocked upon the door. It was opened by a fair girl, who started as she saw him. She looked upon him silently, and the blood rushed to her face, until the tint of her cheeks was deeper than that of the Michigan roses she had tended in midsummer. She opened her lips, but, for a moment, did not speak.

CHAPTER XIII.

"THE WOOIN' O'T."

For a moment or two the girl stood silent, still. Then the blood in her fair cheeks sank back to its sources, and she was, in a degree, herself again:

"I am very glad to see you, Mr. Sargent!"

The fear had gone from him, and he had become a man again as his eyes fed upon her. A little more grave of face, a little more stately of bearing, a little more beautiful in all ways was the woman before him, and he wanted her more and more. His eyes told his story demandingly, and she understood it. What civilized woman ever lived, even the dullest scrub-woman of the floors of a public building, who could not understand such language from the eyes of a man?

She, the woodland girl, knew well what the man had done. None better than she knew the life-risking danger of the solitary trip in mid-winter across the unpeopled waste between the settled region and the Straits. He, this magnificent animal before her, had ploughed his way through deep snows, had slept in the forest when a sudden blizzard might have cost his life, had taken all chances just to look again upon her, to be with her! She understood it very well. She understood it so well that, saying all graceful things after she had recovered herself, and bringing him in to her father beside the great open fireplace, she fled to her own room, threw herself down upon the bed there, and pressed her face hard upon the pillow, and wondered what she should do? She could not tell. But what a great, resolute, daring boy-man it was! What a struggle was before her! She knew that the youth who had come across all those buried miles had not come for nothing. Considering the case of this young woman objectively, it is but fair to extend to her a degree of sympathy. Her problem was certainly a serious one.

What were the thoughts of Barbara? Who shall analyze and make plain in fair print the mind and emotions of a young woman dealing with the love problem? Save in exceptional cases, before the age of twenty-five, the woman is far in advance of the man in keen perceptiveness, and understanding of the relations between them. Yet the man, more bungling, has a certain advantage in that he knows just what he wants, while the girl does not. The girl has dreams, the man has purposes. Her reasoning is all of the abstract, his of the concrete. He is in love with a particular woman, and is resolved to have her and no other woman. She has a sort of vague ideal, she is in love with love, so to speak, and not so much with the one particular biped. He is certain and she is uncertain. The more definite goal in love comes to her later. Her course is most doubtful. The old Biblical gentleman who described as one of the things which could not be foretold, "the way of a man with a maid," one would think might have improved upon it. Why didn't he say "The way of a maid with a man"?

Thoroughly delighted was Judge Sloan over the unexpected advent of the young man whom he had learned to regard so highly. He asked no questions about the perilous trip, for his thoughts now ran in somewhat narrow channels, and it did not occur to him that there was anything extraordinary about this sudden appearance of a visitor from the outer world. He settled back in his easy chair and lit his pipe and began talking with the young fellow who could understand him so well. Sargent was at home in a moment.

Michael, who was lounging by the fire, fingering the strings of his fiddle, thrumming out half-smothered music like that of a guitar, cast a swift, piercing sidelong look at Sargent, his small black eyes betraying a world of meaning in the fleeting glance. As the talk began and went on briskly between Judge Sloan and Sargent, the lad played softly yet briskly and with unerring snap and emphasis—still with his fingers alone on the strings, the bow lying idle on the floor by his side—an ancient Norwegian wedding march. The blood mounted to Sargent's cheek as he heard the smothered laugh of the strings; he looked sternly at Michael, but the dwarfish youth seemed totally unconscious of all around him, except perhaps of the hound which lay at his feet, for he caressed its head with his moccasined foot occasionally.

The bustling Tilda came in now, and began preparations for a mighty refection for the traveler;

and she roused Michael from his dream of laziness
and sent him flying to the spring for water, and to
the great pile of wood for fuel, and to the cellar
for vegetables, and to the loft for frozen spareribs
and dried venison, and so kept the Troll, as Sargent
inwardly called him, chasing about and leaving
doors open, and being called back to shut them,
until, in self-protection, the lad fled away to the
barn, where he had a warm nest in the hay, in which
he spent a good share of his time, remote from the
sharp commands of his mother, and from all other
calls of duty.

And now began a series of bewildering days for
Sargent. There was a trial of skill at love's fencing
between the two young people from the first. The
one purpose of Sargent's life was to declare his love
to the girl who, from the time when he first saw her,
had held his heart as in a clasp which could never
be loosened. The one purpose of Barbara seemed
to be to keep back from the lover's lips the story
he was struggling to tell.

As for Barbara, she felt the currents of her being
setting toward the young adventurer of the snow-
shoes, and she made a brave struggle not to let the
current get too strong. Barbara Sloan was a girl of
great purpose and ambition, loving and unselfish,
and she had not planned, as yet, to fall in love at all.
In her dreams, she had thought of a lover, of course,
and although such dreams were unacknowledged,
the real trouble was that Sargent did not look like
the somewhat stiff and august creature of the
young girl's fancies. And then, Barbara, when she

had returned to stay with her father, after her latest absence from her home, where she had lived among men and women of more than ordinary ideas and ideals, had found her father much broken in spirit and strength, and, saddest discovery of all, she was forced at last to see that his mind had lost, in some degree, its practical tone, and his will its strength of direction, so that he was floating passively, and somewhat aimlessly, along on the stream of life. Barbara passionately denied this discovery, even after it had become a conviction, insisting to herself that it could not be true, but unconsciously she was already shaping her whole existence in such a manner as to hide the lapse from active, virile life which had come upon her father.

The girl's anxiety and apprehension extended to financial matters. She saw complications in the near future brought about by certain ventures of Judge Sloan's in buying timber and mining lands. She clung ever more and more fondly to the gentle, learned, kindly old scholar as she saw his fortunes failing, and recognized the unfitness of his nature and training for the rough struggle for wealth which consumes the energies of strong men without due reward, and in which men of gentle blood, high ideals and scholarly attainments almost invariably fail.

And so, in the girl's ardent soul, had been formed a scheme of life for and with her father. The dream of a lover did not disturb this plan at all, but the real lover did; the real lover, so young, so new to the world and all experience, fresh from college and all the jejune life of college, so masterful, too, and sure of himself, and even of her!

And so the lover and the lass wavered along, one advancing with a heart on fire, the other retreating, but looking back. It was like a Spanish dance, thought old Tilda, as she looked on silently, taking note without appearing to do so, and soundly boxing Michael's ears whenever he became too much interested in the young folk.

One morning the two went out for a walk over the hard crust of the frozen snow. It makes ideal walking, the snowcrust; only, as Barbara said, "You want to run all the time."

They ran a race along a chain of play mountains formed by drifts over the three-cornered fences. It was a mile to the pine woods, in whose shadow the snow lay perfectly level, and they ran across the hard surface, with just a little dust of new-fallen snow upon it, with such ease that it seemed like flying. Barbara was a fleet runner, but of course she was no match for Sargent, and, as he heard her skirts rustling along behind him, and the "pat-pat" of her little feet, he turned suddenly and caught her hand.

"Oh, let's not race," he said, running along by her side, "let's run together."

And so they ran, hand in hand, until just as they were leaving the mimic mountain chain Sargent broke through the snow crust and, with a flounder or two, sank waist deep.

Barbara saved herself by darting with lightning quickness from Sargent's side, and then she stood afar off and laughed at him. When she saw him emerging from the drift covered with snow, she started running again, and reached the woods before him. Then they had a game of hide and seek, dodging about among the trees, until at last Sargent caught the laughing girl again by the hand—well gloved, you may be sure, and not in kid either—and they walked among the sighing lanes of green trees with the frozen waters of Honey Creek for a pathway.

"You make me follow you, Pied Piperess that you are," said Sargent, "and now that I have caught you I am going to quarrel with you."

"Oh, is that what you came up from below for, in the depth of winter? Why, we could quarrel very well in writing."

"But that is one of the things I want to find fault with you about. Your letters are unsatisfactory,—not like yourself."

"You are talking in a double-edged style, trying to cut and salve the wound with one sweep, Mr. Sargent. Pray, to what do you object in my epistolary style?"

"It is lifeless and cold," began the poor fool of a boy, but she interrupted him—

"It is cold up here, you can see and feel for yourself—and then I don't see why you complain—you are unjust. Didn't I thank you with enough warmth for the books you sent me Christmas?"

"Why talk of trifles?" this indignantly. "Well, no, I don't care, your letter was cold, perfunctory, ending with that simpering 'Again thanking you,'

and so on—Why will people write that? They never
say it; fancy a man or woman saying 'Again thanking you'; the straight-out ending of a child's letter
is better, 'As I can think of nothing more to say, I
will close.' "

"Aren't you making a lot of fuss over a little
thing?" asked Miss Barbara Sloan, tying the blue
ribbons of her fur hood anew under her chin with a
certain far-away dignity in the simple action.

"Of course I am—and I didn't mean that at all—I
mean the tone of your letters. It is frosty, and
gives me a heart shiver every time I hear from you.
And I wait for your letters so!"

"Too bad," said Barbara, gravely. "It would be
better not to write at all."

"Oh, no, don't say that—and don't look so, so
school-teacherish!"

The girl immediately assumed the look and air of
a child of nine years old—how she did it, who can
tell?—but her eyes looked out childishly, she swung
one well booted foot back and forth, as she stood
before Sargent, and with her hands crossed before
her, sung in a sweet childish voice:

'How I love my teacher,
How I love my ma,
How I love my preacher,
How I love my pa!"

And then, why then, Sargent came nearer kissing
Miss Barbara Sloan than he had ever before. She
had a narrow escape that time, but by great self-
possession she did escape.

"Come now," said Barbara, as they turned and walked sedately homeward, along the creek, "let's turn over a new leaf and talk sense."

"Then you begin," said Sargent. "You have taken my senses from me, but while you're starting the ball rolling, I will be turning over the leaf and collecting myself together."

"Tell me your plans," began Barbara, "and don't bring me into them, either," she warned, for she saw a dangerous flash in his eyes.

And then Sargent told about his hopes and schemes, how he was to finish his preparations in Chicago for his work in helping to lay out the route for a great railway across the continent, from the Missouri to the Pacific, and how, before the snow should come again, he expected to be in the heart of the Arizona desert or in the Mexican district at his work.

Barbara entered into the new world thus brought before her with great interest, and, with exquisite tact, she drew out the young engineer's story of his profession until they reached home, where the Judge was eagerly awaiting them, book in hand, and finger between the leaves, to show Sargent something he had found, in which the two men had a common interest.

And Barbara, in the silence and trim order of her own little room, as she looked out vaguely at the white world, through her small-paned window, said to herself softly: "I must take care! I *could* love him!"

Very strong in the make-up of Sargent was the

instinct that the physical Nature we know could speak to what we call Human Nature. Happy those who have this thought and instinct, for they are right! Though the wild things may not always speak in their behalf with promptness for an emergency, they will speak at last, to all save the dull-minded.

So Sargent, hoping, grasping, took Barbara out with him again along the creek, the waters of which ran, swift and black, beneath the pure ice, cleaned here and there by the broom of the winds.

The creeks which run north and south from the divide in northern Michigan, are often spring-fed for miles from their beginning. And so the ice above the water is relatively thin in places, especially where the streams linger and spread into ponds, deep and broad, and here the ice is almost absolutely clear. It was out upon one of those ponds, close to its steep side, where the scrub oaks overhung, that Sargent took Barbara one day. He had with him two huge horse blankets, and an axe, and broom. He swept away the feathery snow which lay upon the ice and exposed an area which looked almost black by contrast. With the axe he cut a hole through the ice perhaps a foot across, and cleared away all chippings, so that the hole opened into the water fair and clean. Then he spread one of the blankets upon the cleared surface, close up to the edge of the hole, and made Barbara kneel with him, looking down through into the waters. Over both of them he threw the other blanket, so that they were protected from the cold and wind, in a sort of little

9

tent. It was very good to be thus close to Barbara in that little tent.

At first, there seemed to be what was almost darkness in the tent, but, as they looked downward into the water, there came to the woman a revelation. There was light below, and there was suddenly revealed to her, what she had never imagined even, the real life of the water-world, the under-world. There she could see plainly all that was going on among the people of the depths. She could see the pebbly bottom, with the funny crisscross streaks made by the little creatures of the sand and slime. She saw huge pickerel drift lazily across, each barely steadying himself by slow fin-strokes, or the black bass passing, all alert. What, beyond all, most attracted her, though, were the shifting groups of speckled trout, brilliantly marked, and graceful of outline, and intent on seeking something, none knew what. There were other things, a score of other things, to interest her, but the shining, glittering trout attracted her above all else. Suddenly there was a scurrying together, a moment of wavering, and then a group darted away, far from her field of vision. Immediately across that same field of vision swept something dark and graceful and dreadful. It was an otter pursuing the trout. So swift and fierce was its lightning dash that it seemed almost flattened out in its pursuit, and, following closely, came another shadow, almost the same, as graceful and as swift; it was the otter's mate.

There were other things, a host of them, to

interest, but this fierce chase of the graceful otter after the trout seemed most to attract the astonished Barbara.   Then Sargent told her of the qualities of this most gifted and graceful of all the water creatures, of their made slides, where they played together as children do on the hill slopes in winter, of their lovingness toward each other, and of the caressings of male and mate when they lounged together in summer upon some rock rising just above the water.   And he tried to tell her how, even among the wild things, with greater intelligence came the greater affection.   Of how love in reality rules all life, and of a verity, "makes the world go round;" but Barbara appeared to comprehend and give heed to only the natural history features of what he said.   His talk about love in the depths of the waters and of the forest she called fantastic, and steered the talk into channels much more commonplace.

It seemed to Sargent as if all nature were mating easily, that everywhere the right female came to the right male upon call.   Only Barbara would not come to him.

CHAPTER XIV.

A WINTER FESTIVAL.

"We are going to be very gay," announced Barbara, jauntily, as she poured the breakfast coffee one cold, glittering morning. "I have accepted an invitation on behalf of father and me and our distinguished guest from 'below.'"

"I shall be glad to go anywhere with Judge Sloan and his daughter," said Sargent, "but it's uncanny somehow—this constant reference to the depths from which I come."

"Up here, Mr. Sargent," Judge Sloan interposed, with the entirely unnecessary information, "Up here, every stranger is enevitably located as from 'below'—meaning south from upper Michigan."

"Nothing could come from above," said Barbara, "nothing save the north wind, for there is only Lake Superior."

"As you very justly remark," the Judge spoke with his usual slow dignity, using one of the forms of words which had become habitual to him—and somehow they were interjected into ordinary conversation with ludicrous effect—"it is embarrassing to be continually spoken of as from 'below,' but I assure you no offense is intended."

"Or taken," heartily assented Sargent, "but about that gayety, Miss Sloan? The idea of going anywhere with the thermometer from ten to twenty-five below zero appeals to me with force. Will you tell me what is in store for us?"

"We are going to an entertainment in the Fletcher District," answered Barbara. "This evening at early candle light, the Fletcher mansion, the first house built in all this region, will be opened to entertain the neighborhood. All the beauty and chivalry of the surrounding country will be there, to say nothing of such strangers as are visiting us. And," continued she, "we will take Michael and his 'wee wicked fiddle' along with us so that we may have a dance, if the Court please," turning prettily to her father and making a comic gesture of homage, and laughing as the two men at table smiled, for she had the august Judge completely under domination.

"I fear the evening will be somewhat tedious," said Judge Sloan, glancing longingly toward his chair by the fireplace, and his book and pipe on the table near it.

"But, father," Barbara expostulated, "Mr. Sargent has never been at the Fletchers', nor seen anything so perfectly typical of our Northern Michigan life, as is their home. I think it is but due to him as a guest that we should give him opportunity to see, not only the Fletchers and their house, but our social surroundings just as they are. Mr. Sargent has not stirred from our place, except for walks in the woods, since the day of his arrival."

"Your observations are quite justified, my dear," the Judge confessed. "We must take Mr. Sargent to Fletcher's; the visit will certainly interest and amuse him—for a time at least—''and the good man sighed the sigh of the patient parent of a grown-up daughter.

And so it came that the sound of sleigh bells called the little group of well-wrapped people to their door that frosty evening, just as the red glow was fading in the west. Michael held the reins of the restless horses, and Michael's fiddle was under his seat in the sleigh. Fur-booted and fur-wrapped, veiled and hooded, Barbara sprang into the sleigh like a wood sprite weighed down only by her weight of garb. And Sargent sat down beside her. Judge Sloan, a mere bundle of comfortable clothing, under his daughter's watchful care, occupied the seat in front beside Michael. Heavy buffalo robes were tucked about the party, and the horses gave the bells a shake.

"They feel good, them horses," said Tilda, as she stood in the door holding a lighted lantern of tin with holes bored in it, to show the light through, the pattern being wrought to imitate the befeathered head of an Indian chief. The road was tolerably well broken for the sleigh, and it seemed but a short ride over the eight miles which intervened between "Honey Creek," Judge Sloan's place, and the old house of the Fletchers.

The moon "shone fair on field and fell,"as the sleigh dashed up in front of the great log Fletcher house. Beside the road, beyond the house, extended a long, low, open shed, already fairly occupied by teams which had brought guests in sleighs, "jumpers" and bobsleds. Attached to one of the bobsleds was a yoke of oxen, and from the shed came the sound of much snorting and stamping of feet, varied by an occasional bellow. The bells had announced the arrival of the new party, the door of the house opened, a flood of light streamed out, they were welcomed hospitably and hurried inside upon a scene which was certainly inspiriting.

It was a fine old log house, that of the Fletchers, the main part of it long built, but built exceeding well. It had been, originally, but a rectangle, its side facing the road, with a big doorway in the middle, and a big window on either side. There had been partitions then, the large room with a fireplace at one end, and two bedrooms and a kitchen at the other. As time passed and children and prosperity came to the pioneer couple, an addition had been made to the house in the form of a wing set against its rear. In this wing were all the bedrooms and the big kitchen. The house in its new form was a "T," but this did not show from the road. The partitions in the original house had been removed, and it was now one great room with the enormous fireplace at one end, and was the general sitting-room and living-room of the big family.

The fireplace was just as it had been twenty years before. In front of it the wide brick hearth extended far out into the room, and from one side of the huge chimney still swung the iron crane from which, before the wing and stove stage, had hung the kettles in which hulled corn, and frumenty, and samp had been cooked, and all the stewing and boiling of the old days had been done, to gain a flavor not excelled by any product of the stove in the new kitchen. Upon the hearth before the fire and in the tin oven which formerly stood there, had been cooked such "johnny-cake" and bread as the older men said they could get nowhere nowadays. From the crane had once hung the griddle, where big buckwheat cakes were baked, and on the hearth above the raked-out red coals had once stood the three-legged revolving gridiron on which venison steaks were broiled. To the left of the fireplace the old-fashioned dye-tub, with its indigo dye and its soaking yarns, still occupied a place, making an excellent seat for any of the younger members of the family, and on the right stood the pile of fire-wood, such as had been brought in nightly for nearly a quarter of a century.

There is art in piling up the firewood brought in at night. The great backlog, of hickory or hard maple, must be lugged in first, for it is first to be utilized in the morning. It must be laid three or four feet from the wall, and the space between it and the wall filled with the split ash and beech and smaller logs used for constant replenishing of the fire. When this space is filled about even with the top of the backlog, the forelog, smaller but also of hardwood, must be brought and laid well in front of the backlog. Above this and heaped high up against the wall the remainder of the fuel necessary may be laid without any order. All this is because of the fire building of the morning, when he whose duty it is to get up and build the fire with the thermometer away below zero, half dresses hurriedly, rushes to the fireplace where nothing is visible but white ashes, pulls out the heavy andirons, seizes the great iron shovel standing ever at hand, scrapes the ashes away from the back of the fireplace and exposes a great mass of huge living coals, the backlog of the day before. He pulls them to the front, clears out the hollow at the back, heaves into the place so made the backlog brought in the night before, covers it with ashes, shoves the andirons up against it, one on either side, heaps the blazing coals between them, throws on a bit or two of light wood, lays the forelog in front squarely across the andirons, and then, between it and the chimney back, above the already blazing fire below, lays more or less criss-cross, so that air and flame may circulate, the sticks which make the ordinary fuel. There is a roaring, warming, comforting fire in no time.

Six or eight inches from the floor, in the jamb at the right of the fireplace, there was a space which shone whitely of deep abrasion and indentation; this was where a generation had kicked its frozen cowhide boots on in the morning. In the heavy oaken floor, a little at one side, was a smooth dark hollow, charred in at one time; this was where a "smudge," made in a tin pan to drive away mosquitoes, had, some summer night, burned too fiercely and fired the floor beneath.

Above the fireplace was a mantel shelf, black with smoke and age, and upon it were various articles in common use. At the other side of the room was another shelf, well elevated. Upon its middle stood a high clock with an imitation mahogany frame, the lower part of the door ornamented with a painted flower-pot holding a tremendous bouquet of red roses and other flowers. On one side of the clock stood a big green camphor bottle, and on the other a bottle of "cholagogue," a sovereign remedy for fever and ague, as malaria was still designated, danger from which yet lurked in the swamps, in the spring and fall. Further along, on each side were coal-oil lamps, though formerly candles, made by dipping, had occupied their places. To-night there were blazing lamps on each of the two shelves, and on brackets set in the wall. At each end of the clock-shelf stood a vase with more flowers upon it. Never, even in summer, were real flowers placed in such vases. They were purely ornamental; and not to be desecrated by use. Upon the walls were pictures, two colored prints, one of Henry Clay, the other of Frelinghuysen, and there was another, "Washington Crossing the Delaware," and one of an old English landscape. The overflow to northern Michigan had been mostly from New England and New York. There were chairs and rocking chairs ranged about the sides of the room, and in one place stood an old cherry "bureau," in the top drawer of which was kept the smaller finery of the girls, in the second that of the men and boys, while the one beneath was locked and belonged to "Mother," as one of the children told Barbara during the evening, telling her also that in it was a little baby's cap which had grown yellow, and that there were some old dresses and ribbons, and pressed flowers and a red-stone breastpin, and a little book, and that "Ma" cried some times when she went there.

The beams of the low ceiling of the room came down almost to the heads of the tall young lumber-men and farmers and wood-cutters, who, dressed in their best and awkward in consequence, were paying their court with bashful zeal to the beauty and grace of Fletcher's District.

When Judge Sloan's party entered there had been a moment of confusion, but the measured chant that could be heard outside very soon began again. A young man and woman stood at one end of the room with their hands clasped higher than their heads, and under the angle formed by their arms, the merry-faced girls and strong-featured, laughing men marched one by one, singing to an air certainly older than the settlement of America:

> "The needle's eye,
> It doth supply
> The thread that runs so true.
> There's many a lass
> That I've let pass,
> But now I have caught you!"

The song and march went on monotonously over and over for a few minutes, and then there was a great shout of laughter, a little pause, and the song began again, with a new girl blushingly holding up the hands of the young gallant who had chosen her. In her turn she must now choose a partner—and a

kiss was always exchanged between the two—the
signal for the shouting and the laughing.

Sargent glanced at Barbara as she stood by the
fire demurely looking on.

"Let us join the players," he said. "Had I known
about 'The Needle's Eye' I should have begged
that we might start for this place before dinner."

But it would have been easier for the camel to
get through the eye of the needle, or for the rich
man to obtain the Kingdom of Heaven, than for
Sargent to secure what he craved from this
particular needle's eye. Barbara promptly introduced him to a blooming maiden with saucy black
eyes, and sent the couple helplessly on their way
around the room. Joining her father, who was duly
installed in the place of honor on a pine settle by
the side of the pioneer and host, Barbara watched
the play with a delighted sympathy which had in it
no shadow of condescension or mock modesty, and
yet she seemed to Sargent to be far away from the
joyous laughing circle in which he found himself.
He gave himself up to the moment, however, and
soon became the center of the riot and fun of the
merry-makers. It could not well be otherwise, he
entered with such zest into the spirit of the
occasion, and as he towered even above most of
the stalwart woodsmen, his magnetic personality and
his striking, laughing face won all at once. They
liked him, and he felt it and was very glad of it.
If he could not have Barbara, he could, at least, be
a thorough boy for an hour or so. Besides, the
black-eyed girl was certainly very pretty.

Soon the song was changed, and the company took hold of hands and began circling around a pink cheeked and pink gowned girl standing alone in the center of the space made by the singing players. It was a long time before the play ended.

> "So the farmer sows his seed
> And scatters far what he may need,
> Stamps his foot and waves his hand
> And turns around and views the land!"

So sang the chorus of careless young voices, the lines which have later wandered even into the kindergartens, suiting the action to the words, the great feet of the men, shod in cow-skin, coming down on the bare floor with a loud bang, and the more lightly clad feet of the girls making a pattering noise by their side. Round and round they whirled, the bright faces flushed in the lamp light, and "clap! clap!" went big brown hands and smaller ones as the game unwound itself, always coming to a climax of kissing and then beginning all over again.

Barbara went with the young women of the Fletcher family into the new kitchen, and helped them set out the supper on long tables made of boards set across wooden "saw-horses" and covered by coarse, well-bleached linen. Here, from time to time, came trooping admiring elderly women, doing homage to the wonders of the Fletcher cuisine.

There were two immense game pies, cold, as was everything on the table excepting the boiling coffee, a boiled and roasted ham, with cloves stuck all over it, and roasted chickens and turkeys, great platters of bread and butter and pans of doughnuts, plates of pickles and glasses of jelly and jam, and on every other space a pie of mince or apple, or a cake of famous construction. Pitchers of coffee stood along the middle, each with a smaller jug of rich cream beside it, and the table was, when the girls had finished setting it, a cheering sight.

At eleven o'clock the whole merry group came pouring in, and the supper was no play. When the company returned to the big room there sat Michael, dreaming away over his violin, playing snatches of strange old minor tunes, mingled with "Sir Roger de Coverley," and other dancing airs. Then, with a flourish of his bow, he was off with the enlivening strains of "Money Musk."

And now Sargent caught the hand of Barbara for just a moment in his own, and begged her to dance with him. And she consented and they stood up opposite each other and went down the middle together and outside alone and wound their way from one end to the other in breathless and joyous abandon, and, although there was no kiss to this play, it was nevertheless the most enjoyed of all that evening, by these two young people, at least.

There was much bustle and merriment when the time came for departure. Team after team was driven up before the door, and load after load of merrymakers hid themselves between the robes. The horses came from the shed, frost-fringed and prancing, and dashed away impatiently for their distant stables. Even the solitary ox-team, draw-ing a jumper, was full of fire and the oxen clashed their white horns together impatiently and started off in a cumbrous trot; while the log-chain jangled and banged from the yoke to the iron pin at the other end of the sleigh-tongue, and the bright night was full of clamor in all directions. The Sloan party left with the others, though more quietly. From a sleigh behind them came a chorus of voices joining in the singing:

"Buffalo gals, ain't ye comin' out to-night?
Comin' out to-night! comin' out to-night!
Buffalo gals, ain't ye comin' out to-night,
To dance by the light of the moon?"

By contrast, as they passed a cross road, there came floating to them across the field from another sleigh, the words of Toplady's wonderful old hymn:

"Rock of Ages, cleft for me,
Let me hide myself in thee."

Close together beneath the warm robes Sargent and Barbara sat silently. His arm stole about her, but its pressure was a farce. He almost dared, but dared not. Her head was close to his, though, and her warm breath was upon his face. It was an hour of bliss. All the way back that night, the bells sang a sweet song to Sargent, and who can tell what they said to Barbara?

CHAPTER XV.

"THE CAVE OF SILVER."

And the days passed. Happily unhappy or unhappily happy, was the deep chested and splendid youth who went perplexed about to woo the young woman of the woods. It was curious, but by no means new. It is only what happens to young men of good brains and good blood—that which came to Sargent throughout this period of watching and waiting and hoping and dreaming and planning and much fooling and much brave silliness.

Take a young Anglo-Saxon male of decent heritage and qualities, and then send him through a university, and, queerly enough, he ordinarily cannot at first reason with that degree of practicality which adapts most easily the means to the ends desired. It does not matter much whether the end to be attained be the hand of a young woman, with her feet and her head and the rest of her likewise, or control of the stock of some railroad which might be made dividend-paying in time. The young graduate has yet to learn that learning is but the hammer with which rocks may be split. But the rocks can be split only when the blow is delivered with a certain impact and at a certain angle. The impact and angle can be learned only by attrition with other human beings in the world of men and women.

So Sargent reasoned bunglingly. He said to himself—this was in a fretful mood, and his fretful train of reasoning had become almost constant—"What is the reason that I cannot get what I want? Here I am, I who have worked hard and have become a good engineer, and who am in love with a woman, and who feel within myself the ability to care for her as a woman should be cared for and to protect not only her but her kith and kin. She doesn't care for anybody else, that I know. She cares for me, that I know too, but there is something queer about her caring. She ought to know. She does know. What's the matter with the red-haired reed of a thing? What's the matter? What am I to do?" And he would take a gun and plunge off into the woods and make a circuit of fifteen miles or so, and come back with a couple of ruffed grouse and a rabbit or two, and say he had been having a fine time. He was a liar, and yet the good-blooded youth would not have stood and told a lie knowingly, even to gain for himself the girl he wanted. It was but the old story of a woman of younger years being older than the man. Doubtless when Clive and Hastings were seizing India there went often into the Eastern world other young men of similar blood and quality, who said good-bye, among their other good-byes, to girls who did not grasp the situation with all its relations as pertaining to the young male animal. The fellows who went

10

out with Clive and Hastings probably came back with more or less of wealth and honor and a thousand tugging fancies in their young hearts when they sought the girls again.   As far as the record goes they found most of their old sweethearts married, and all of them full faced and thick-waisted, having married young, and being more or less happy or unhappy until they died, while the young adventurers found for themselves new sweethearts, without trouble now, and thought no more of the old ones.   They had become men.

All sympathy, however, is not to be bestowed upon Sargent alone.   Barbara had her troubles, no less serious.   She could not but understand how this young giant loved her, and there is no better saying among all the proverbs than that "love begets love."   There was a wealth of clean loving and strong affection in the creature, and here was a good object for its expenditure right at hand.   What should she do?   There were nights when the young woman did not sleep well.   There was night after night when, like those of the man, her own fancies ran away with her, and she dreamed of how the struggle might be made with him to be begun then and there and carried forward, on her part at least, as it should be done by a good wife.   But there was logic in her and much filial quality, and after all, though not as years go, she was older than he, so maybe it was the best for her, but her course is not to be recommended to all the world.   She resolved not to be "carried off her feet" by Sargent.

He must wait, she said to herself. If he loved her in reality he would come back, and while he was away she could make up her mind whether she loved him well enough to be his wife. He must wait. That the girl decided and she vowed to herself to stand by the decision.

There came a moment when Sargent could no longer keep his tongue from speaking out of the fullness of his heart. It was just before his going away. The two young people were seated by the western window of the cosy sitting-room, watching the reddening of the snow on the pines and on the hills as the sun set in a cold, clear sky.

Barbara was talking earnestly. With an effort, Sargent made himself take notice that she was commenting on Thackeray and his creations. "His men are all right, but how I hate his women!" declared the fair critic, and, right then and exactly there, literary subjects were dropped from the conversations of those two people for some time to come.

There was nothing else in Sargent's world; he had no thought or care for anything but for the girl who sat facing him, her hair shining in the fading light. And this the young man told her, with such earnestness and power that Barbara paled as she heard his words. She became serious instantly, and listened to him quietly until his eloquence had spent itself, and then he stopped suddenly, frightened by her silence and seriousness. Could it be that she for whom he was as molten lava, was but unyielding ice? His glowing heart turned cold. A moment ago he had begged her to speak. Now he was afraid to hear her, and he began again to urge his love and plead for himself. At last he stopped in his wild torrent of talk, and then, answering him in a gentle voice, with a manner new and strange for the imperious Barbara, she said that she could not give the lover cause to hope that she might love him enough to be his wife.

"Why? why?" urged the stricken man.

She told him he was young, with all the world before him, even as she was, and that it was too soon for either of them to talk of marriage.

"My life seems pretty well laid out for me here," she said with a little note of sadness in her voice, "but yours is all before you. It is better for you to go out into it free; you have to win your spurs. You do not know what trials may be ahead of you, or what triumphs, or, perhaps, defeats."

"In short," interrupted Sargent, smarting under the pain of it all, "you refuse me because I am young and inexperienced, poor, and so, uncertain as to the future. You do not love me nor even care deeply for me, and you wish me a very good ten or twenty years in which to win my spurs! I tell you, Barbara Sloan, you are my spur,—you shall drive me on to fortune, and so that much of you I have won! No more, I know,—but without your love I care for nothing!"

And the poor fellow dashed out of the room and plunged out of the house into the drifts, for a walk in the snow and the almost arctic cold.

It was a cruel blow; its effects grew worse and worse the more he thought of it. But, at last, Sargent remembered that he was a man, and so must be reasonable and strong, and tender toward the woman who had inflicted the wound he was suffering from, and he floundered back to the house.

At the early lamp-lighted dinner, Barbara was a shade more sedate than usual. That was the only change in her from her usual buoyant mood. She proposed, after dinner, as it was the last night of Sargent's visit, that the evening be spent in the "old house," as the kitchen wing was called, with stories and songs for entertainment and with cider, nuts and cakes for refreshments.

"The house should be more pleasant
And the guest be more contented."

This last Barbara gave with the sing-song of Hiawatha.

Two hours later, when the bustle of Tilda's "clearing up" was over, all of those who dwelt under Judge Sloan's roof were gathered around the great hearthstone—Tilda, and Michael, too, with his fiddle, by Barbara's special invitation, for she meant to have some Norwegian music to lead up to the story-telling and talk which was sure to last until midnight, long after the hard-working Norse people were in their beds.

To begin with, the Judge, who was an enthusiastic and accomplished student of Norse lore and literature, told a blood-curdling werewolf story, and, when it was done, Michael took up his violin unasked and began to play. His music was made of that of the folk songs of Norway, with his own strange fancies woven in between. There were slow minor love songs, and odd, crashing, short-breathed dances, and funeral dirges, and frolicsome wedding lays, all coming from the little red fiddle with Michael's black eyes shining over it. At the waving of his wand of a fiddlestick, the minds of the little audience were full of the images set before them by the fantastic young-old wizard. By and by, as he played a slow, melancholy strain, his mother, Tilda, began to sing. Michael at once dropped into an accompaniment, and the two finished the song. They were urged to continue, and then their old Norwegian songs, grave and gay, followed in quick succession.

Barbara asked for a song in English. "Father has translated two or three of Tilda's songs, and she has learned the English words," she explained to Sargent, who had often before been a charmed listener to Michael's music, and who well knew Tilda's Norwegian songs, from hearing her as she sang at her work about the house.

"Please sing 'The Cave of Silver,' Tilda, and in English," she asked the old woman, who was pleased and flushed with the joy of singing her national songs to three admiring hearers.

Michael at once began playing a strong, low-toned, monotonous strain. He drew his bow with vibrat-

ing force across the strings, and swung his ungainly
body from side to side.

Tilda swung in her high-backed rocking-chair.
She closed her eyes, listening to the long wail of the
violin, and, when she opened them, she seemed to
look out beyond the walls of the house to the
distant snow-covered hills. Her eyes had in them
bright lights, but they seemed not to see anything
but the pictures drawn in imagination by the words
she sang.

The air of the song was one of those unchanging,
long-drawn tunes of the people, dwelling on one
note throughout a line almost, to fall in a minor
interval at the last word,—a sort of music which
grows as naturally among primitive peoples as does
the moss upon the beech tree.

There was a wild yet melancholy power in the
strange contralto voice which poured forth the old
Saga without a tremor of age or weakness. The
sturdy form of the singer rocked slightly backward
and forward, as her chair rocked. Her hands were
once or twice raised a little with the impulse of her
song, and then dropped carelessly in her lap. In
the pauses between verses, the violin took up and
continued the unvarying strain with piercing itera-
tion and strenuous power, and then, as the singer
resumed, dropped into a simple, harmonious
accompaniment.

This was the song they sang, old Tilda and the
violin:

"Go, seek me the Cave of Silver!
Go, find me the Cave of Silver!
Go, seek me the Cave of Silver!"
    Said Hilda to Brock the Bold.
"And then you may kiss me often,
And then you may ring my finger,
And then you may bind our true love
    With a round hoop of gold.

"For Hilma, the witch, has told me
That up in the wild Lapp mountains
There lieth the Cave of Silver,
    More precious than caves of gold;
Beyond the purple pastures,
Beyond the shining meadows,
High up in the wild Lapp mountains
    Seek ye, oh, Brock the Bold!

"Bring me no skins of foxes,
Bring me no fur of otter,
Boast not your fighting vessels;
    Hear me, oh, Brock the Bold!
For I would lie upon velvet,
And sail in a golden galley,
And naught but the Cave of Silver
    Will win me, Brock the Bold!"

"I go," said Brock, right proudly,
"I go to the far-off mountains,
To seek the Cave of Silver,
    More precious than caves of gold!

But when the wild Lapp arrows
Have pierced the heart that loved you,
I leave my curse on the woman
    Who slaughtered Brock the Bold!"

And Summer passed, and Winter
Came down from the far-off mountains,
But back from the Cave of Silver
    Came never Brock the Bold.
And the maiden Hilda waited,
And sat at her door at evening,
And watched the gleaming lances
    Of the North so bright and cold.

"Oh, wild Norwegian gallants,
Go, seek for my lonely lover,
Go, seek for the Cave of Silver,
    Where tarries Brock the Bold!"
But the wild Norwegian gallants
They laughed at the cruel maiden
Who away to the wild Lapp arrows
    Had driven Brock the Bold!

And she mourned for the Cave of Silver,
And she mourned for the purple pastures,
And she mourned for her lonely lover,
    Till her heart and her face grew cold!
But back from the shining meadows,
Or back from the wild Lapp mountains,
Or back from the Cave of Silver,
    Came never Brock the Bold!

Long afterwards Sargent, humming the ancient air to a sympathetic musician, contrived to get it in written form as it appears here, a wild spirit imprisoned behind conventional bars at last:

There was a long silence after the song was finished, and the wind blustered about the chimney and sung its own wild song. And then Judge Sloan courteously thanked old Tilda and her son and during the conversation which followed they disappeared from the room. After a time the Judge went to his book-room to get a volume or two of the old Norse literature he loved, to show to Sargent, and the two young people were left alone. Sargent sat looking into the fire, and, at some slight movement or remark from Barbara, he looked up at her, for she stood by the table, the lamp shining on her face. Sargent, too, arose and came close to Barbara. There was in his eyes a bright, steady look, and his face had in it a new firmness and resolve.

"The maiden Hilda was not the last woman to send a poor fellow out into the world," he said. Then his face changed. "I am going to-morrow, but I am afraid there will be no mourning or watching for me"—and his voice broke, for, as has been said before, he was but a boy, after all.

Barbara grew rosy and then pale. She remained silent, except for an inarticulate murmur of sorrow or regret—who can tell?—and Judge Sloan re-entered the room, his arm piled high with precious books. There was a long evening together, of legend, story and song, and then they all said good-night.

In the morning, after the three had breakfasted cheerily together, Sargent took up his homeward journey, this time with a party of woodsmen, with dogs and sledges, and the journey was quickly made. The youngster's heart was heavy, but he was buoyed up by hope. Somehow, it would not fade out of him. And he hummed the old song of the Northland, and thought how he would force a different ending to the tale of the "Cave of Silver."

CHAPTER XVI.

IN A NEW WORLD.

In all the world there is nothing so unconsciously helpless as a young man, without means or friends, in a great city. Especially is this true where the young fellow is smarting under the first real trouble of his life. In seeking shelter and food, he of necessity must make acquaintances, and being youthful and hungry for society knows no better than to accept such companionship as comes with the routine and machinery of daily living.

Sargent, on the lookout for a room, called one morning at a tall house of stone and brick on Wabash Avenue. He had found the house in which he had formerly lodged when in Chicago calmly moving down the street in a manner as dignified as could be expected from a large frame building at the end of a rope wound around a windlass. Sargent was impressed but disappointed. He must begin anew his search for a home. The wide avenue looked like a village street, with its houses set back from the wooden pavements, with green plats of grass surrounded by painted iron or wood picket fences, beside wide sidewalks, with grass plats between them and the roadway, and spreading trees on either side. Mrs. Graves' house was an exception to the general rule on Wabash

Avenue. It had no green grass plat—its basement
rose from unsodded ground, carefully graveled, it
is true.   There was an iron fence and gate, and iron-
grated windows all around the basement story.
Two clanging doorbells alarmed the house whenever any one sought entrance at the basement, or
stood on the landing at the top of the steps leading
up to the double front doors of black walnut.   A
scared-looking, shabby young girl always opened
these doors.   She admitted Sargent, on the day of
his first call, and, after closing the door, amused the
caller by standing with wide admiring eyes looking
at him very approvingly before she disappeared,
leaving the visitor standing upon the polished floor
of black and white marble looking helplessly at the
high narrow walls and stairway, and the massive
ugly hall chair and hat-rack of black walnut, the
sole furniture in sight.   No one ever sat down on
the chair, or hung his hat upon the arms of that
truculent-looking rack.   One's instinct was to keep
hat in hand and person in readiness, as with one
foot uplifted, for instant flight.

Yet Sargent did not run when he had been
admitted to this hall of silence and decorous gloom.
He stood there waiting for the proprietress, having
told the "slavey" who opened the door that he
desired to look at a room for himself.   As he waited,
he felt a presence, and, looking up, saw a beautiful
child, or rather a young girl, coming down the stairs.
She glanced shyly at Sargent as she turned the
corner and ran down the basement stairs which were
directly under the main stairway.   Sargent had a

sheepish feeling that the pallid serving maid had
sent this lovely child in to take a look at him. If
he had before any inclination to run, the sight of
that sweet, childish face framed in wreaths of dark
hair, and that graceful, slender figure, would have
checked him. He decided, at once, to be suited
with the lodgings provided by Mrs. Graves, whose
house had been recommended to him by a young
man at the office. Of course Sargent had no serious
intentions, nor any even tinged with gallantry,
toward the beautiful stranger—he was only attracted
by that irresistible loadstone to a young man's fancy,
a fair face.

Mrs. Graves, noiseless of step, downcast of eyes,
quiet and black-clad, with a widow's bonnet and
a veil casting additional gloom over the place,
appeared, and with her Sargent arranged to have a
large square sleeping room on the third floor, paying a not unreasonable sum for it. His meals he
had chosen to eat at restaurants. In Mrs. Graves'
house no table was set for boarders. She rented
her rooms, most of them by the year, to men of a
sort of regular irregularity, so far as hours were
concerned, but certainty as to pay, and knew and
cared no more about them. Her name, Mrs. Graves,
probably caused the uncanny suggestion, but her
face reminded Sargent of one of the long, narrow,
white marble headstones which mark so many
graves in the cemeteries of the West. Her countenance was long and narrow, with a square forehead and chin, and she was always pale. Her
features were regular. Her hair was dark, and

rich in color and profusion, but her eyes and lips were colorless and her look was still and expressionless.   She was always dressed in black, her gowns fitting exquisitely her graceful figure, but only once or twice did Sargent ever see her without her widow's bonnet with its long crepe veil streaming down her back.   She was often pulling on or off black kid gloves, out of which her white hands came with startling effect.

All work in that house, from answering the doorbell to carrying up and down stairs and putting in place heavy furniture and trunks, seemed to be done in solitary struggles, with which no one interfered, by the slender, shabby girl, whose abbreviated name, "Em," was called out all day from various parts of the house by whoever had a task for her. On the day after Sargent took possession of his room, when he was coming downstairs in the morning, he met the undersized, thin-armed Em bringing his trunk upstairs. The young man from the country was surprised at seeing a girl laboring in this manner.   He seized the trunk, as the panting woman creature stopped for breath on the step where she was laboring, and, unheeding her protest, shouldered it and ran up to his room, setting down the heavy thing with a bang which shook the house.

"Em!" called the voice of Mrs. Graves from the basement, "Em! what are you doing?"

"Nothing, 'm," the tearful voice of Em replied over the banisters. "It's the new lodger, a-openin' his trunk."

The pitiful figure now came to Sargent's door, and stood with a hand upon each post. She was a young creature, stunted in growth, broad-shouldered, with skinny arms, and she was bent and thin. Her face had the pallor of a prison, almost, but her eyes were bright, with an expression of mingled audacity and fear, which was the surprising feature of her otherwise commonplace face.

"Oh! Mister, won't I get it!" she exclaimed.

"Why? Is that what I get for helping you?" said Sargent, laughing.

"Oh, but you might a' jarred the plaster off the second front's ceiling, and then what would happen to me? I'll never dare tell Mrs. Graves what you did! Why, that's nothing for me. I tug and I lug and I fetch and I carry all day, and purty nigh all night sometimes and nobody ever cares or thinks anything about it. Say, Mister, what's yer name?"

"Sargent," was the reply, and evidently not at all to the satisfaction of the energetic Em, for she expostulated:

"Why, that's a common name—excuse me, I don't mean any harm, but, somehow, I thought you might be a Montmorenci or Llewellyn, or some one of a more romanticer name than Sargent, but of course a Montmorenci would never a' carried his trunk upstairs, I might a' known."

Sargent laughed again. "I imagine you have a taste for novels," he said good-naturedly, drawing out the eager mind which seemed caged in the frail body leaning against his door-posts. "What is your name? I hear you called 'Em.'"

11

"I am called Em," said the girl, earnestly, "by those that know no better, but my name is 'Grace Emily.' Any one that is really my friend calls me 'Grace Emily.' That's what Elsie calls me, but she is the only one."

" 'Grace Emily'; why, I'll call you that, from this time on, and then you'll forgive me for making all that noise, won't you?"

"I had already forgiven you," said Em, with a stately emphasis not before employed by her, and infinitely laughter provoking it was, "but now, since you name me aright, you are thrice forgiven."

"Em!" shrieked a loud, musical voice from the attic, and, without further parley the magnanimous heroine disappeared to the upper regions.

CHAPTER XVII.

THE PITY OF IT.

Sargent was immersed by day in his round of duties and studies at his office, but in the gloomy house on Wabash Avenue he began to feel an intense interest. The people in it attracted him from the first, and soon his keen, alert sympathies became aroused and then thoroughly enlisted upon the side of the weakest combatant in a struggle which, at last, became the supreme subject of his thoughts.

He soon learned that Mrs. Graves had but recently returned from a visit to England, where she had been to settle the affairs of her dead sister, a burlesque singer, Kitty Romaine, the mother of Elsie. Later on he was to know that at the time of this visit the yachting nobleman who was Elsie's father, though unacknowledged, had settled upon the girl, under the control and management of Mrs. Graves, a sum of money sufficient for the education and ample support of his unfortunate child, and he was to learn in time, too, that Mrs. Graves had her own ideas as to how this money should be expended, and for whose benefit.

That Elsie was destined for the stage, Sargent knew from the first. He noted with curious and delighted interst all the new life around him, and in a few weeks had become entangled in its meshes, but in his own honest and fearless and clean-going fashion.

The only woman lodger in the house was Rosie Clyde, a passé beauty, who had won money and praise during the brief summer of her reign on the burlesque and variety stage, and who seemed to have some sort of a claim on Mrs. Graves. She had been a white terror in her day, but was now harmless enough. Sargent looked with the astonishment of youth upon her, for she was the first member of the theatrical world that he had ever seen at close range. A woman with fewer claims to beauty or style he had never seen, and yet half a dozen years before she had turned the heads of the gilded youth of New York and of London. There was, though, a good-natured, happy-go-lucky way about the overblown stage rose which was mildly captivating to the lonely youngster in a strange city, and many a long talk he had with her in Mrs. Graves' economically lighted, stuffy little parlor, with Elsie sitting listlessly by, content but entirely without interest in the lively tales of accident by flood and field, and adventures rare and bizarre with which Miss Clyde regaled her auditors. The actress seemed to have a sort of careless regard for Elsie, and for this the poor girl was so grateful that she rewarded her with a kind of adoration.

In pursuance of the settled plan of Mrs. Graves, that Elsie should go upon the burlesque stage, the girl was taken regularly to her dancing master, and she spent hours daily practicing her voice before piano and mirror, for it was essential that she should look pretty and sing in time with her accompaniment, whether she had any real singing voice of attracting quality or not.

The girl's figure was the embodiment of grace, and her face was "alone her fortune," as Miss Clyde enthusiastically told her again and again. Dressed in shabby black, without any aid from the filigree of toilet, she, in truth, could not appear anywhere without giving delight to all who saw her. It was like the carrying along the street of some flower to see her go and faces lighted as she walked. But there was so much unconscious goodness and gentleness in her that no one ever spoke to her or even looked upon her too boldly in the strident Western city, even when she was in company with Rosie Clyde, brave in cast-off stage finery skillfully made over, with bleached hair and a complexion not her own. Elsie was often chaperoned by the burlesque fairy, and, as a matter of fact, she was a veritable dragon. Both she and Mrs. Graves well knew the pecuniary value of modesty and virtue in a young candidate for theatrical honors. Once on the stage it would be different, but now the slave girl was being prepared for the auction block, or for more such sales than one.

As the weeks passed, Sargent found from his talks with Elsie, when the older women were not by her side, that Elsie herself had no relish for the programme laid out for her. This surprised the young man, for, to him, knowing as he was in many ways, there was a certain fascination about everything con-

nected with the theater. In those days he spent
every evening when he was not at work, at some one
of the play houses, but always before the curtain.
He had sense enough to cherish his illusions. He
never dared let himself go to the stage door. He
dreaded to see Pauline turn into a commonplace,
well-dressed lady getting into a hack, or little Eva
eating pink and white candy, or Ruy Blas in a silk
hat and trousers. But to his mind there was, after
all, a glow around the names of theatrical folk and
he could not see how a girl of such striking beauty
as that of Elsie could, though he had clean doubts,
wish for any career except that which would give to
the whole world what it worships, in its most
dazzling form, but as he came to know Elsie he
found that in nature she was timid and shrinking to
such a degree that the rude regard of strangers was
a positive agony and that the thought of stage life
was abhorrent to her. When realization of this condition had found a firm seat in his mind he could not
keep from speaking of it to Rosie Clyde. One night
in June, while they were sitting on the piazza, Elsie
being away with her aunt for the evening, Sargent
opened the subject.

"She isn't fitted for the life of the stage world,
and I don't believe any one can make a successful
actress out of her," he said.

"Oh, yes, we can," said Rosie Clyde, easily, while
she ate cherries and snapped the stones at Sargent.
"She's so pretty she'll go, anyway, no matter what
she does."

"But she doesn't like it," urged Sargent, "she's

too retiring and not fond of that sort of thing, you know. It's all right, of course, for those who are fitted for it, but Elsie isn't, and never can be."

"Oh, stuff and nonsense, Mr. Sargent! What is your first name, anyway?" and without waiting for his slow-coming reply, Rosie Clyde went on: "Why, she'll be all right as soon as she gets going. One or two champagne suppers and she'll be as gay as the gayest. A little Dutch courage, and she'll be as jolly and successful as her mother was! Why! Are you going?"

"Good night," said Sargent from the gate, and its latch clicked behind him. He fairly swayed as he walked rapidly along the broad sidewalk, and turned down a street leading to the lake shore, and, under his breath, he was cursing with such fierce vigor as he had never exerted before. It was some time before he could bring himself to talk with Miss Clyde again, but that easy-going person soon won him over to being civil to her, by her perfect ignorance of his antipathy and by a thousand little sallies of good-natured talk to him and any one else who happened to be in the same house with her. Most of all, he was reconciled to this feminine monster of morals by the evident love with which she was regarded by poor friendless Elsie, for from her aunt the child knew nothing but cold, hard displeasure and task-setting, and so to her even Elsie's gentle nature could not cling. In the kindly-mannered Rosie Clyde the girl found something to care for, and upon her, who was inwardly as cold

and unfeeling as Mrs. Graves herself, the neglected
creature lavished her affections.

So, as the summer passed, his surroundings took
hold of Sargent.   Interested and drawn out of himself by Elsie and her future, he studied Mrs.
Graves with profound attention and found her a
creature new, strange, and, finally, awful to him.
Her voice was an astonishingly deep contralto, low
and well controlled, except when she was very
angry, when it was harsh and threatening enough
to frighten any one.   In excitement Mrs. Graves
was a marble-white, black draped, raucous voiced
feminine demon, whose whip of scorpions was her
tongue.   The awful eloquence of the ancient bards
and orators of the Irish was hers; she excelled in
vituperation and in denunciation of such bitterness
as seemed to blast the understanding while one
listened to it.   Blighting curses flew from her lips
like those envenomed arrows of the Indians of the
tropics, which leave festerings in the flesh of their
victims, and so cannot be robbed of their prey even
when withdrawn from their bodies.   Poor little
Elsie trembled and shrank under the affliction of her
aunt's displeasure, and it was small wonder.   There
was no man nor woman who was content to hear
Mrs. Graves' recital of her unveiled thoughts,
opinions and desires.   These paroxysms of passion
were not common with Mrs. Graves, and even with
all their terrors, the mood which followed them,
lasting for weeks, was more unbearable to those
whose misfortune it was to live under her dominion.
These unhappy mortals she treated with a cold,

unbending displeasure, with sharp censoriousness thrown in for seasoning, no matter how obsequiously and carefully the poor subjects of her wrath strove to appease her.

Sargent studied and looked upon the gradual unfolding of this malevolent character with unmixed astonishment. At first he could not credit his own senses nor conclusions, but, finally, he became convinced of the reality of the vicious nature with which he had come in contact, and from it his soul recoiled in horror. To him the ideal of womanhood had been formed in an ideal home and society, from the high standards which are constantly held up before young Americans, and he had been used to attributing everything that was good and beautiful to women and expecting nothing but high aspiration and counsel, or harmless merriment and spirited conversation from them.

Mrs. Graves was a revelation in human wickedness made additionally astonishing by the fact that she was a woman. At first he had not been able to believe the evidence of his own senses. He thought there must be some extenuation, some unknown softener of what seemed so hard and cruel. He came finally to see that the human heart can be as relentless as the unbending laws of nature herself, that there are human beings with whom one can come in contact with as much safety as one can put a hand in the fire.

CHAPTER XVIII.

THE ROOM OF DEAD VANITIES.

One evening at the end of summer, on his return from his office, Rosie Clyde met Sargent at the street door. "I was lying in wait for you," she said. "I have something to show you. Prepare to be dazzled."

By Miss Clyde's freedom of speech and movement, Sargent divined that Mrs. Graves was out of the house, as, when she was there, no one spoke naturally; and he was right in his conclusions. Mrs. Graves had gone to consult her attorney, leaving Miss Clyde to a task which pleased her very soul. This was to make a list of the contents of seven huge boxes from London, containing the wardrobe and belongings of poor Kitty Romaine.

Mrs. Graves had packed the boxes before she left England, after her sister's death; following her, they had been shipped to her by a sailing vessel, so that they had arrived long after her. They had, after some delay, been unpacked, and now all the finery, the jewelry, and dainty belongings of the belle of the footlights were to be sold for the utmost penny that they would bring. Miss Clyde had herself unpacked the boxes in a large room just then unoccupied by a lodger, and so available for the purpose; the variety singers' butterfly possessions were arranged to the very best advantage, for the benefit of those who should come to buy.

Sargent looked around him with a feeling of mingled dismay and admiring curiosity. He was reassured by the sight of Elsie sitting in one of the windows, looking delightedly at the gorgeous array of velvet, satin and brocade robes spread out on tables and chairs. A pang shot through his heart as he noted the brightness of the girl's eyes, and the flush on her face as she cast fairly adoring glances at the finery around her. He noted the longing eyes, with their slumbering covetousness awakening, yet could not understand their language. To him they were perfect in beauty, those gray Irish eyes, shadowed by black brows, and made bewitching by long dark lashes, but something in their expression now frightened him, without his knowing why.

"Just see there," Miss Clyde exclaimed, going up to the mantel shelf upon which, from end to end, stretched a line of the most dainty and fanciful shoes, slippers and sandals in the world. Spangled and overlaid with gold and gems, of every extravagant shape, color and material, the fairy footwear was set out ready for inspection.

"And look," said Elsie, designating by a glance a table upon which were heaped fans of every size, rainbows starred by jewels, Sargent thought, as Elsie took them up, one or two at a time, and waved them around her, and over her head, as she danced slowly and rhythmically around the table.

Over one sofa lay a cloak fit for royalty, splendid

in crimson and ermine, and over another trailed a long court train of cloth of gold. There were filmy gauze skirts in bright colored heaps upon the floor —flame-colored and blue and green, yellow, black and snow-white, and upon the dressing table blazed jewels, the real indistinguishable from the false gems, but making a show that rivaled any jeweler's showcase that Sargent had ever seen.

There were endless fripperies of linen, gauze and lace, and ribbons, for which Sargent knew no name. He sat down, pleasantly entertained, while the faded burlesque beauty and the fresh, budding maiden displayed the gewgaws and draperies of the dead singer.

"Sophia La Belle is coming to dinner to-night, with her manager, Simon Strauss, and you may be sure Sophie will never leave without some of these things," said Miss Clyde, at last, when Sargent began to tire of the show.

Elsie came and sat down on a chair near Sargent, unmindful of the rose-colored silken gown hanging over it.

"I'm to be all dressed up to show off, too," she said, with a half smile, and a tremor in her voice.

"To the manager?" asked Sargent.

"Yes, and if they like me they may take me with them in their company," said Elsie.

The town billboards and fences were all plastered over with glaring advertisements of "Sophia La Belle's Paralyzing Blondes," and as Sargent heard this announcement he felt sick at heart, and desperate.

He left the room of cast-off splendors without more than a word or two, and sat in his room brooding, silent and savage, until dark. When the street lamps were lighted he went out on the steps, brushing against an oily-haired, obese, be-ringed and highly perfumed personage, with small ferret-like eyes, clean shaven face, and a large hooked nose. He recognized the theatrical manager without trouble. He was nauseating, but Sargent was glad he had escaped the "Star" of The Blondes; she had evidently preceded Simon Strauss, as there had lingered a strong smell of patchouly all the length of the hallway, and a high voice could be heard in Mrs. Graves' parlor.

Who can tell the disgust with which Sargent thought of the company surrounding the beautiful girl who was beginning to fill all his thoughts, that evening? He walked through the streets until long after midnight, for he knew the house would not be rid of its visitors until after the return of the whole party from the theater and supper. When he ventured to go there toward morning, there was nothing to remind him of them but the smell of sour beer about the house.

He slept uneasily. There came before his eyes, in his dreaming, a red-crowned head and scenes of a cleaner life, as they came to him hourly throughout the day; but here was another life of the present, and his sympathies and emotions were all roused.

That one who had been so earnestly and clearly in love should so soon love elsewhere and anew seems strange, but human nature is human nature, and this was, in fact, not the love with deepest roots. There is no suffering so acute as that of the young, because they do not know that there is "balm in Gilead." To them darkness shuts down on the world as if never to lift. They cannot hope; their faith is too gossamer-like a thing to stand the storm. It is only when one has reached middle life that faith and hope have grown robust enough to endure the world's convulsions.

The cruel early blow to Sargent's dearest hopes had found a helpless and bewildered victim. He suffered silently and deeply. Work and new environment brought a sort of benumbed relief, and slowly the outer world pressed in upon the morbid consciousness.

It was certain to befall a youngster in Sargent's case that the pulse of life should seek to some way sustain itself by creating new interests, and that from those who lived near him some should be attracted to him.

The bruised and sore spirit inevitably seeks to adjust itself to its fate as surely as does the broken and anguished body. It is human to crave and gain relief. He who laughs at the renewing of interest in life in one whose affections have suffered, may as well laugh at the efforts of the sufferer from bodily wounds to obtain comfort. The disconsolate young soul looks and leans toward happiness as the parched plant yearns for rain. Unconscious both sufferers may be, but they surely seek relief, and God has so made the world that to most of his creatures relief comes, when their extremity is reached.

To be able to take an interest in another human being than himself, to think perhaps he could be of use and help somewhere in the world, was to bring a thrill of renewed life to Robert Sargent, and inevitably these experiences and thoughts came to him, after months of brooding over the torn fancies and ideals of his life. Feeling had not died within him—he was alive and the great world was whirling around him. Gradually it came about that he thought less bitterly of Barbara Sloan and his wasted love; by degrees he began to live again.

CHAPTER XIX.

SHOWN THE DOOR.

As Sargent turned to go up the second flight of stairs the door of the Room of Dead Vanities was softly opened, and he heard within Em's hushing "Sh!" He quietly walked over to the half-open portal. Em's hand swiftly drew him into the room, and as soon as the door was closed a blaze of light flooded the room. On a table, her hand at the chandelier, stood a radiant creature; she was not recognizable at first as Elsie, but it was she.

Now with her finger on her lip she stood like a statue, wide-eyed and half smiling at Sargent's amazed looks. She was dressed in a cloud of filmy, lace-like black, her bare neck, shoulders and arms rising out of the silky, shining jet-colored gown like snow. Jewels blazed in her ears and around her throat and upon her arms, a golden girdle encircled her waist, and upon her feet were golden sandals glittering like gems.

Suddenly, before Sargent could speak, the bewildering vision moved. Elsie sprang lightly to the floor and ran up to him as he stood by the door with Em, too surprised to speak.

"I sat up to show myself to you in my finery," said Elsie, softly. "I wouldn't take off so much as a bracelet until you had seen me! And am I not gay?'

The girl drifted like a leaf before a breeze over in front of a tall mirror, and began to dance before it noiselessly and with a light grace which made her look more than ever like some creature from the land of sprites.

Poor Sargent! It was all over with him now. From indignant pity to infatuation is a short step, and he had taken it before the dancer had looked around at him from her posing before the mirror. It was not long; all in a moment she turned from her own bright reflection and ran, this time straight into Sargent's open arms. He touched her reverently and gently, taking both of her hands in his, and leading her to a seat. There was the innocent coquetry of a child of three years in the girl, and that was all. She looked at him with the pride of a baby who wears its first red shoes.

"Elsie," said Sargent, his voice trembling, "don't go with the theater people! I love you. Let me take care of you. Let me make you my wife and then you can go away from here with me and live with me always."

"Hush!" said Elsie. "Em hears you—Grace Emily, I mean."

"Never mind Grace Emily, Elsie, I want to say I love you before the whole world. Will you marry me?"

The girl held her face in her hands for a few moments, then she looked bravely up.

"I have never hoped that you would love me, or imagined it," she said, "but I have wished it from the moment I saw you, and I have prayed that you

12

would, and now I am happy!" Then she began to
sob, but checked herself immediately.

"Take off those jewels, and that dancing dress,"
said Sargent, "and remember, dear, forever. I am
a poor boy, and you will be the wife of a man who
is struggling for himself and you in the world. You
shall have all that my love and work can give you,
—no more—you understand?"

"I understand," said Elsie, "and I will love you
and obey you always. I don't want anything but you!"

Sargent took up the girl's little white hand and
kissed it. She trembled and held up her lips to
his, and he kissed them; and then they said good
night. The girls softly stole away, and, after
standing a minute in the dark room, Sargent went
upstairs.

Mrs. Graves was never visible before noon, and it
was the evening of the next day before Sargent
could see her. Then, as she sat in state at her
table, entered to her Sargent with Elsie by his side.

The young man began at once the business of the
moment, and asked in the most matter of fact
manner for the hand of Elsie. Then, after a
moment of frozen surprise, Mrs. Graves gave the
intrepid man a very bad quarter of an hour. She
told him anew her plans for Elsie and declared her
unalterable purpose of carrying them out.

To Sargent's attempted expostulations she made
the unanswerable rejoinder of curtly ordering him
out of the house.

"Go at once," she said. "I give you half an hour
to pack your trunks and get out."

Then Sargent turned upon her. He poured out in an irresistible volley all the anger and disgust which tormented his soul. He advanced as she shrunk from him until he stood over her as she cowered against the wall, and he rained down bitterest denunciation upon her until Elsie crept to him and plucked his sleeve and begged him to desist.

"Come with me, Elsie," he cried, trying to take her hand. "Come now;" but Elsie, looking at him helplessly, was bodily taken in hand, and half-pulled and half-carried away by her aunt, who had rallied as soon as Sargent turned his attention to Elsie, and now she withdrew with the young girl to her private room.

Sargent was stunned. He looked at the closed door of Mrs. Graves' sitting-room and rushed to open it, but found it locked. He shook it, and finally hurled himself against it with all his force, but the barrier was unyielding. Suddenly his reason asserted itself and he stood still. He was acting like one demented, and, as he realized it, he slowly turned to go.

"Hist," came a sharp sibilant sound as he walked along the second floor landing on his way to his room to pack up his belongings ready for instant removal. He looked all about him, and, as he mounted the next flight of stairs, he saw leaning over the banisters in the half light of the hall, the figure of Em. She grasped Sargent by the coat sleeve as he came within her reach and hurried him into his room, shutting the door softly behind her. Then, in a loud whisper, she said, "Trust her not!"

"Who?" said Sargent, surprised out of himself.
"Not Elsie?" "No! No!" emphatically whispered
the tragic Em; "Miss Clyde! Trust her not, she is
an enemy and will basely deceive you!" Here
in somewhat stilted phrase was confirmation of
Sargent's own premonition, and therefore it was
strong.

"But who am I to trust?" he muttered, half to
himself—

"Trust me!" said the small slavey, laying her
thin, bony hand on her hollow chest. "I love Elsie,
and I am determined that you shall rescue her from
this palace of hate!"

Sargent lost all thought of amusement over the
girl's grandiloquence, in his intense anxiety, and his
hopeless hope for help from some source. He
looked at the pitiful little work-worn figure, with its
earnest, beseeching face, and it came upon him with
a feeling of self-pity that here indeed was the only
being in the world to be depended upon to keep
him in communication with Elsie.

"Trust me," repeated little Em, and Sargent did
trust her. Hastily writing a letter of promise and
comfort to Elsie, he gave it to his new-found friend
and ally, with strict commands as to its secret
delivery. The girl looked ecstatically at the billet.
It was the first bona-fide love letter her eyes had
ever beheld, even on the outside, although in the
pages of story books, complete letter writers and
"Dream-Books," they were her favorite study.
"Remember I trust you, Grace Emily," said
Sargent. She did not reply, but stooped down, hid

the letter in one of her shabby shoes, and with a look of farewell, and the words, "Be of good cheer!" she left the room.

Within ten minutes Sargent's trunk, locked and strapped, ready for transfer, stood in the middle of the apartment which he had already left forever. He saw no sign of life on the stairs, or anywhere, as he went. He left the money for his week's lodging on the hat-rack table in the dismal front hall, and went out into the street. There was no face at any window or door—no signal nor mark of interest from the house which held so much that was dear to him that it seemed to hold all his world.

Elsie's imploring, loving face haunted him. He did not blame her for not coming at once to him. He knew well the shrinking, dependent nature which could not avoid yielding passively to the strong hand which had drawn her away from him just at the moment of decision, before the real situation had become clear to her, but he could not keep from raging at the thought of the deserted girl, left without help or love. But even momentary quickness and strength of will on her part might have given her to him and made an end at one stroke of all her troubles.

Now he had but one object in life, to get Elsie out of her prison and marry her forthwith, and then what? Visions of his mother's home and of the sure refuge his young wife would find there while he was seeking his fortune in the West, filled his mind satisfactorily as regarded the future. All he had to do was to get possession of Elsie and marry her. The present held the main problem, he thought. The future, of course, was bright, and held no uncertainty.

CHAPTER XX.

THE RELEASE OF ELSIE.

Sargent spent the night at a hotel, that comfortable refuge of the homeless, and, after getting himself settled in a new boarding house the next day —this he knew must be a temporary home, for the surveying outfit he was engaged for was to go West soon—he went out at evening to look for Billy Barnes. He needed a strong friend and helper, and Barnes, who was in a lawyer's office in the city, was just the man his heart craved.

During the past few weeks Sargent's daily life had been one of severe work, often extending late into the night, in preparation for his start West on the railway survey in October. And in addition to what was demanded by his work his attention had been gradually concentrating upon Elsie and her surroundings in the forbidding house on Wabash Avenue, so that, without knowing it, the youngster had neglected and temporarily forgotten the few friends he had in the town. Barnes greeted him with unshaken cordiality, however, and soon the classmates were walking at a great pace through the lighted streets.

Barnes laughed before Sargent had fairly made a beginning to his story.

"Another girl!" he exclaimed. "Has she red hair this time?"

Sargent stopped short on the sidewalk, and by the flaring gaslight his face had for a moment an angry look. Then he walked on in moody silence. He did not hear what Barnes was saying. Before his fancy, stronger than reality, rose a vivid, riant face crowned by glowing hair. A scent as of pine trees was in the air, and all around him the fields of grain and clover seemed to spread. That was reality, he thought, as he strove to regain hold of himself, and this, the city and all the people in it, but a morbid dream.

Barnes took hold of his arm and shook it. "You're not offended, old man?"

"No, of course not, Billy! I may as well tell you, though, that the red-haired girl refused me. Let that end it. Now, as I was telling you——"

And he went on with his story. Barnes was soon thoroughly aroused, and he entered with all his heart into his friend's plans. It was indeed more than could be expected, and as he said, "too good to be true," that he should be concerned in an elopement, for this and nothing less was what Sargent had determined upon. It was the only thing to do, speaking in all seriousness, he explained, and then he set forth his plans in detail.

Elsie went twice a week to an afternoon dancing class, in one of the theater buildings down town. Sometimes she was accompanied by Rosie Clyde, sometimes by Em. Sargent's scheme was, with the assistance of Em, with whom it was easy for him to communicate, to have Elsie slip out of the dancing room some day and meet him in the hallway, and

then, the rest was easy. To Barnes, Sargent
confided all the arrangements necessary for the performance of a strictly legal marriage ceremony
within a few minutes of the time when Elsie should
be safe in Sargent's care, at the doors of the dancing
master's rooms.

The two friends discussed every detail of their
enterprise. Sargent and Elsie, immediately after
the marriage ceremony, were to be hurried into a
carriage, Barnes being the driver, to Barnes' office,
where they were to await the time of departure of
the train which should carry the young pair to
Sargent's Michigan home. All that remained to be
done now was to get word to Elsie, so that on the
following Thursday, at the time of her next dancing
class, she should be ready for her wedding and
flight. Sargent and Barnes parted late that night,
having arranged it so that each could find the other
easily or communicate with him at any time, day or
night.

When Sargent met Em, the third conspirator, the
next evening, that romantic damsel's spirit was
swollen with such pride as no one could well depict.
Here was she, the despised and persecuted Em,
walking along the avenue upon the arm of a tall,
handsome young gentleman who bent over her
solicitously and talked in lowest tones. She
fervently wished that some acquaintance might pass
by, only to see it, even in the uncertain light of the
September evening, with only a street lamp now
and then to make the darkness visible. It was true
that the low-toned voice discoursing on themes of

love and adventure was vibrating with emotions
inspired by another than herself, but Em did not
mind that. The situation was full of romance, and
was intoxicating. She was, inwardly, a little disappointed at the prosaic meeting planned by
Sargent; it all seemed a little tame, to her fancy—
the dingy place down town, the office of the Justice
of the Peace and the railway station, and all in broad
daylight, too. Em had formed visions of a midnight
escape, with a rope ladder, fashioned, who knows?
but by her own hands, and Sargent's practical
arrangements were so different from her dreams!
She said nothing, though, but concentrated her
attention, very faithfully, upon remembering exactly
every direction, and every message she was to
deliver from Sargent to Elsie.

Just at parting, near the house, Em said, and
somehow it sent a stab to Sargent's fast beating
heart:

"Don't be too disappointed, Mr. Sargent, if we
aren't there, Thursday. Elsie has not been out of
her room or able to sit up since yesterday; she can't
eat or sleep, she says, but Mrs. Graves says she is
only 'playing sick,' and she won't believe there is
really anything wrong with Elsie's health. I think
myself she'll be all right when she has heard from
you."

"But, Em," said Sargent, "you must tell me to-
morrow night how Elsie is—or—be sure to be up at
five o'clock to-morrow morning, and meet me at the
door. I'll be there; I can't ring the bell, you know,
but you come to the door at five, Em! Do."

"Of course I will," promised Em, and then she ran down to the basement entrance and disappeared.

So little Elsie was sick. It pressed upon him like a smothering nightmare. He feared, he knew not what. Certainly it was unreasonable, "as all fear is," thought the young man, but he could not shake off the foreboding which oppressed him.

Before sunrise in the morning Sargent was at Mrs. Graves' door, and promptly at five o'clock came Em with brush and hot water, ready for her morning task of scrubbing the high white stone doorsteps. She set down the heavy pail she carried, and stood, pale and red-eyed in the morning light, looking at Sargent.

"Been up all night with Elsie. She's very sick. I'm scared about her," she said simply, with an appealing look, and pitying too, at the great fellow standing there helpless.

"Em!" he said, "call Mrs. Graves, and tell her she must have a doctor for Elsie. Tell her I shall come at noon, and if she has not called a doctor before then, I shall bring one, and he shall see Elsie, too! Run, Em, run!"

At noon Sargent rang the door bell—he had an hour from his office at noon—and Rosie Clyde opened the door. She would not admit Sargent, but she spoke kindly to him, telling him that Elsie was ill, but not seriously, and that a physician had been sent for, and would soon be there. To Sargent's imploring look she only said, "Impossible. You can't see her!" Hearing footsteps on the stairs she abruptly closed the door, leaving

Sargent standing there staring at the heavily carved black walnut barrier which had just shut him out.

Sargent had never dreamed of such an abyss of uncertainty and misery as he now began to endure. Day followed day, and for a week he never saw Em, or even the half-friendly Rosie Clyde. A sour-faced, unkempt old Irish woman opened the door when he rang Mrs. Graves' door bell, ordered him from the steps, and slammed the door. Night after night he haunted the place, and only once he met Mrs. Graves. She was coming home from some evening excursion, and to Sargent's appeal for news of Elsie she curtly warned him away, and threatened him with arrest if he continued to haunt the vicinity of her house.

The next night, while he was keeping his vigil near the house, a big Irish policeman slowly approached him, and laying his heavy hand upon his shoulder, said, "Is this Robert Sargent?" The poor fellow thought the threatened arrest had come.

"My name is Robert Sargent," he said very stiffly, shaking off the large hand from his shoulder.

"Then I think I have a little business with you," said the policeman; "walk along wid me, will yez?"

Sargent reluctantly paced along by the side of the blue-coat for a few yards, until they stopped under a street lamp. The policeman slowly drew from his pocket a letter and held it up between his finger and thumb so that Sargent could read the superscription upon the envelope. It was his own name.

"Take it, me boy," said the unexpected messenger, now grinning with delight over

Sargent's astonishment. "She's not a beauty," he continued, "but there's none keeps her doorstep whiter on Wabash Avenue!" And, with a playful thump on Sargent's breast from his big fist, the honest fellow went lumbering off upon his beat.

The cramped writing on the envelope betrayed the hand of Em, and Sargent tore the missive open with an impatient hand after he had run a few steps to thank his new benefactor and returned to the lamp-post.

Em's short letter, ill-spelled and evidently written with much labor, showed that Elsie was desperately ill, and that a doctor was in attendance who gave but little hope for her. A nervous fever, the medical man said, had prostrated the delicate girl, and she had scarcely strength enough to rally. "But, of course," wrote Em, "wile thers life thers hope. Elsie calls yure name all the time. Wish you could see her."

Sargent was at Mrs. Graves' door early next day, and never left it until he had waylaid the doctor when he left the house after his morning visit. Dr. Hamill was a kindly man, bluff, humane and sensible. It comforted Sargent to talk with him, and, as for the doctor, he, of course, saw at once what the anxious inquiry by the haggard young fellow meant. He spoke reassuringly, and Sargent blessed him for the first gleam of assured hope that he had enjoyed for days.

Why prolong the story of what followed? the story of days and nights of lingering anxiety, indignation, savage desperation, hope and despair for this young man? The end came, and came before many days had dragged their slow length by. One morning— Sargent had been sitting at the door all night, and had seen the good doctor go in and come out, look- ing thoughtful and grave, after midnight—though he gave a word of hope. Sargent was sitting in the morning chill, at that hour of dawn when the world looks either its best or worst, when Em suddenly appeared from her door in the basement under the front step, and with a cry, and a look, gave him instant news. Elsie was dead!

The poor lad staggered away after the first few words, words he did not hear, for in Em's face he had seen what had happened. Afterwards he learned only that Elsie had died with his name upon her lips. That was all.

And so the strange, pitiful little love story came to an end. Barnes, who had of late gotten into a way of seeking out Sargent every morning, and, after giving him his breakfast, taking him to the surveyor's office and setting him to work, where he went on mechanically until night, came at the usual time, and, finding Sargent gone from his usual place of vigil, sought and found him at his lodgings.

It was a day of September winds and rain when the two friends saw the open grave waiting for the fair body of Elsie. From a distance, over the wave-like surface of the place of graves, the two watched the simple burial. They said nothing, but when the people who had come in the short funeral train went away, Barnes went away with them, as he knew Sargent desired.

And then Sargent stood over the new-made grave, and as he noted the shabby hearse followed by two carriages driving away, he thought of that other burial in London a few months ago, when Elsie's mother, already forgotten before she had ceased to breathe, had been hidden in her obscure grave in an alien land. But, after all, he mused, the difference between the two was as wide as the ocean and the lands which separated their humble graves. One had been the plaything of fortune, to be dizzied for a day by flattery, and then thrown away like a broken doll when her charms faded in the blight of sickness. The other, neglected and bruised in spirit all her short life through, had found in death a refuge from what she instinctively loathed and repudiated.

Even then, above his own anguish and above the storm of indignation which shook him, Sargent was conscious of the merciful end, which had come to the girl he had pitied and loved so much. It made not much impression in the stress of sharp, newly inflicted sorrow, but the sense of it was with him from the first, and gradually, afterward, it grew in him until he could estimate with some sense of proportion what had befallen the girl whose life he had declared should be one with his own, and also see something of his own part in the simple drama of suffering which had ended, for her at least.

As the wind blew the wet leaves from the thinning elm trees around him, and a light rain fell upon his bared head, Sargent felt that he must rouse himself as from feverish, restless dreams. He was overpoweringly homesick standing there alone, and he found himself complaining to himself and lamenting silently that he could not go home and lay his head on his mother's knee. He needed the restful comfort of home before he started West on the railroad survey work, he thought, but could not have it. Then he walked slowly away, to find Barnes waiting for him at those gates where so many heavy hearts pass in and out each day. The two friends went back to the town together in the close companionship of silence.

CHAPTER XXI.

THE LAUNCHING OF A MAN.

To men of a certain caliber there comes, when sitting in a rushing railroad train, an increased clearness of thought—maybe it comes from the earth —but the fact exists that when he is dashed along on the train with the vibrations beneath him and around him, the man of a type seems to think things and see things more clearly. He knows better what his prospects are; he knows better what the one woman is; he knows better what he ought to try and do in the world to make his prospects better and the one woman's prospects better, and to help the other people in the world who ought to be helped. Of course this effect of riding upon a railroad train comes only to a few men. Maybe Mother Earth gives some things to only a few of her children. We can't tell about that.

As he rode on the train from Chicago westward, Sargent thought over what had passed—Barbara and Elsie. It was all "mixed up," he thought. Barbara seemed brilliant, fascinating and hard. Yet somewhere about her there seemed the ruby, the greatest and richest of all the stones; possibly the association of red hair had something to do with that. He had thought that in Elsie could be found the loving, clinging, dependent creature to whom he would be

13

all in all, and that in her he could forget the eyes of Barbara questioning from so far away, but the glowing, expressive face of the red-haired girl had been in all his dreams, and he still saw it on the morning when, his railway journey ended, he and his peons were getting things together and doing the packing.

It was all odd, it was all strange; it was a leap from one thing to another; it was a leap from something feverish and heart-touching in a great city to another climate and other conditions and other men to meet with, and no woman, for the present at least, and only those things to eat and drink which are provided straitly, but which, after all, will make one clearer of mind mentally and morally; all which is exceedingly good for a man. He was clear headed now. He was getting gaunt, which is excellent for one. He was handling the men about him and thinking of the two women who had formed part of his life; the smaller, for whom he had done all he could, and the other who really, as he even in his half-boyishness knew, owned him pretty fairly. There was much to come yet before Sargent could understand how great the woman was and—then, God bless him—there is good air up the mountain slopes and it is not bad for the Anglo-Saxon if he have occasion to knock another man down in the early morning merely because the other man hasn't belted a mule properly, and when rebuked has drawn a knife. He knows more of the relations of things. He sticks to his friends more faithfully and loves a woman better.

He would not, when he was fairly at the end of the city story, standing upon the edge of a new experience as he was, acknowledge it; but, deep in his heart, lay one thing out of all the years had brought him—the thought of Barbara. It had been so all the time. He and she seemed left, the two real things in the world. And he hummed under his breath the old song of "The Cave of Silver."

Over him rushed the thought of Elsie, often and often, but she seemed already a dream. He saw her fragile, graceful figure, poised before him in her gauzy robe of black for the dance, or he saw her face, wistful, sweet, trusting and pathetic. He knew, even now, that it would have been a question whether he could have delivered this beautiful soul from its surroundings, and made the poor child into a happy woman. It was all unreal —all but the pain of it; that was at least real. The rest was a dream.

The life of a man upon the Southwestern plains of America in the first years of railway prospecting and building across them, made in itself a rugged story. Sargent entered, with a sensation of relief, upon the new and stimulating experience before him. Hardships he laughed at; bodily fatigue he welcomed; work which severely taxed mind and body he rejoiced in; and the wholesome tonic of his ceaseless labors and of continuous outdoor existence in the wonderful elixir of the air of the high plains and mountains, in a few months, made him over. Every trace of the youthful Squire of Dames soon vanished, and a hardy young man on the alkaline soil of the half desert stood ready to front the world.

The rough, squalid life of the mushroom towns which sprang up along the road as it grew, fascinated Sargent by the study it gave him of naked human nature, human nature shown without constraint or any reserve. Here men and women showed themselves with character on view as plainly as are revealed the bones of a skeleton. Vice glared unrebuked from the eyes of whites and redskins. Avarice clutched with ready hand the wide-flung money of the careless adventurers, laborers and engineers who led the onset of the iron road. Men showed their virtues, too, as well as their vices. They were full of rude kindness and their hands were ready to help in all emergencies and dangers. The workers who were fortunate gave freely to those who were sick or poor, and many a roysterer proved a tender nurse by the couch of blankets on the floor upon which tossed feverishly a suffering comrade.

There were few women in these towns of uncouth shelters of pine boards and canvas and "dug-outs" in the hillsides, and such women as were there, save a few rugged wives of the petty contractors, were of the sort into whose personal history one does not go at length. They had, as a rule, the virtues and the vices of the men except that they did not gamble. It is odd, this thing about women. It is only an abnormity among them who gambles for money. They gamble, of course they gamble, just as men do, but, as a rule, they gamble only for men. This was shown quite as much in the shanty town over the crest of the iron snake crawling toward the Pacific, as it is in great cities where men are richer and women plan and do things in a more graceful way.

Was it the proverbial parsimony, or speaking more kindly or more flatteringly, the economy of their sex which kept Moll and Jenny from the poker table, or was it that trait which is strangely despised in a man while it is praised in a woman, fear? Sargent never reached a conclusion any more nearly than to feel that women could not gamble where men are, because, in the end, women could not sit at the table with them. Gambling and violence, rising passions, possible personal assaults and death go together. The very idea of a woman in the neighborhood would be grotesque. And so the man, growing daily sterner of face, harder of muscle, and harder, too, of thought, it may be, pushed forward with his engineering associates, leaving the builded road behind them, and far behind them, as it chanced; for there was new work to be done in a surveying and directing way over the route toward the Pacific, which must be outlined with more definiteness.

The little group of men, leaving the building road, strove along over plain and desert and mountain rises, making their camping places where best they could, never resting in their work while the sun was in the sky and energy for the toil remained, or from their watching under sun or stars, for they were in the land of the Indian, of the Apache, or those who were his kindred. They were but a small party and must ever be upon the alert. Quite truthful was the captured Indian of the far south-west, who said, "If you see Apache sign in these mountains, look out; if you don't see sign, look out more!"

Many a night when Sargent was standing on watch under those stars which in a clear desert atmosphere seem like great lights swung down from the far vault of heaven, he pondered over the short drama of his life and read new meaning from it, now that he was so far away from what had been. Only objectively comes good reasoning. Droll fancies came to him in the midst of it all. He would look at the gloriously lighted sky and the glooming waste, and it would seem to him that it must have been some other boy who had grown up in the Saginaw Valley among the trees he could scarcely believe in, as only memory recalled them in this treeless waste. Even when, in the mountains, trees appeared, in all their worshipful beauty, they were unlike in form and growth to the savage trees of Sargent's knowledge. Upon these western mountain slopes they grew apart without under-growth, and in groups which gave to the landscape an effect which was almost park-like. Indeed the people of the western slope have named their forests parks. But it was not of landscape or sur-roundings that Sargent thought alone or first. Never grew a tree since the world began, not even the greatest of the great conifers, whose height exceeded that of the woman a man might be in love with. Sargent thought often of the slight and graceful girl, of the beautiful, childish face of Elsie; and over her, ever, he wondered was she real; had she, had Mrs. Graves, had Em, and all the rest of that street and that city by the lake been real? And could he have been the youth who shivered and shuddered upon that city doorstep, while the poor girl was dying within? But ever, there is something dominant. It may not be the mountain crest which we can see; while we never see the living, volcanic fire beneath. Ever in the midst of all his thinking existed in the mind of Sargent overpowering comprehension of the glowing woman of the North, and she, he knew, was real; when he remembered her, he felt himself recovering the sense of continuity of existence. While the rest of his life, while even his doting mother and proud father and his sisters, friends and college chums, seemed shadowy and unreal in his new, strange existence, Barbara was as vigorous and alive to his consciousness as ever. He looked at his sinewy brown hands, and as sure as he was of them was he of her firm white ones.

From the Mexican border Sargent wrote to Barbara—he had been silent to her for more than two years—and after that, with long intervals between, he sent letters to her from the desert places of the world in which he lived and worked. They were letters full of his pulsing life and individuality, and he sent them more as a necessary relief to himself than as a plea of any kind to her. They showed his continuous love of her,—he could not help that,— but they asked nothing in return. He began to

receive letters from Barbara, after awhile; they
came to him in his remote working places long
after they were written, and were the treasures of
his life. They were not love letters, but they were
sufficient for love to feed upon, elusive, piquant, and
altogether charming. They were dangerous, these
letters, for they made him understand more fully
the woman he loved, and the more he understood
the more he loved her. Of all the winged shafts of
love that with a pen at the point is sharpest.

With comprehension and desire would come a
great resolve. He must have that girl! The Indian
might prowl on the flanks of the march, and he
was a very real thing to be dealt with, and had a fell
hand when accidentally triumphant, but he had no
more certainty of clutch when in possession,
thought Sargent grimly, than had the fair Barbarian
of the North upon a certain man. So went on the
work of thrusting a railroad outline down toward
the softest of the oceans, and so among the
engineers, doing that great work and himself
developing into greatness in his field, went Sargent
until the months grew into years, and he became as
tawny almost as the Indians he sometimes faced, or
the peons who were his servants. Wiser, too, and
more practical in all things he grew, even as to his
loving. But his growing practicality did not obscure
his knowledge of a great truth. He began to
realize that true chivalrous love had been like a
wall around him during all the dangerous days of a
youngster's first freedom of the world.

Then there came periods of such work as absorbed

every force, mental and physical.   There came times of stress and danger.   There came times of privation, ending in marches of incredible hardship from the mountain trails to the supply station on the plains, and more than once Sargent stood the sturdy one of a camp in which starvation held rule, and from which the whole party were delivered only by determination, endurance and pluck, such as perhaps American pioneers and pathfinders almost alone know.

And these times of trial and suffering showed Sargent what manner of creatures men are; showed him the good and bad of them.   He learned to tolerate the man who would steal the blanket from his sleeping comrade on freezing nights or cunningly contrive to get more than his share of rations when the explorers were short of food, and he learned to know the man who gave up his sheltering cover or let the cup of coffee in all its unutterable value pass him by for a weaker or ailing member of the party.

And in other ways the young man learned to know his fellow men.   He studied with amused interest the new type, to him, the "Greasers" who occupied much of the country.   Many a lazy hour he spent sitting in the shade of an adobe house haggling over a calf or bullock with an ancient Mexican, whose dark face was wrinkled until it looked like a map of a city.   He learned to read cupidity and avarice in the strange faces of these aliens as they lounged about in apparent ease and carelessness, taking hours to settle upon the price

of a sheep, and months to fix their terms for a strip
of land; for the prospectors bought a few acres from
time to time, as they saw chance of future values in
these forgotten places of the world, and Sargent,
looking forward to the day when the road should
come into being, made more than one shrewd guess
and expended certain small sums of money in
evidence of his belief in what was as yet to be only
guessed at.

"It is my way of gambling," he said to himself.
"It is in the air out here, the spirit of staking to
win or lose, but I am sure that it is not lose with
me!" and, in reality, Sargent's ventures were
founded upon somewhat more than chance; upon
his knowledge of nature and of the ways by which
nature determines the movements and lines of men.
He knew where the railroad must go, because he
knew where it must cross the bed of a stream, one
of those channels which, dry one part of the year,
contain full currents of mud-colored water during
certain weeks or months; or he knew the pass it
must make far over the mountains, or the cañon it
must cross and its most available crossing by high
network of trestle. And the sites of certain future
railway towns were purchased, and in due time
their titles were drawn to the name of one Robert
Sargent, late of Michigan, but now of the Great
Central Plains of the United States and Mexico.
Thus the foundation of the young adventurer's fortune was laid.

During the two years of his first prospecting and
surveying journey into and around in the strange

lands of the far Southwest, Sargent made two hurried journeys East on business for the great railway corporation upon one of whose projected branches he was at work. He visited Boston and New York, and remained for a few weeks at the National Capital, where he had such a glimpse of American political life as gave him much food for thought when he returned to the far-away lands of plain and mountain where his immediate work lay. And he dreamed of days of power in the time to come, feeling the strivings within him to take his share in the public work and weal which characterizes the American citizen, but he could not reach his home.

Later, after years of striving and stress on the Pacific slope, came a sort of period to Sargent's especial branch of work, and he joined an exploring expedition which would take him to the Pacific ocean, and thus he saw the western edge of the continent, and looked out into the mysterious ever-flying West. Then he set his face homeward. It was a strange sensation, the return journey over the first great railway line from the salt seas to the fresh inland waters of the great central valley of America.

Sargent could count the cost of such a road as he came easily along, for he knew what those long miles over deserts, mountains and barren plains had meant to those who, farther north than his work had been, had toiled across before the triumph of the meeting of the locomotives, and the driving of the golden spike which celebrated the uniting of the two roads, could be effected.

One day, he recalled as he journeyed along it, in the time of rain and flowers and such grass as grows when the rain falls in the far southwestern arid districts, how, as the prospectors had wended over the level plain, they had come to a yawning gash in the earth, and, looking down a thousand feet, saw in the deep black shadows a stream flowing at the bottom of the cañon. Sargent, planning with the others how this desperate fissure should be bridged, had afterward thought how a certain chasm in his life must be crossed, and he had sung over to himself the song of the Cave of Silver, not in desperation, as he had sung it once in a camp of starvation high in a snowy mountain pass, when the fate of Brock the Bold seemed to be his own, but in a mood of contradiction and contest.

And now the man coming home from his toil to a well-earned rest, felt within him the spell of the love of woman more deeply than ever, and with it a certain fixed and manly resolution.

CHAPTER XXII.

AT THE HALF-WAY HOUSE.

"This town is but a great half-way house between the mountains and the seas," said Mr. William Barnes, attorney-at-law, as he sat at ease and looked across the table at his vis-a-vis, Mr. Robert Sargent, fresh from the Far West.

"Just sit here, and the world passes by," continued the speaker. "Everybody seems to be chasséing east and west, north and south. We catch 'em all."

Sargent had reached Chicago that morning and had found Barnes at once. They were not effusive when they met—that's the way with the American —but they were glad. The junior partner, and the hardest working one of a flourishing legal firm, spoke briefly to his associates, shut the door of his office with a bang and lugged his friend out into the street. "Have you eaten yet?" he asked.

"No," said Sargent, "and I'm hungry."

Barnes grasped him by the shoulder and dragged him into a glittering place. "I don't care what I eat to-day," he said, "but let them do their worst."

"But I care!" announced Sargent. "What to eat is a matter of importance to a fellow who has eaten from the tables of the wilderness for many weary moons—and suns too. Many a bill of fare have I conjured up as I fasted out there on the plains and now I mean to see what reality there is to one of them;" and he gave an order to the waiter which startled that staid functionary while it excited in the breast of his friend emotions of mingled envy and alarm.

Sargent was lean and brown, but the very personification of healthy, glowing manhood. His powerful frame was yet clothed in the easy dress of his active outdoor life, and so, unmarred by the work of fashionable tailordom, was as graceful in every pose and movement as he was strong and manly. His eyes shone with joy and love of life, and his face revealed the presence of a spirit, strong, studying, yet playful, rejoicing in health of body as well as mind.

"He's a man," thought Barnes, "to be proud of."

"It is a great moment," exclaimed Sargent, interrupting Barnes' inward comments. "It is a great, a glorious moment when we sit down to a square meal! Poets may rave over the joys of the muse, but give me the pure, unalloyed and unimpeachable happiness of a well-cooked meal! Homer may twang his lyre and Dante sing his lay, and all the other fellows do all sorts of things, unenvied each by me." And, with a flourish, he lifted the cover of the dish before him.

"Tell me first about yourself, Barnes," he continued, as he began his soup. "You look as content as a friar of the middle ages, so rosy about the gills, so white of hands and generally well-fed and well-kept. 'Property! property! property!' I'll bet

that's what your horse's feet beat about, to the confusion of Tennyson's farmer!"

"It isn't 'property,' Sargent, that makes me look
so prosperous," expostulated Barnes; "I am doing
fairly well, no more, but I'm very happy—" and the
honest fellow looked a bit confused.

"Billy   Barnes,   you're   married!"   exclaimed
Sargent.

"There's no 'denygin' ' of it," the Billy of ancient
days confessed; and then Sargent had an excuse for
ordering a bottle of wine, for, so far, the two were
following the almost universal American fashion,
eating without wine or beer.

"We must have wine in which to drink a health,"
said the returned chum. ."What shall it be?—Ye
gods! Whitefish; broiled whitefish on the shores of
Lake Michigan! Have I lived to see this day!
Billy, look at that wine card and see what will go
best with whitefish in honor of Mrs. William Barnes;
God bless her!"

The wine was ordered, and the toast drank, and
Billy told his story—a short, honest story, and made
Sargent promise to go home with him to dinner that
night, and remain at his house during his short stay
in Chicago.

Then the two talked as men great enough to
remain boys will talk, and Sargent heard of many
of the college friends he had lost all knowledge of
in the years of his distant work. "The worst privation of all," he told Barnes, "was the want of
letters. I have been months without a word from
home, or from anywhere else. It made one feel

as if the world had dropped away from under his feet."

"Oh, but I'm glad you're out of the wilderness!" said Barnes. "This is a red letter day, to be marked with a white stone. How are things at home? Have you heard yet?"

"Oh, yes, vaguely, at San Francisco, for I came around that way, and later at Kansas City, but, tell me about the old boys, about Lathrop, Mayo and Snow, and all of them."

"There's nothing but good to tell of the whole lot," said Barnes, enthusiastically. "They've good stuff in them, as you know; they showed that long ago; and it stayed right with them, as good stuff does when it's in the original package."

Then began the comforting reminiscences. Perhaps men laugh too much at women who do gossiping. It may be that the fact of gossiping is sometimes but a manifestation of interest in others' welfare, and that if there be venom anywhere it comes from the individuality. Of course, men do not sit and talk of other human beings for long hours as women do, but men have bread-winning to do and so the time is taken up. But for real comfort give to me a good reminiscent talk between two strong men.

And then began the stories and the news, how this one was a rising lawyer in his native state, and that one a noted professor doing good work in a Western college, while another Sargent himself had news of, having met him on the Pacific coast, and so the confab ran on unendingly and was broken off in the middle, but to be resumed that night after dinner in Barnes' home after the young wife had, with wisdom beyond her years and experience, left the two chums alone over the last fire which was lighted in the library grate that summer. Barnes would have a fire, though the windows all stood wide open, and the glow and blaze was not uncomfortable that cool June night, and morning, for it was morning when the two men, having smoked the last pipe, said good night at the door of Sargent's sleeping room.

"Give him strong coffee, Lucy, and with plenty of cream and sugar," said Barnes to his wife at breakfast, looking approvingly at Sargent. "If you should ask him which dish he would take at dinner, digestible or indigestible, he would probably choose indigestible, to such an extravagance have his spirits risen!"

"Of course," said Sargent, "I would choose the indigestible anything, knowing it would be the best. Everything particularly delectable is dangerous, if not wrong."

Sargent walked down town with Barnes that morning, and as the two men, leaving the lake shore residence region, came southerly along Michigan Avenue and crossed a street, Sargent looked toward Wabash Avenue and said:

"Have you paid any attention to Mrs. Graves, or heard of her since I went away?"

"Yes," said Barnes, "I have heard a little about her. She has evidently grasped permanently and utilized for herself the fund provided for Elsie by Brockhurst. I doubt if the father knows that his

14

child is dead.   He left her entirely in Mrs. Graves'
hands, it appears, being convinced that she was
devoted to her sister's child and to her happiness,
and now the miserly instincts which were well at
the fore when you knew her have completely
absorbed her.   She still lives in her house over there,
and is known as one of the hardest, coldest, most
rapacious of mortals, to the few who know her at all.''

"Poor Em!" muttered Sargent, "I wonder what
has become of her!"

"Em!   She was the little slavey, wasn't she?"

"She was, poor girl!" answered Sargent, then
suddenly seized by impulse he stopped, and turned
back.   "I am going over there," he said, and
Barnes went with him

The house looked just as it did in the old days,
grim, closed up, forbidding, yet well cared for.
The neighborhood was now fast changing, having
fallen from its first estate as a fashionable residence
quarter some time ago, and the prim house had some
undesirable surroundings.

They asked the slipshod servant who opened the
door for them for Mrs. Graves, and were left standing on the well remembered black and white marble
floor of the hall until the mistress of the house came.
She recognized Sargent at the first glance, but chose
to conceal her recognition; with a slight bow she
stood looking at the two men, and, as neither of
them spoke, she, in her soft "company voice," asked
what they wished to see her about.

"I came to see Miss Grace Emily Ferguson, Mrs.
Graves," said Sargent.   "Is she still here?"

"You mean my kitchen maid, Em, I suppose?" Mrs. Graves asked.

"Yes," Sargent replied. "Your servant, Em. Please call her."

He opened the door of the small parlor, and held it open for Mrs. Graves and Barnes, then followed the two into the room, and they all sat down.

"Kindly ring the bell," said Mrs. Graves, looking sourly at Sargent. He pressed down the indicated button on the wall near him, and when the servant answered, Mrs. Graves commanded her to send Em up at once, and then sat rigidly in her chair while Sargent looked at her curiously.

She was still an attractive looking woman, at first glance, still clad in that widow's uniform which blots every city landscape, but her face showed plainly the marks of her consuming passion, avarice, the ugly thing which had set the seal on the fate of the shrinking, quiet-souled Elsie. Sargent had studied the world since he had last looked upon that hard face, and now he understood only too well what had once baffled and so puzzled him.

The door opened and Em appeared. Thin, round shouldered, with great eyes staring out of her homely, honest face, she stood looking at the visitor who had summoned her, not even noticing or comprehending the sharp remark addressed to her by Mrs. Graves. Sargent set a chair near the window for Em, and, standing between her and Mrs. Graves, began talking quietly to the poor girl, while the tears rained down her cheeks.

Now Billy Barnes rose to the full height of his mental powers.

Moving his chair close to that of Mrs. Graves, Mr. Barnes, attorney, began to discuss the weather, but soon passed from that topic to one which plainly arrested the entire attention of his listener. He spoke of the house in which they sat, and asked confidingly if its owner had ever thought of selling it? Had she thought of it? She would never have said so, but in reality to sell her house at a good price was now her one immediate object in life, dreamed of by night, planned by day; and well the astute Barnes divined all this. Values were falling all around her, and it was little short of agonizing to Mrs. Graves to see, as she had to see, that her property was worth less at this moment than when she bought it.

Soon Barnes had the ungracious hostess deep in a discussion of possible and impossible sales of the particular piece of real estate in which the woman's soul was wrapped up, and Sargent continued his interview with Em unmolested. At the end of a few minutes he spoke: "Barnes, give me your business card," and when Barnes handed it to him he gave it to Em, saying, "Two o'clock, remember."

He had made Em promise to be at Barnes' law office at three o'clock that afternoon.

"Ugh!" shivered Barnes as they left the close-shut house behind them. "That woman is uncanny! There's nothing the matter with her, though, but the root of all evil, love of money! She's got it bad, though!"

Before Sargent left the city he had found Em a home and a kind protecting friend in the house of Billy Barnes, for he easily interested Barnes' young wife in the poor, friendless creature who had been taken when she was a little child, an orphan, by Mrs. Graves, and made into a joyless toil-worn dependent, as much a slave as was ever any black-skinned human being in the time of slaves.

"She has such a square-toed little face," said Billy Barnes, speaking of her to his wife, "and she is alone and without happiness in the world!"

"We'll make her happier!" declared the whole-some, joyous woman who shared Barnes' life and made it bright for him, and Sargent's heart felt warm and light whenever he thought of the relation which was soon established between two women of such differing characters and fortunes as Lucy Barnes and Em. They had one point of resem-blance. A great good heart beat in the bosom of each, and as the years went by, Em became the confidential, petted and deferred-to counselor in all domestic affairs in the Barnes home, as well as the faithful, tireless helper, to be trusted in every strait.

Sargent's stay in the "Half-way House" was brief. In a few days, having attended to affairs of business of his own and for the great railroad com-pany, and after certain soul-stirring meetings with old college friends contrived by his host, he took his place in a railway train. The Wolverine was "headed for home."

CHAPTER XXIII.

THE HOME COMING.

When the youth who has gone out into the world and changed and become a man of forcefulness and reserve, he is not unlikely, as he nears his home after the long absence, to become a boy again, with all boyish fancies as to what he will see and what may happen. It was so with Sargent, and there came, as there has come to so many others, a half-delighted shock at the changes he found in his own family, and in all surrounding nature.

The father and mother were changed least of all, and Sargent found them still in the old house, a house overrun by his sisters and their children, and he found himself called "uncle." To be called "uncle" for the first time gives a man a queer sensation, as it doubtless does a woman to be called "aunt," because, when those titles are applied there attaches a certain suggestion of family dignity and, sometimes, the less desirable one of increasing age.

The old home was still controlled by the potent father and the dear mother, that is, it was theirs nominally, but, practically, it belonged to the grandchildren, who, Sargent soon declared, were all of them being spoiled. But, though changes had come, he found no change toward him, and his

loving reception was all that he had dreamed of in
the far Southwestern deserts. His father grasped
his hands in the same old way, and the two
men, the younger affectionate and the elder proud,
were glad to meet each other. As for the mother,
well, she came out as he ascended the steps to the
old doorway and she came with a certain beaming
dignity, but, as she looked into the eyes of this
great brown man who was born of her, and saw in
those eyes the light which only the eyes of a great
lover-son can give to the eyes of a mother, why,
then she burst out crying and he leaped upward to
her and enclosed her in his arms of something very
much like steel, and there wasn't any dignity or anything else save the mother-love to speak of. As for
the girls—brothers always call their sisters "girls"—
they crowded around and laughed or cried, and
Sargent was introduced to his nephews and nieces.
Even Bessie, Sargent's sister-sweetheart, had
married, and he was glad that it was to the one
man in town whom he liked best. And the baby,
who could already walk and talk too, though in a
most mumbling and incoherent manner, was there
to meet him.

Sargent declared that the child was too bow-
legged and that its nose was wrong, but it so
chanced, a few days later, that, when that wobbling
young person was not brought over by Bessie to be
around the house with him, Sargent announced that
he was an injured being and neglected by those of
his own blood. It is doubtful if there ever lived a
man worthy the name in the best sense of the word

who could keep himself from falling in love with a baby-thing.

As to his mother, the man who had lain under strange skies and far from humanity of his kind, wondered at his own good fortune in finding face to face with him again and where he could put his hand upon her shoulder or pat her cheeks, the elder being who had given birth to him and to whom he was now almost as a child again. There came to him in those days an overwhelming understanding of what the world is, of what woman and man-child are, and of what the child grown should ever do for the one who nursed him. He took his mother upon trips with him, just little pleasure trips, as he would have taken a woman of his own age, and he made her tell him about her own young being and of her life before he was born, and it was all wonderful to the two. The woman of sixty, gray-haired and, under other circumstances, stately, looked often into the face of her son and then showed very little sense for a firm lady of her age and social standing. She would occasionally repeat the exploit of crying a little and then her big son would hug her, if the occasion offered, and "brace her up"—and that was all.

In later years, Sargent thanked the good Lord that there had come in time to him what comes to fewer than it should, the happiness, in manhood, of falling in love with his own mother.

But all this was but of the life of the household. Outside there were a thousand things which gave to the man a keen enjoyment. He met his old schoolmates again, the fellows who had licked him or whom he had licked, men of his own age, and they exchanged confidences and compared experiences in the world. He would sit in this office or that one and smoke and talk with the man of business, or he would sit with dangling legs upon some lumber pile and talk with some sturdy laborer who had also been his playmate in the old days. He sought out his sweethearts, too, and was received by them and their husbands most hospitably, and passed reckless opinions upon their children, as he had upon those of his own sisters.

Perhaps, though, there came no keener delight than when he went out to the old farm beyond the town, where he was born, and revisited the old places in company with an uncle, who owned the adjacent place, and who, being much younger than Sargent's father, had been a half-way companion to him in his youth. The uncle, remaining on his farm, had kept in close touch with the nature of the region, and though, when they separated, they had been but young man and boy, they were now two men together. Sargent was excited and his kindly, keen-sighted uncle became sympathetic and, in a degree, enthusiastic himself as they wandered through the old haunts and talked over former exploits. In some ways the experience had a degree of pain for Sargent. Where once was a forest of beech ridges where ruffed grouse had been most numerous and where they had wagered as to which would do the better with a snap-shot as the fall covey rose from the shelter afforded by the branches of some fallen tree, Sargent saw now only a great wheat field, a green sea of verdure harboring no single grouse in all its area. They visited together the site of some woodchuck hole, where, long ago, they had dug out its inhabitant and witnessed, as a reward, a most delightful fight between a small terrier and one of the largest woodchucks they had unearthed in all their diggings, but there was no woodchuck hole there now, and, as the college song says, "the green grass grew all 'round." They visited the old deer-lick and, where the little pond in the woods was brackish for some reason, Sargent saw no trees nor pond, but only a buckwheat field not yet in bloom. In a way, it was almost oppressive to the visitor. This had been the most comforting scene of his imagination, but all had changed. The cutting away of the forest had affected the rainfalls, and at one place upon a roadway, where there had been a little bridge beneath which the creek ran, and where Sargent had caught minnows with a pin-hook when a boy, there was no bridge at all. The creek had disappeared. They went into the low lands through which a larger creek ran and where there had once been a muskrat pond whereon ducks alighted in their spring flight North, and where the blue crane found in midsummer sunfish and other delicacies, and where there was a great fringing border of pond-lilies. But there was no such border now; the big creek had degenerated into a slight one and the pond was little more than a mudhole, ploughed by cattle hoofs. The tiger lilies still rose, blazing and luxurious, in the long grass of the bottoms, but the scene was changed.

Throughout all the Northern country the pioneers, as they cleared away all the other forest trees off the land, left standing in the fields of the lower slope one or two great hickories. They left them because the hickory tree furnished the nuts which made part of the enjoyment of a winter evening, and because, as those practical men reasoned, the hickory, being a slow growing and, when left alone without surroundings, a somewhat wide-spreading tree, would afford a shade for cattle feeding in the field about it. Sargent thought of the time of the ripening of the hickory-nuts, when the inefficient youngsters gathered about the trees and picked up such nuts as nature and the red squirrels threw down to them. He thought of the later time, when he was a few years older, when they threw clubs up at the limbs and obtained their fullest harvest. He and his uncle lingered long beneath those hickory trees, standing solitary in the lowland meadows. Sargent pondered queerly, and doubting himself, upon the difference between the boy who had been born upon and who had known and grown up on this spot and the one who had come back again. That hickory tree had once seemed to him one of the largest trees in all the world. He and his cousins had struggled in the season to get the nuts from this same giant of the forest of that time. Now he saw but a symmetrical, tough old tree standing in the midst of the meadow, of about one-half the height he had, in his imagination,

given it.   It was so with other things; all distances
seemed shorter.   It was but a step from the house
to the barn, but a step from the sheep field to the
spring—all things were belittled.   He went with his
uncle to the flats where once, bearing a tin pan, he
gathered mushrooms in the early morning, and to
the place in what was in his time a buckwheat field
where the wild turkeys found good feeding, and he
found nothing reminding him of the past any more
than a view of the mouth of the Orinoco River would
remind one of the mouth of the Minnehaha.   The
sky-line bothered him most.   In his time the sky-
line was defined by something of a blue-black hue
lying between it and the landscape which started
from his feet.   Now it was all different.   That
blue-black line had been the forest surrounding
every farm.   Now it was all changed and the wheat
fields and the other fields ran into the sky
blurringly.

There were other buoyant enjoyments, reminiscent
all, into which this exile of some years plunged reck-
lessly.   One day, walking along the street with one
of his sisters, one of the elder and ever comprehending, he met a woman, a widow reasonably well-
to-do, who had once been a schoolmate and sweetheart of his.   She had been hot of temper, piquant
in all ways, and just a white, natty little personage.
They met and all three strolled down the street
together and the two, Sargent and his former
sweetheart, drew somewhat close together in their
chatter.   They came in sight of the spire of a
church which was perhaps a block away.   Now it

so happened that once, in his boyish days, Sargent had met this girl upon the sidewalk and, seeing the door of this church open and knowing that there was no service at the time, had half-way pulled her up the steps and into the vacant entrance and there kissed her with much earnestness. It was a social tragedy between the two—for she was much more in love with another youngster—and he had never kissed the young lady again, but neither of the two had forgotten the incident. As they walked up the street together, he said to her:

"Jane, do you remember how violently I once pulled you up this church portico and kissed you?"

"I remember all about it," said the fair widow, looking up impertinently into his face.

"Jane," said Sargent, "do you remember what the Governor of North Carolina once said to the Governor of South Carolina?"

Now it so happens that perhaps throughout the United States the bit of nonsense best known between the seas is that which occurred at an unknown date between the Governors of North and South Carolina. It is grotesque and absurd enough to be thoroughly American. There is a flavor of mint juleps and laughing conception and good fellowship about it all. What the Governor of North Carolina said to the Governor of South Carolina was, "It's a long time between drinks."

The fact that his fair companion admitted that she remembered this also was enough for Sargent. They were nearing the church now, and there was

no one inside and the outer doors of the portico
were open as they had been years before, while the
discreet sister had turned aside to do some shopping.
The small widow, a slender, knowing and most lov-
able small widow, was lifted up the steps and a little
aside from the doorway of the silent portico, and
there she lifted up her lips again, and was kissed
again, this time without a tremor. Sargent thought
he might as well take advantage of the occasion and
did so with perhaps too much earnestness. A civil
engineer, one who has to deal with floods and
changes, gets into the habit of improving every
opportunity. Perhaps he rather overdid the thing.

"That's too many at once," said the widow.

"I don't know," said Sargent. "How can there be
too many?"

But that was the end of this episode, for each of
these two people understood the other, and while
kissing is a serious thing—far more so than is
thought by some nine-tenths of those who kiss—
there was nothing to it all; it was but a sort of jest;
they were only great friends. These were fine
times for Sargent in one way, but never, in the
midst of all the happiness of home, was he really
content. Ever like a strained cable was there something dragging him to the North. There was a
tugging, with a woman as an unconscious power at
the end of it, toward the land of swifter summer
growth and lower temperature.

Of course the man knew what had brought him
home at this time in defiance of what chanced to be
his own monetary interests and his relations with

the great railway company, of which he had become almost a part. He knew that he had hungered for his father and mother and his sisters; he knew that he wanted to look upon them, and his own skies and his own grass again, and to meet those who had been the companions of his youth and to be more or less close to them again as their varying conditions might determine. He knew all that, but underneath it all—and he thought of something else.

One of the cleverest and sweetest writers in all the world once wrote a little poem called "The Bells of Shandon," and they still sound throughout the resonant atmosphere of intelligent humanity. They're pretty good bells, those "Bells of Shandon." They're good bells and there have been hundreds of other as good bells, built in blood and metal throughout the centuries, summoning some one to come somewhere, but the ruffed grouse of the North has a wing-beating bell, as good, and it mattered little to Sargent, anyway. The woman has the best bell of all, and the man, however she rings it, must come. And these are all similes mixed, for it is almost impossible to tangle up a cable and a bell.

One morning a big, brown man shook hands with his father and talked with him on business matters, while the elder man's eyes gleamed satisfiedly and proudly, kissed his mother perhaps half a dozen times more than was the ordinary practice, and then, because of the tugging of the cable, took a train for northern Michigan. The look in his eye was very different from that of the eye of the junior from college who had made the same trip some years before.   The eye of the Cæsar who left Rome to gamble with his legions was very different from the eye of the Cæsar who, on his return, did not ask, but ordered them to cross the Rubicon.

CHAPTER XXIV.

IN THE NORTH AGAIN.

The northern summer is late, and its woods looked like the woods of May or early June when Sargent took his way through them toward the center of all his hopes, before the summer's sun had begun to show its full power, even in the Southern Peninsula.

The years had contributed toward ease and rapidity in traveling over the way Sargent was taking. New settlements had sprung up, the roads were at least clearly defined, though they were rough and almost wholly unimproved since their first rude laying out, and here and there a settler's house sent up faint smoke wreaths from its wide chimney.

All along the way were evidences of the new work of man. At times the rugged highway would pierce and twist its way into and through a forest or cross what looked like some vast clearing, with the work upon it but half done; but this was only where the pine and hemlock had grown so thickly that there were few other trees among them, and so it chanced that the lumbermen or bark-gatherers had in certain areas accomplished almost the first work of the farmer pioneer.

At other places along the route smoke could be
15

seen rising on the distant hillsides.   Men had learned that beneath the hill-crests of the Northern Peninsula of Michigan lay perhaps the greatest copper deposits of all the world, and the area of search had widened and shafts were being sunk at a venture.   The transformation, crude enough, was somewhat striking.   Certainly five years brings more about of change and striving forward in the newly developing portions of America than in a "Cycle of Cathay."

Whoever said that "it never rains but it pours," had assuredly a degree of sense with some nonsense about him; really, though, there should be a sort of counter-maxim, something to the effect that "the sun never shines but it shines more."   The good luck packages seemed to be saved up and sent, ordinarily, together.   It chanced that Sargent, as he rode from Conway on a hired horse, on nearing the homestead he was seeking, overtook Judge Sloan walking along the shaded road a mile from Honey Creek.   The younger man fairly tumbled off his horse as the two came together,and reached out his hand to the old Judge, who recognized him in a moment   The years had seemingly not affected the aged jurist's eyes nor his memory as to those he liked, and his reception of Sargent was all that the younger could have desired.   It was glad and cordial, and Sargent leading his horse, the two walked together and finally up the slope to the homestead.

The horse was given to the astonished but grinning Michael, who was almost unchanged in every

particular, and who, by some accident, chanced to be
where he could attend to work, and the two men
entered the house—the well remembered, hospitable
house—but Barbara was not there. Then they
strolled out toward the big barn, builded since
Sargent's going, whose great sliding doors stood
open, allowing the summer breeze to play through
the building unobstructed, between the scented haymow on one side and the grain-mow with the stables
underneath upon the other. Sweet was the fragrance still lingering about the barn soon to be
filled again with the product of the fields, and sweet
was the air, coming scented from the woods, which
flowed through the vast hallway across the big
farm building. There, as the two men turned in
their walk to where they had a view across, seated
in the swing which hung from the lofty cross-beams
and which in midsummer is an adjunct of almost
every barn in the Northern Peninsula, was Barbara.
A book was lying in her lap, her hand was folded
upon it, and she had leaned back with half-shut
eyes, her head resting against one of the ropes,
while one dainty foot just touched the floor and was
keeping up from time to time a softly swinging
motion.

It seemed ever afterward to Sargent that there
was in Barbara's beautiful, thoughtful face as he
saw it then a look of stillness, a haunting,
indefinable expression of slight but inexpressible
sadness. He hardly realized it then, though it came
to him afterward. The photograph was made upon
his mind at the moment when he looked upon her

hungrily and eagerly as she sat there in her self-forgetfulness, before she had seen him or her father. They were talking as they walked and as they turned in upon the log-built sloping bridge leading upward to the barn doors, the woman heard them and straightened up and saw them.

When she so looked up, her face changed, and—so Sargent thought, at least—it changed forever, so vivid was the light of welcome in every line of it,— a light which grew and grew and never died out. There is much in the eyes that see, so much that where one man sees heaven another will pass by indifferently, seeing nothing, but in truth Barbara Sloan's face was never again quite the same, and Barbara herself was never again quite the same after that minute of surprise and joyous greeting on a day in summer when Robert Sargent stood before her, hat in hand, greeting her as if he had but left her yesterday.

A woman's face—beautiful as it is to her lover— is never so beautiful as when she becomes a lover herself, and love leaped up and held the fair woman's heart and looked out of her eyes all in an unguarded moment, as she saw before her the bronzed face and changed, yet unchanged, figure of the man who had been sent away humming the old Norse song on a winter day.

The Judge, worthy, restless man! muttered something about letters to write and went away. And in some way Sargent found himself seated in the great swing on the wide seat by Barbara's side.

Neither said anything for a little time and then

Sargent began to talk to the girl. The words were what he might have said to her when they were last together, but how different the inflection! With all their lovingness and all their sweetness there ran unconsciously through the words of this lover outpouring his heart the steel cable of the man who knows. Apropos of nothing, this is the best lover in the world, and all women should know it, though, unfortunately, there are not enough of the class to go around, not more than perhaps about one man to a thousand women. The majority of the other fellows are pretty good, though.

Barbara understood. She was as great in her way as the man beside her was in his, and she understood. She sat silent for a little while, but she had what one of the hack phrases well describes as the "courage of her convictions." She was a woman who had thought, now, and she was not afraid to say to the man beside her that she loved him:

"And she longed for the Cave of Silver!
And she mourned for her absent ——!"

She began the old air bravely, her sweet voice vibrating with feeling, and then she broke down, and, in a moment, she was cuddled in the man's arms and there followed the old story of two human beings who have found themselves, the story which has probably been told some thousands of millions of times since the world began, which we laugh at but respect, and without which this lump of earth floating in space would not be decently habitable for human beings.

Sargent told the story of his love and longing, of his faith and hope and work, and all that had inspired and held him up during the years of his absence. And Barbara, replying, said a little of what her own heart dictated, the gist of it all being that she loved Sargent, and would love him always, —and was not that enough? What more is there to tell of the meeting of two crystal streams held long apart and fretting, too, now at last rushing together to become one stream? Once hand in hand here in this Northern country on this summer afternoon, both knew that nothing could part them again. For good or ill they were one. The very dogs saw it as they walked to the house, the birds saw it from nest and airy perch; old Tilda, fussing over her milk pans on the kitchen porch, with one swift glance over her shoulder saw it, and Michael, lounging along the lane with his string of freshly caught trout, saw it through the brown mist of a misty being who had never himself known what he never-theless recognized. As for the Judge, though dim the eyes of his mind in some ways, he knew all about it at once, with the perception which is one of the kindly things of good old age, and when the lovers came into his room and stood by his chair, he only looked at them and said, "I'm glad." Later on, when he sat down opposite Barbara at the dinner table, he remarked, his eyes comprehending her heightened beauty, "How much you are growing like your mother, child!"

"I'm afraid you will have to be content with the 'skins of foxes' after all, Barbara," Sargent had said, as they sat together on the porch, for a little time. "Are you willing to give up your dream of 'a golden galley?' I have found work in a world that needs what I can do, and I can take care of you, if you will come out into the West with me, but I don't know about your lying on velvet, or anything of the sort!"

"Don't harp on that old song," said Barbara laughingly and lovingly. "I trust you for all time to come."

Now if any one imagines that there is going to be an explanation of why Miss Barbara Sloan fell in love with Robert Sargent—and confessed it—all in one moment of time, on a still summer's day, she who some years ago had sent this same young man out into the snow in the dead of winter to search for a "Cave of Silver" or on some equally foolish errand—it seems as if she did say something about "spurs"—if any one imagines that this story is going to be encumbered with the reasons, arguments, entreaties, protestations and allegations of this young woman who was very well in her way, that rash imagination and expectation is doomed to fall; he or she who essays to reason upon certain high and mighty mysteries is wasting time. Taking Miss Barbara Sloan at her own word—and whose could be better?—she loved Robert Sargent in that moment when he returned to her, on that day of July, and engaged to love him evermore. Why need we give ear to all she said about her thoughts of him in his absence—of her growing appreciation and understanding of things in the world, and of

people, and, incidentally, looking backward, of that
lover she had in such innocent truthfulness sent
away from her, cruelly wounded if not slain? The
two talked for hours over all the time while they had
been separated, and neither of them tired.

The story of Elsie, told in time, made a tender,
heart-stinging diversion, and Sargent had to tell it
all over more than once, at Barbara's command,
though she said, herself, that it never failed to
make her heart ache, and she owned that she did
not like to hear it or think about it. Sargent himself had a sense of pain whenever he thought of
Elsie, but, after a time, he discovered that Barbara
was always especially tender and loving to him after
a talk about the fragile, buried flower that had
withered before his hand could reach it, and so he
found some compensation for dwelling on an unwel-
come theme. So Love triumphs over Death, over loss
and pain and all the ills of existence. The flowers
which grow on graves have an especial, an appealing, poignant sweetness of their own.

CHAPTER XXV.

VAGARIES.

He had his foolish, teasing moods, and though Barbara professed much indignation at such times, her eyes and lips betrayed her. He would demand, occasionally, if she loved him as much and as well as she did a quarter after three last Thursday; not that he remembered with any definiteness what they were doing at a quarter after three o'clock, but he wanted to know whether or not he was holding his own in her affections. She would reply as her fancy might dictate, sometimes admitting that his condition had become perilous and sometimes declaring, with much graciousness, that she believed there had been no jot nor particle of change in any of her feelings. Then he would become more or less indignant.

"You believe," he would say. "You only believe! Why are you not sure? My dear girl, I regret to say that you lack mathematical accuracy, as so many of us do, and if ever mathematical, accuracy is needed it is surely in a love affair such as is ours. For instance, you, just now, very sweetly, I'll admit, used the expression "jot." Pardon me, but how much is a jot? Can you tell? I'll venture to say, my sunbeam, that you cannot even repeat the Table of Minimums!"

She expressed the opinion that there was no such thing as a "Table of Minimums."

Shocked and surprised was the lover at such ignorance in one so fair and, in most things, well informed. He explained ponderously:

"The word 'jot,' just employed by you, my woodling, is, in itself, one of the terms of the table. I'll tell it all to you," and he repeated in a sing-song way:

2 Iotas	make 1 jot	
4 Jots	" 1 tittle	
4 Tittles	" 1 smitch	
2 Smitches	" 1 smithereen	

"And, oh!" he burst out as he finished the sing-song, "you don't know, dear, what a comfort it is to thus improve your mind! Of course, I don't mean that you've not a fine mind—one far superior to my own—but there are little things where I can help you so! Aren't you glad of it all?"

And Barbara, laughingly indignant, said that she had long suspected the existence of streaks of harmless madness in him, and was now more than ever convinced that her perception had not been at fault. Take, for instance, this foolish Table of Minimums. What silliness it was! What did it all mean? How could he justify this outbreak of the court jester.

And then he became sad-faced and earnest again: "Doubt the soundness of the Table of Minimums! Why, one would be as abandoned as Sidney Smith's man who could speak disrespectfully of the Equator!" He would tell her all about it, he said, and his disquisition on the subject was intended to be most thoroughly convincing.

"Now," said he, "take the Table of Minimums—honestly, I wonder you don't see all its significance. I wonder that you don't just gasp with happiness. Just think of it—think of it for a minute or even for a particle of a minute. You're engaged to the man who invented this Table of Minimums! Now, I'll try to tell you about it:

"My child with the red-head, just look me in the eyes and listen thoughtfully to what I am saying. I am going to do you more good within the next twenty minutes, that is in a purely mathematical way, than ever any man did to a girl since all of us had to climb trees to get away from things. I'm going to tell you about the Table of Minimums."

But Barbara interrupted his opening remarks of explanation with the announcement that it was time to go to dinner, adding that she was not sorry to close this interview and dismiss the subject of conversation.

"It was rather small, that's a fact," assented Sargent; but he could not be prevented from engaging in a disquisition illustrative of the relative sizes and shapes of the quantities in the table.

"Now, Barbara, turn your head just a shade to the left—the sun hits your red hair that way and I like it better. Now, my dear, to repeat, and by the way, I rather like to repeat, Barbara, my dear Barbara, we will proceed," and he went on with the nonsense, concluding grandiloquently, "Now, Barbara, do you understand? There's one comfort in explaining a thing to a red-headed girl. She's impulsive and hot-tempered, but she can generally see things. I'd rather have something sharply comprehensive than dully non-comprehensive, and I'm hungry and it seems to me that I've done you so much good to-day that, for the time, I shall try to do no more."

And so they went up from the woods and along the pleasant pathway to the house and there was dinner—the mid-day dinner of the North—and after that, talking between Sargent and the father of Barbara, for these two, one in his waning and the other in his waxing, kept getting closer, as it should be ever where gentlemen are concerned. Then, of course, Barbara was dragged off again by the fond and foolish lover.

The young man was not this time occupied in mind with the idea of the Table of Minimums, which is a most beautiful table—but was full of other varieties of foolishness and new manifestations of lovingness. He informed Barbara in a lofty way, as they went down one of the wood roads, that he believed he was the only man who had ever lived who really knew how to fully appreciate a girl of the best of the North Michigan sort. Here he somewhat blundered. The woman looked at him charmingly but quizzically.

"When did that wonderful and exceptional appreciation begin?" she asked.

He was at ease and confident: "Oh! seven or eight years ago, or whenever it was I first met you. It has not varied since."

"But," said Barbara innocently, "though I am not scientific, nothing but a poor woodland creature, yet I've learned the regulation things. I've learned, for instance, that the body changes every seven years, and so that this is only another girl, anyhow, and you needn't fret for the love of the girl you met at the University. Necessarily, that girl is all gone somewhere, I don't know where, but she's gone!"

"Yes, I know it," he answered, "but, you see, I'm in love with that particular arrangement of particles and it is understood that the arrangement is duplicated, after a fashion, in the successive years of the individual."

Of course there was no answer to that. There would be other moods and varieties of conversation between the man and the woman. On another day, after dinner, when nothing had been decided on for the afternoon, and it was rather probable than otherwise that all would be lounging about the house, Barbara came down arrayed somewhat finely, that is, she wore one of the best of all her gowns, and above the stately ruffle about her neck the warm hair and the milk-white skin were potent. It was not surprising that Sargent's pulse exerted itself and made a trifle better time:

"She does be a sumptuous lady," he said laughingly.

The girl blushed and was glad, because she knew what he meant. They were alone in the room and she asked him if he would come and sit with her upon the sofa. It was one of the old-fashioned, haircloth kind, and she advised him, incidentally, to sit at the farther end.

"Will you come?" she asked.

"Will I?" said he. "I'll come to that sofa as blithely as the meadow-lark drops into the clover."

Then — this was one of his more or less maudlin days — he told her how fair to look upon she was in the garb she wore, and how often in the hot Mexican nights he had dreamed of her sleeping or thought of her when awake, and of what hopeful comfort there came to him in his imaginings.

"It was wonderful and it was good for me," he said. "I thought much of the home, of the home of soft luxurious things for my love, and of books, and pictures and music, of a pleasant literary atmosphere in which we would rejoice together and work together, we are so alike in tastes, and how you could achieve what was in you and how vain of it I should be and proud to have you meet the others of the world. I thought of you, the stately, gracious, tactful little woman who would receive her friends there and rejoice in the fact that she had such a home for them, and that she would make it a privilege for them to come to that home, although she would never know it. And I thought of our love life and of how a woman should be cherished, how I should always be thinking of her and make it so for her that it would hardly seem like living when I was away. And I thought of all that might come after and the greater, broader happiness of it, and the rounded-out life with her lived faithfully.

Oh, I dreamed, dear, and I worked, too. And here we are! The dream is coming true.

"Be mine, give yourself to me literally, and obey me. Let there be in all your life just an abandonment of your entity for my sake. Try the experiment and you will get more for it,—for the responsibility and the delicacy and the thoughtfulness will be thrown on me,—than you would in any other way. You are a woman of ambition and intellect, but it is only one such as you who would do this thing. The weak woman would be petulant at times and not steadfast in purpose, and would yield to some passing trouble. I want you to be great enough to lose yourself. I do not say that it is right, nor that it should be the rule in marriage, for it would be evil were the right man not involved, but, in such case as comes sometimes, it is the perfection of dual oneness."

And to these sentimental outbursts, the crystallization of desert thoughts, the young woman had much to say. She was not afraid, though. Since the world began, despite what some of the weaker romances say, never has man been feared by woman in an earnest love-making. And this woman had no fear in her, though she had a certain timidity which puzzled Sargent and even puzzled herself. The intensity and masculine force of her lover startled her, but her own high-strung nature, while it responded to his, protested at the same time against this power which seemed to be taking complete possession of her.

She was a thoroughly self-reliant human being,

too, and revolted at the word "obey," as savoring of
servility and old-time notions of domestic rule, and
thought that to give herself to the young man was
enough, and, deep in her heart, resented his thinking it necessary to instruct her at all as to her
attitude toward him. But the strong love which
had grown up in her overwhelmed everything else,
and, silently, she thought that she would do better
than was asked of her; that, with her, for duty, love
should always stand in her relations to Sargent and
rule all and, as for obedience, she was certain that
love never would have to issue orders. "Where
Love puts on the uniform of a general, discards his
bow and arrow for a sword, and calls out 'Present
arms!' he has become a new sort of a god." She
ventured so to comment once when the man had
been talking somewhat loftily in his innocence; and
the old Judge, who was sitting near them, half
entering into their talk, smiled to himself and
whispered to the same respectful listener, "He
will learn! He will learn, in time!"

Barbara was perfectly happy, the more so
because she knew how happy she was. Love
brought to her the crown of her existence and she
could think of nothing more perfect than this
cloudless summer of the present, with an adoring
strong lover to love.

It troubled the ardent man a little, the very perfection of Barbara's content and happiness in the
moment; for happy as he was he ever longed for
the completion of it all in marriage. He could not
think with patience of ever leaving her again. He

had inwardly vowed to take her with him when his time came to go back to the world of work. "I will take my heaven with me," he had resolved.

And so, sometimes, Sargent chafed while Barbara lingered delightedly in the charmed present of love and dreaming, loth to cross the invisible yet potent line which separated her from a husband's arms.

They were two foolish people, but not the only ones in the world; not the first nor the last. On the whole, they were happy as some human beings deserve to be, as do all really true lovers.

CHAPTER XXVI.

"WHERE THE BEE SUCKS, THERE SUCK I."

It was at the crest and prime of the year, when flowers and leaves were fresh and young and bees were droning all day long in Barbara's garden.

It was almost too early for it, there were too many blossoms lying atop of the lush openings in the forest, or where the weeds grew beside the fields, and the buckwheat lot was just blossoming with its wide blown offering of all that was best for them to all the bees in the world, but one day Sargent, aided and abetted by the swart Michael, prepared for a hunting expedition. Barbara was to be one of the very select party, and the prize was a bee tree. Barbara was delighted to be able to reconcile her tenderness of heart for once with a hunting trip, and was as joyous as a robin as they started on their way, making straight for the wooded hills and across country to Gibb's clearing. They passed by the cabin where the farm hands, wandering men from Canada, mostly, lived in summer, while work was to be done, and the three adventurers, climbing the three-cornered rail fences, were soon in the woods.

As they walked along in the welcome shade Michael ran ahead of the lovers, or explored the forest on either side, returning to them from time

to time much as a dog runs around and comes
back to his master when a free walk is under way.

"Michael will never grow old," said Sargent,
looking after the active figure as it wound its way
in the woods ahead of himself and Barbara. "He
is not changed, he will always be a boy."

"He seems happy," returned Barbara, "and yet
there is something almost tragic in his fate. He
has stopped growing, in mind and body, and cannot
get beyond a certain point, but in all his senses he
is almost abnormally acute, and with him instinct
seems to make up for a lack of intellect."

"He is a faithful soul, too," Sargent said,
"although he is full of mischief. He confided to
me the other day, that although he hates the sight
of a book he longs to read, just to please his
mother."

"Poor martyr!" laughed Barbara, "he has to go
to the district school every winter, and I don't
know which to pity most, Michael or his teacher!"

Just then the object of their conversation burst
out upon them from a hollow tree, in which was one
of his own special hiding places, and as they came
to a creek he pointed out to Barbara another of his
haunts, a great soft maple, leaning far over the
water, and covered with wild grape vines. Running
like a squirrel up the gray trunk, he beckoned
Barbara, and would not be content until she had
swung, for a few minutes, in his vine-wrought cradle.
The delighted fellow laughed and clapped his
hands, and sung in a voice, musical, with a wild
note in it: "Rock-a-bye, baby, up in the tree-top!"

Then the stalwart form of Sargent had to take its turn in the airy hammock, and the two left Michael crooning to himself in his swing as they resumed their way. Soon he darted by them, for the thought of the bee hunt had returned to him in the midst of his swinging.

Michael knew bees. Sargent knew bees, too, but not as Michael did, and so it came that Michael was made the head and front of this vast undertaking of finding a bee tree in the forest at a season somewhat too early for the work.

Michael was almost a part of the woodland. He loved his mistress, Barbara, because she was good; and because he understood that she now belonged to him, he was henchman to the brown man, Sargent. It is hard to trace the reasoning of such a mind as his. He knew as friendly beings, his mother, and Judge Sloan, and Barbara. He knew and hated the inoffensive school-teacher who vainly tortured him with those small black figures on white paper which meant so much to many folk, but nothing to him. And he knew horses and dogs and cattle, and could sit so still in the forest that the birds and squirrels grew bold, and came to his hand to be fed. But best of all in the world to Michael, most loved and cherished, was his red violin. But of all these things he never talked, at least in words. Something of his soul he poured out in music, a music as simple, yet as freakish and baffling as his own personality.

"Oh, luckless wight," exclaimed Barbara, when Sargent showed himself splashed, and with one foot swinging wet, after a slip on the stones as he crossed the creek.

"Why wight?" queried Sargent. "What is a wight, Coppercrown? Tell me out of your garnered wisdom. And when you have described your wight, pray explain why he is always a 'luckless,' 'weary,' 'foolish' wight."

"I don't know," said Barbara, "what a wight may be; I seem to have a picture of him in my mind— but I do know that a wight has to be a somewhat unfortunate being, and though I said 'him' I really think there is such a thing as a feminine wight."

"Of course there is," assented Sargent. "You're one yourself, a feminine wight, with red hair, and a white dress, and a straw hat in her hand instead of on her head, where anybody but a wight would carry a hat, and one of your misfortunes just now is that you look so that you have to be kissed!"

And he kissed her then and there, before Michael came up with them. They stopped at the edge of Gibb's clearing, and looked out upon the sunny patch of greenery, while Michael busied himself about his bee-catching enterprise with some advice from Sargent thrown in now and again.

There are half-way pioneers as there are half-way poets, generals and statesmen. So it comes that in the shearing into the forest of a new country there are some who venture but for a year or two and then depart. All through the wild Northwest with the drift of those who cut away things came those who worked hardily for a brief time and then, being deficient in the lower jaw, abandoned the hard task. No one can tell why these certain strong men made clearings and then abandoned them; it may have been that the girl in the East had written to the young man that he might come back again; but adjacent to all the drift of civilization throughout northern Michigan were deserted "clearings," each a space hewed by some one in the forest and made fit for cultivation and then abandoned. These rare open spaces, little farms begun and then left, were, necessarily, well known to all the people on the really developed farms of the surrounding regions. They were oases in the forest, great bright places where the sun smote down over areas it had not seen before since the trees which once covered it had begun to grow. And there, upon the soil where great timbers had been felled and burned, upsprang a growth of such things as the land had never known before, a growth such as the shrewdest and most far-thinking of all the scientific men of all the world cannot yet account for.

There lay one day, as the suddenly happy or unhappy pioneer abandoned it, a burned area in the forest looking upward at the sun. One would think that the acorns or beechnuts which had been dropped for centuries on the soil might have become embedded and would sprout, and that there would uprise an infant forest of the same families as those which were all about, but this did not happen. From the beech-burned soil even the weeds which first grew were different from those which had existed in the region heretofore. Whence came this seeding? No man can tell. For there were

none of them in the region until axe and fire had
come. But the gross, rank, high-growing fire-weed
made first harvest. And as young trees sprang
upward they were not beech, nor maple, but poplars
growing thickly as in some flourishing nursery.
How were sown, and who sowed, these seeds?
From what comes that which appears when forest
land is cleared?

But there were great open spaces, where, somehow, the common grass of all the North which wins
its way eventually, had found a foothold and seized
upon certain territory, and where white clover grew
and many flowers and weeds rejoiced in its society,
where dandelions flourished in their season, and
the wild violet, and the wild phlox, and wild roses
in the damper places, with honeysuckles often.
And a little late in this region, in the higher and
dryer places where the grass grew more or less
gingerly, like the beard of Petruchio's sexton, the
wild strawberry, knowing better how to reach down
with its roots to the life juice beneath, flung out
great broad lush leaves and broad white blossoms,
and lived very well its life. A great place for wild
strawberries, the Northern Peninsula of Michigan.
There were half a hundred other honey-offering
things, blossoming sweet-scented in spaces of these
clearings. And the wild bees sought them, and
found what they wanted. There were two of these
clearings but a short half hour's walk from the Sloan
homestead; one, the Gibb's clearing, and the other,
Donahue's clearing, and to emerge from the forest
upon either one of them in summer or early

autumn was to come into a bright world of short
white clover exhaling a sweet fragrance, and a world
of droning and humming, and of a life which we
call beneath us, but the quality of which we can
only guess at.

There was an open area of perhaps two hundred
yards each way, an area somewhat lighter than the
main clearing.   Michael began his preparations for
the beguilement of the bees by building a little fire
toward the southern end of this space, and Sargent
and Barbara rested in the shade, not far away.
They were sitting in a part of the new-springing
forest, so that the little wood-encircled world was all
before them open to the eye.   Together they saw
much.   Barbara would have seen little, for she did
not know; Sargent saw more, for he had learned
some things; but how little have the most scientific
and woodcrafty of us learned as yet of the under
world which may perhaps be the upper world!
They heard the droning, which was sweet, and
through the laden air came to their senses the floating breath of the overflow of the growing and
blooming things about, which, for aught we know,
may feel and see in their own way.

The two sat and waited.   Near to one side, where
the open area cut sharply into the denser wood,
there stood an elderberry bush, vagrant, encroach-
ing, with one outstanding topmost limb of a foot or
so, with leaves only at the end; down, from somewhere, descended and perched upon the vacant space
of this bending, swaying twig a king-bird, and its
mate alighted near it.   Then before the eyes of the

two onlooking human beings, themselves full of
their hopes and fancies and darings, occurred the
every day exploiting performance of the brave and
fortunately skillful. An insect, it might be one of
the bees, would rise and wing its way from some
flower of the open area toward the forest, and
darting at right angles toward its quarry with such
infinite swiftness as can hardly be described, one of
the king-birds would catch the insect in midair, and
there was an end to one insect life and a partly
gratified appetite in a light-breasted and slate-col-
ored thing of the tree and air and perch. Then
suddenly from somewhere came the wild, generously
alarming cry of the ever-present bluejay as a hawk
swooped downward toward the thicket where song
sparrows were in sight. As the cry sounded, each
bird about the open space dived into the safety of
the greenery, the sentinel bluejay having led the
way, and the descending hawk, missing the prey,
dipped as a wave dips, and rose again toward the
sky, but not alone. The two king-birds dropped
from their perches with a curve so insignificant as
scarcely to be noticeable, and then shot upward close
together toward the hawk, which was seeking the
upper air. Fast he flew, but they flew faster, and
soon overtook him. Either one of them would have
been scarce a mouthful for him, but their lightning-
like swiftness placed him at a disadvantage, and he
knew it well. They flashed about and pecked and
belabored him from above, and though they could
not kill him, his strait was sore for half a mile away.
Then the two king-birds darted back over the

intervening distance and alighted, calmly insolent
and protective, into the tree where their own nest
was, and into the branches where no other bird
might venture safely.   Barbara looked on amazedly,
and Sargent explained the qualities of this little
bird, called the bee-martin in some parts of the
country, but whose name—the king-bird—fits it as
neatly as does the shell of an acorn its nut.

Sargent and Barbara, sitting at ease and speaking
in but low tones according to Michael's plea, were
amused to see the eyes of the swarthy bee-hunter
fixed upon them from time to time with a wondering, mysterious questioning in his dark gaze.   He
was fumbling over his little box of honey, whisper-
ing to himself, and then casting puzzled looks at
them until Sargent asked, at last: "What are you
thinking of?"   But he was only importunately
motioned to by Michael for silence.   This started
Barbara into a laugh and Sargent took the infection
of merriment, before long to be joined by Michael
himself, and the three made the wood ring with
happy, causeless laughter.

The lovers never heard from the lips of Michael
the gist of the thought which lay behind his speculative gaze, but he confided the secret to his mother.
Michael was thinking in that darkened mind of his,
of the old and decent custom of "telling the bees"
when death enters the family, and was wondering if
that ceremony were not as important when a marriage is celebrated.   He had his own thoughts and
opinions about the canny bees, and on no account
would he have omitted any attention to the hive or

more of them in the Judge's garden which he guarded as his own special property, captured as they were by him from their wild forest home.

Often in summer twilights, lengthened in these northern latitudes, Michael sat on a convenient log in the garden near the bee-hives he himself had made from a hollow basswood log, and played sleepy tunes to his small black and yellow friends. He talked to them, and crooned old songs and rhymes to them, and was sure that they understood him better than did the people around him—and who shall say that they did not?

When the laughter was over for a moment, Michael bestirred himself for his adventure and Sargent explained to Barbara the scientific lines upon which bee-hunting is founded. It is true that successful bee-hunting comes as a gift to certain unlearned folk, but there is science back of it, nevertheless.

Barbara watched Michael now, having previously examined at close range his outfit for capturing a few of the swarming marauders who were rifling every flower in sight.

He had a little box made of thin pine board, the cover of which slid easily back and forth in a groove and which had let into it a piece of window glass enabling the observer on the outside to see what was going on within. Michael drove a stick in the ground, and, somehow, so managed things that it stood there safely balanced at the height of a man's head, so that one watching anything flying from that box could get a fair sight from the start.

Then he picked up a flat stone and laid it near the bottom of the stake upon which the box was placed. In the box was merely a bit of honey in the comb, and in his pocket Michael had brought some bees-wax. In his fire the stone was heated, and upon it the beeswax was placed, where it melted and ran about. There arose then the beeswax odor which all the world knows, and it called the bees.

They came—only the good Lord knows the ways of the bee and the ant—but they came from the surrounding forest, drawn by the scent or fragrance or whatever you may call it which told them in some inscrutable way where was the sort of sweetness upon which their brief life must depend.

They came dipping toward the burning wax, but lifted upward and settled into the honey-laden box, and there having found a small fortune for the hive, began loading themselves to the utmost.

There were perhaps four or five bees upon the honey when Michael shot back the glass cover and left the gorging inhabitants imprisoned. Michael now cared no longer for Sargent and Barbara. He was as the gambler is, absorbed in nothing but his game, for your bee-hunter is as great a gambler in his way, though honestly and unknowingly, as any man who ever threw dice when the army swore terribly in Flanders, or who in later times has taken his chances in Monte Carlo or Baden-Baden. Michael but watched the bees. One by one each became surfeited or rather fully laden and essayed to leave the place wherein he had become imprisoned. Michael, the watchful, waited until all were full and impatient and bumping against the glass which seemed but sky to them, and then he drew back the slide suddenly, and yelled to Sargent:

"Watch! look where the bees go!"

Never was word better devised than that which is called a "bee-line," for straighter than bullet from its powder bed—since its trajectory is not inclining—flies the bee from its loading place to its home. What superhuman instinct enables it to do this no one can tell, but the fact remains.

The bees flew from the open box across the clearing, one after the other, all in the same line, which showed that they all belonged to the same lofty hive, while the keen eyes of Michael and Sargent followed them, noting the direction of their straight course. Barbara looked on amazed and interested. Twice and thrice was the experiment repeated, Michael becoming oblivious to all else in the pulse of his search, and Sargent himself getting almost as much involved in the interest of the thing. They had a "line" and a promising one, because the great number of the bees indicated a hive of magnitude, but how far away from them in the forest was the bee-tree was another matter. They knew how to settle that question, though. The bees had flown northeast, almost directly. But a short distance east of them was the Donahue clearing, and there they went. Again were repeated all the pioneer enticements for the bees, again all about the trio were the wonderfully sweet blandishments of the summer life of the region, and again came the bees to sip to their full, and cloyed, to fling themselves away in a straight line through mid-air to the hive in some great lofty tree bole. Before, they had flown northeast, and now they flew northwest, to Barbara's bewilderment; and Sargent and Michael, the man of the world as excited as the creature of the forest, discussed the matter, but not with hopelessness. The two men, each in his own way, knew that the two flights must have met, and that where they met was the bee-tree. Uprising above the general sky-line of the forest was a gigantic pine which was agreed to be a little to the north of where the lines must intersect and, since this particular pine happened to stand in an open space, and to have been a landmark for many wanderings, they could estimate as to where within a radius of not many hundreds of yards must be their bee tree. They bolted away all three together, Michael a little in the lead, trotting with head down like a beagle, and Sargent running along after, hand in hand with Barbara, laughing also, but running, as a matter of course, as the hind follows the hart.

They reached a place near where they thought should be the bee-tree, and in a little open space they found Michael repeating the exploit of the clearings. Little time was required now. As soon as the wax burned there was a descent, not of one, but of a host of bees upon the honey in the open box. No longer were they imprisoned at all, but were allowed to fill themselves and fly away. They were too near home now to toy with other sweets before carrying their conquests to the hive. They came in hosts and loaded themselves greedily and then flew up with a slant so steep that the half barbaric Michael danced about excitedly.

"We've got 'em," he said.

They moved the lure a few hundred feet to the right and the bees came as before, in hosts, and thus they gained another locating point, a close one this time, and again making an estimate and again moving, they came into an opening in the midst of which stood a gigantic red oak, dead, apparently, on one side, from a growth of fifty feet above its roots. The bees flew straight upward now, and keen eyes soon detected the opening to one of the great hives of the wilds. Just above a vast dead limb there was a little black hole into the huge brown trunk, and about this opening weaved and buzzed a coming and going swarm of little black workers, as numerous as about the hives of the ordinary homestead where bees are kept. The bee tree was found.

There is a custom, which is also a law, which gives to the discoverer of a bee-tree a right to it if into the bole of the tree he cuts, squarely and cleanly, initials, indicating ownership. Sargent knew this well, and taking Michael's little axe he hewed into the vesture of that not altogether prosperous forest monarch the outlines "B. S." "It's an ancient compliment," he said. "Youths say it when they give some caramels, but, 'Sweets to the Sweet.'" So Barbara owned a bee-tree.

As for Michael, that elfish young man was lost in anticipation of the night when he should come with full authority, and men to help him, to take and carry home the sweet spoils of this summer day.

As they walked slowly homeward through the woods, Michael fairly flying on before, the lovers went hand in hand, like two school children.

"I can hardly believe in this happiness of ours," Sargent said, earnestly. "I have dreamed a hundred times of being by your side, secure in your love, as I am now, and it has come true. To be happy, and to know how happy one is—that is wonderful."

"Yes," Barbara said, "children are happy, but they don't know it. We know just how to be thankful, don't we?"

CHAPTER XXVII.

"MORE."

The wise lover has occasion frequently to pay almost as much attention to some man as to his sweetheart. He becomes interested in the welfare of the males of the family with which he may become connected. So it came that Sargent, sympathetic and strong, was attracted anew to the father of this Barbara. The men came to care more and more for each other and the elder to lean on the younger. It was fortunate that this was so, for a man young, forceful and resolute was needed on the scene.

It is a proverb that shoemakers' children go unshod. This may or may not be literally the case, but it appears to be a generally admitted fact that not one lawyer or even judge in a dozen is a good business man. His advice to others upon business subjects may be perfect, but, like the physician, the lawyer does not seem capable of healing himself. Conditions are neglected in theories. So it happened that Judge Sloan, wise and just jurist, owning, because he had paid for it, a large and valuable tract of land in northern Michigan, was in danger of losing his estate. He, who as a judge had passed upon the quality of a thousand titles, had neglected, in his own buying, sufficient inquiry into the clear-

17

ness of a title the quality of which was much to him. There was a weak spot in it. Some miles distant from Judge Sloan's place there lived a queer and not altogether reputable old person named John Tisdale, half hunter, half trapper and about one-third drunkard, who, in earlier days, had secured from the general government a patent on the land which was now Judge Sloan's. The hunter had, long ago, sold his perfect title for some small sum, but had never properly transferred it, though the one to whom he sold had, in all honesty, given, when he in turn had disposed of it, a warranty deed of usual form. From that had come the transmission to Judge Sloan, but the title was not flawless.

Old Hiram Slade—it is odd how regions and conditions breed them—old Hiram Slade, smooth-haired and pallid, and gray-bearded with shaved upper lip, the land cormorant of the big, wild county, had, in his seekings among the books of the recorder's office in the little county seat of Conway, ten miles away, discovered the nature of the flaw in Judge Sloan's title and had sought out disreputable old John Tisdale in his hut and bought from him a quit-claim deed to all the property involved in the original patent. He paid only twenty dollars—for old Tisdale, when extremely thirsty, would have sold his soul's prospects—and there might have been a profit on the trade—for half the sum.

So began the work of Hiram Slade; but, later, it so happened that from the same money so transferred came what might mar the scheme, for Tisdale, squandering most of it in a debauch in Conway, became too talkative and told of how his sudden wealth had come. His chatter reached the ears of Judge Sloan upon his next visit to the town, and he, listless though he ordinarily was, became sufficiently impressed to himself seek out John Tisdale in his fastness and get from him a quit-claim deed as old Hiram Slade had done, for the Judge had discovered that the Slade deed had not been yet recorded. The irresponsible and thirsty Tisdale would have given quit-claim deeds, as he had a legal right to do, to any one to any piece of property in all the Peninsula of Northern Michigan. Much depended now upon the exhibition of energy in the recording of a deed, but neither of the two most interested knew of the imminence of things.

As related, Sargent and the old Judge were drawing more closely together, and so it came that the older told the younger, in a general way, of his monetary difficulties, but failed to give him details. Trouble and stress would have been avoided if he had but told more. The Judge had himself almost forgotten that his deed had to be recorded to make good the title which was his in equity. And the days passed by and the young grouse were getting feathers in place of down, when matters became serious. The details of what happened then must come a little later.

After all, there is no such thing as smooth sailing, with a woman in the boat, thought Sargent, when he came to press upon Barbara the setting of the time for their marriage. Sargent was anxious to convey his bride home with him before the fall of the

leaves, but he found little encouragement to enlarge
upon this dream to Barbara. Whenever he approached the subject with an air of practical determination Barbara whirled away into the universe
anywhere for a subject of talk except in the line the
lover was taking.

Once, when fairly at bay, she turned on the young
man, and reproached him for intruding the topic of
marriage upon their little lover's heaven.

"Marriage is so prosaic," she cried. "Why,
you'll be calling me 'My Dear,' and talking about
rents and taxes to me, when once we are married.
I can just hear you say: 'My Dear, have you seen
the morning paper?' Ugh!" And she shivered over
the anticipated horrors of the bleak and humdrum
matrimonial existence she had conjured up.

At another time, when the great question of the
hour had been craftily sprung by the perplexed
lover, Barbara gravely explained that she had
serious fears about certain details of their marriage.

"You see," she said, "whom could we get,"—and
here she had the grace to blush,—"to perform the
ceremony? The only clergyman in the woods here
is Elder Goings, a good man he is, but a toothless,
and, if he can read, he can't speak one sentence
straight; I mean as to grammar and pronunciation."

"What difference would that make?" said the
infatuated lover.

"Difference! Why, I simply will not stand up—I
could not, and keep my countenance,—while he said,
'Barbary, do you take Robe-r-r-t to be' "—but here
the mimic was hushed by force of arms.

"The only other possible man," she continued, when she had caught her breath, "is Squire Fletcher, —the young squire, but he stammers so I should die! I could not stand it! We'll have to give it up! But, don't you think we are very happy as we are?"

"Barbara," said Sargent, "you mean to marry me, don't you?"

"Oh, yes, some day," was her reply, "but mind, no cold-blooded, set, ordained, and duly elaborated wedding shall we ever have! You shall come some fine morning like young Lochinvar and ride away with me on your saddle, or like the lover in St. Agnes' Eve you shall steal me away some bitter cold night and together we will ride through the pelting snow! That would be something like!"

Here she was brought to an end of her discourse.

"Now, by my halidom, fair shrew!" thundered Sargent, springing to the open doorway! "Married thou shalt be without delay, even to me and by bell book and candle! I'll saddle the snow-white roan and prick to the Straits, and eftsoon bring back a sleek priest, an' he can urge his ambling palfry from a walk! And then, scornful though thou art, the blessed rite shall join us ere set of the morrow's sun!"

He tightened his belt around his waist, as for the journey, but a momentary diversion cleverly executed by his fair enemy and enslaver delayed him, he hesitated, and the mad ride in search of a parson was postponed.

One day—alack the day! It must come even with true lovers—the two quarreled. Sargent, intoxicated with the new wine of assured love, was very buoyant, and had just told Barbara as they walked in the woods together, that nothing could ever trouble him, now that he was sure of her. Then Barbara, echoing back his happiness, at first, lapsed into a dreamy silence from which she emerged to announce that she had something "serious" to say.

"That is almost as bad as if you said you were going to speak plainly and tell me the truth about something," said Sargent, "but go on, sweetheart, and be as serious as you may, if you only aver, to begin with, that you love me well!"

The declaration of undying love was duly made with appropriate ceremonies such as lovers know, and then Barbara proceeded to unburden her mind.

It was nothing but a young woman's tender thought about the father she was to leave while she followed the fortunes of a husband in his roving life; and Sargent met the loving heart half-way, and unfolded plans he had already made to secure the comfort and happiness of Judge Sloan when his child should leave him.

They had an hour of quiet, loving talk together, speaking of the widowed sister of the Judge, who, with her daughter, was to come and live with him, and of other family affairs. Barbara was anxious, not only over her father's future, but his present troubles, of which she knew enough to make her uneasy. To-day she was, in consequence of this unspoken worry, a little out of tune with the world, tender of feeling, and easily ruffled. The talk drifted from personal matters after a while, and then some little word of Sargent's, it might have been about the moon or stars, or how the bark grew upon a tree,—it happened to be the character and possibilities of the American Indian that they were discussing—neither knew how or why, but a spark of anger leaped from Barbara's eyes. Sargent blunderingly fanned the blaze, and, in a minute, the two were flaming in angry debate. Sargent was the first of the two to regain himself, and he tried to laugh the whole episode away, but in vain. They walked back to the house in moody silence, and Barbara kept herself out of the light of her lover's eyes during most of the day, while he resolved never to boast again of complete happiness and was quite miserable in a protesting, impatient way, having completely forgotten what the whole wretched quarrel was about; indeed he could only recall that Barbara was angry with him, and declare to himself that he was doubtless a brute.

He went about like an uneasy ghost, and, at night, was stalking moodily out into the moonlight for a walk, just as the family were retiring to their rooms.

Barbara, in her white dress, came to the door, and seeing Sargent standing on the pathway, stepped upon the porch landing and slowly approached the silent, brooding figure near the gate. Not a word was said as the slight figure joined the stalwart one. The man turned toward her silently and the woman took his arm. They walked up and down the pathway together and something was said in a perfunctory way about the luxuriance of the night. Then Sargent broke out suddenly:

"I set a rhinestone in gold. The trouble with me and my family and race is that we cannot pluck out the rhinestone and put a real jewel in its place. It is decreed that way. We must be faithful to what or whom we love, be it good or bad."

The girl did not answer, except to ask him if he thought he had ever seen a clearer night or when the stars hung lower, even in their northern country? He answered courteously but stiffly. So they walked up and down and through the garden until the time came when she said she must go in and parted gently from him.

This was good night, he knew, and, furthermore, he began to realize that he had made, in some measure, an ass of himself, as men deeply in love do easily. Yet he was stiff in his repentance, as men sometimes are, and when, as she turned to go away, he took her hands and drew her toward him, he kissed her very lightly.

The girl drew back with the moonlight smiting pleasantly on her fair face. She looked upward into the face towering above her and lifted up a pair of lips not of the sort to be resisted.

"More," she said.

CHAPTER XXVIII.

JOHN HALFDAY'S ERRAND.

Judge Sloan seemed to be quite easy as to the designs of Hiram Slade upon his property, and after he had unburdened his mind to Sargent he settled back into his usual abstracted yet genial mood, delighting to be interrupted in his reading by any conversation upon abstract subjects, but rather resentful if topics of every-day import were thrust upon him.

Barbara, keenly alive to all which touched her father, and full of youthful ardors of love and hate, had become intensely interested in the character of Hiram Slade, who was, as she said to Sargent, the nearest approach to a villain that she had ever seen in her quiet corner of the great world, and it was not surprising that such conclusion had been reached by her.   Cupidity is the most inexplicable of vices to generous natures, and to inexperience it is incredible. The lovers reasoned and argued much, as is always the wont of ardent young folk, over the puzzling problems of the never-ending study of man in this world.   They were, fortunately, not touched by the rage of religious or doctrinal dispute, being content to rest unquestioningly in the quieting arms of the faith into which both had chanced to be born. They, in their happy mood, were full of love toward

God and all his creatures; and they had no arrogant idea that they were right in all their religious beliefs, while all who differed from them were wrong. They simply rested in loyal faithfulness to the high ideals which are, after all, discernible in every branch of the Christian religion, and which had been held up to them wisely and lovingly in the impressionable years of childhood and of youth.

But there were the endless themes of human virtues and failings, aspirations and defeats, and all the wondrous turns of character and incident to talk about and wonder over, and there were the allied fields of literature and art to compare. The two found sympathies and antipathies in common, and sometimes they found themselves firmly opposed in likes and dislikes—and as the days passed by, they delighted more and more in each other.

Barbara, for example, rebelled at the more insisted upon forms of the doctrine of heredity, and brooded in awed pity over the saying of her father in one of the talks of the three together, that "every man is what he must be." Sargent, fascinated by the theme, drew from the Judge tales of his judicial experiences, and certain stern conclusions which had come from them.

The Judge averred that the grasping man—Slade was the text of his homily—was seldom a thief. "Worldly wisdom will not allow outright theft," he declared. "Of course he who cheats his neighbor out of his property is as bad as a thief," continued the Judge, "but he is not, after all, a thief. The thief is another kind of man, has a different head, differing eyes, hands, feet, and entirely different make-up, from that of the sharper and swindler or grasping land shark we know of. But neither of them can help, once he has yielded to his bent, being what he is." And then to these thoughtful, speculative human beings, educated and understanding, and more or less contented together, came what disturbs life swiftly.

At one side of the garden, underneath where two maple trees grew close together, there had been made a long seat and upon this seat the three, father, daughter and lover, had been accustomed to idle and talk together after the mid-day dinner in the shade of the early afternoon. It was very pleasant, this communing, but there was, too, the almost inevitable jostle which shows the quality of such human beings as may be affected by it.

One day as the three sat quietly in the garden after dinner, their talk running on this very theme of human failings and their almost fateful inevitableness, Michael came running like a line of blue in his jeans overalls and "jumper"—which is a sort of jacket—across the fields from the encircling trees. He came from the direction of the road which ran a short distance from Judge Sloan's boundaries, from the woods toward Conway, the county seat and town eleven miles away.

Instead of making for the barn, his usual goal, or the kitchen door, where Tilda stood looking at him, and ready with an errand for him, Michael came straight to the little group under the maples, and without removing his cap, worn summer and winter, the swarthy youth began a hurried, half inarticulate tale to Judge Sloan in which John Halfday, the Indian runner, at whose cabin by a lake in the woods near by, Michael spent much valuable time loafing and talking about fishing, and Hiram Slade, and Conway seemed mixed in inextricable confusion.

Sargent, at the first word, sprang to his feet, and Judge Sloan, as he gradually realized what Michael was telling him, became as one fixed in despair and self-reproach.

From Michael's confused talk it was at last gathered that while the lazy youth was lounging about the cabin of John Halfday, the Indian runner who was known over the whole State alike for his habitual indolence and his great feats of occasional running, Hiram Slade had appeared, on foot, and engaged the Indian to go with the utmost speed to Conway with a paper, which must be handed in at the Court House before five o'clock that day. The Indian had at once made ready to go, as it was then long after noon, and it was eleven miles by the road to Conway. Michael had not been noticed by Slade until the Indian started on his way, when Michael came from his seat on the chopping-log back of the cabin, where he had heard the bargaining between Slade and Halfday. Slade caught the black-eyed Norseman's cub roughly by the shoulder, and threatened to "skin him alive" if he said anything about John Halfday's errand, and Michael, twisting himself out of Slade's hands, had run for home with such speed as was in his spindle legs.

Slade, as he saw him go, had shouted after John Halfday that he must run for his life. The Indian looked back, uncertain of Slade's meaning, and stood still to hear what he had to say. "Run! Run for your life!" yelled Slade. The Indian at last made out the words that were being hurled at him. He straightened himself up, tightened his belt, and set off on a dog-trot, a gait he could keep up for hours, along the road toward Conway. All this the keen eyes and ears of Michael noted as he skirted along the road which swerved by one side of the Sloan homestead, and all this he told gaspingly, for, somehow, this combination of keen and dull wits knew that Slade and Judge Sloan had differing interests, and by some instinct such as simple natures sometimes have, he had connected the errand of John Halfday with a threatening of Judge Sloan's peace and happiness.

"Father, what troubles you?" anxiously asked Barbara.

Judge Sloan explained: "Hiram Slade has heard that I hold a quit-claim deed from Tisdale; he has secured another himself and has sent John Halfday to record it. This will cause me endless trouble, and I may lose the property altogether."

"But, Judge Sloan," said Sargent, "your title is all right! You were saying only the other day that you had in your hands John Tisdale's quit-claim deed to all the property of the original patent."

"I have never had it recorded," Judge Sloan said, in a voice of anguish. "I have neglected it from day to day—and now it is too late!"

"Father," said Barbara, "send Michael for my pony; I know your horse is lame; and let him ride to Conway and record your deed before Halfday can get there."

"The horses are out in the woodland ranges, Barbara,"—the Judge spoke in a dejected tone— "and your pony is with them. It would take an hour to find them."

"What time is it?" asked Sargent, suddenly.

"Past three o'clock," was the answer.

"See!" cried Michael, pointing southward where the road reached the crest of a hill, and as they looked they all saw John Halfday hurrying along the road as it disappeared upon the wooded hill-top.

"I will take your deed to Conway," said Sargent to Judge Sloan. "I can go across country, saving a mile's distance, and possibly reach the recorder's office before Halfday. If I am there half a minute first it will be all right."

Then, seeing Judge Sloan hesitate, he turned to Barbara. "Please run and get the paper," he said, "while I make ready for the go. I think I can win in a race with any Indian, even with Halfday, who has won more prizes at running than I have. Anyhow, I'll try it."

Barbara, directed where to look by her father, sprang into the house, and returned immediately with an official looking envelope from which Judge Sloan took and examined the quit-claim deed before giving it to Sargent.

The young man was dressed in the easy costume of his western work, with blue flannel shirt, leathern

belt and corduroys.   He had thrown off his coat and
looked well to his shoes, which were broad of sole,
yet well fitting his feet; he had sent Michael flying
to his room for a cap in place of the straw hat he
usually wore, and now he stood ready for the start,
a tall, sinewy, well-knit figure, with energy and
determination showing in every line of his face and
every motion of his body.

Old Tilda, unable to bear the strain of curiosity
longer, was half-way from the house to the
little group of excited people of which her son had
been the center.   What had Michael done now? the
mother asked herself.   Had he burned the school-
house, out of hatred to his place of torment?—a
vision of his crime blazed across Tilda's mental
horizon, for Michael had made dire threats against
school and school-master last winter, when he had
been forced to school, despite his age, for he was
still almost unable to read.   But somehow, as she
approached the knot of four earnest people, standing in the garden, Tilda's quick instinct told her
that her dwarfish son was rather the subject of
approval from his betters than otherwise, and she
stood still, watching Sargent as he spoke quietly and
earnestly to Judge Sloan and then turned to Barbara
for a word before leaving her.   The girl's face was
trustful, and full of pride as she looked up at her
lover.   It was an hour of triumph for Michael when,
a little later, he stood by Tilda's chair and under
maternal authority submitted to her questionings as
to what had occurred.

CHAPTER XXIX.

THE FOOT RACE.

As he stepped down upon the walk that led between the flower-beds, Sargent turned a laughing glance back toward Barbara. "I must hurry," he said, then walked lightly down the path to the gate and, as soon as he reached the slope outside, went forward at a trot. The girl had walked to the house and stood in the doorway watching him and, though he did not intend it should be so, saw him change his gait as he turned the corner down the roadway. As for him, his heart was full of her and his lungs full of the pure air of the region, and, though he was not assured of the outcome of the run, he felt at least hopeful and resolved. He would do the best he could! What man so fortunate as to own her would not do the best he could for the creature standing there in the doorway! Before him was the tremen. dous task of a straight-away run of more than ten miles across a wooded and uneven country, the sort of run that has tested all there is in man's physique since the Olympian days, but he was not distressed. He ran easily and smoothly, even after he had reached the first upward slope. He was in fair bodily condition, because of his so recent hard experiences in the far southwest. And, as he increased his pace, he thought of the college races and of how a trained man of his quality should run a mile in at least eight minutes easily.

But miles are cruel things. It is in the second mile of such rough racing as this that the strongest and best of runners becomes aware that he is running. So after the first up-hill work came the consciousness to Sargent, and it came portentously. He knew within a very little time that he had what was very like a headache, that there was a slight pain in his side, that his feet were burning a little and that his eyes seemed dim in a way, while his mouth was becoming dry. But he made the mile in decent time.

The bodily distresses increased upon him and, while the manhood in him prevented even the slightest consideration of it, the suggestion developed in his mind that it would be delightful to stop and rest. He had an up-hill run now, and that was trying. He went at it resolutely, but his gait became slower and slower as his energy was expended. The upward reaching space was at least a quarter of a mile and near the top he faltered into a walk and so reached, at last, a long level. As he emerged upon the even space the breath came back to him, and the bodily infirmities decreased because the walk had aided him. Into his mouth came back the moisture which is comfort to the human being. His feet had been dry and burning. They also were now moist again. He was less absorbed in the sensations of his own body and reverted more in thought to what it was all about. He thought of that girl of his whom he had left such a little time

18

ago standing there in the doorway and he ran faster all across the level and on a downward grade.

The grade continued sloping slightly and he freshened at every step. Now that he had comparative ease for thinking came keener conceptions in every way and, so, clearer sense of obligation. He worried over the thought of how the Indian might be running. Then in the midst of this anxiety he broke out on an expanse of soggy ground, across which no runner could run with anything like speed. His heart fell then, but there was no pausing. At the end of half a mile, after steps light, well placed and leg-straining, he emerged upon an open, rising stretch of solid ground. What a relief it was to feel what was reliable under his feet again! But now the pains came back and all the burnings and thirst. Then over a slight beech-crested rise he looked forward upon what to him seemed more beautiful than had ever appeared such a common thing before. It was nothing but a creek of clear water running straight across his course. Somewhere in the Bible, some fine old fellow uses as an illustration the expression, "As the hart panteth after the water-brooks," but as compared with Sargent, the hart had little of sensation. As he reached that water he plunged into it half knee deep and his feet were new things in a moment. He bent over and with scooping hands laved face and head, and then pulling back his sleeves, thrust his arms half-way to the elbow, down until they rested on the pebbly bottom, and so stood there bent uncouthly upon "all fours" until hands and feet were cooled together. The rest was brief, but when Sargent strode out on the bank something like normal existence had come again. He stood there for a moment, reached up his arms and stretched them outward and said to himself, "I feel almost as if I hadn't been running," and he started off resolutely and easily at a dog-trot.

The course now lay up-hill for half a mile and in the midst of that wearing trot Sargent found that the water in his shoes and stockings made it necessary for him to sit down and wring out those articles of garb. They were heavy as leaden soles upon his feet. He wrung the stockings dry as could be done with his strong hands and put them on again with the drained shoes. Somehow, even after this little rest, he now felt fagged, and finished the up-hill climb in a simple walk. The crest reached, there seemed to come again the vigor of all his manhood. The water and the walk had freshened him and half his long run was done.

There was a level stretch now and the big fellow inhaled a deep breath and started out upon what was like running again. There was a course of a mile where the obstacles were but slight and the man thought as he ran how easy it would be to beat the Indian if the cross country forest route were all like this. He ran this mile in admirable time, but as he neared the pine-gladed end and saw another hill before him in the distance, there came that sinking of the heart, or, to speak with more absolute correctness, that apparent sinking of the stomach which runners know so well. The straining man was worried.

The physical was attacking the mental with all its force, and Sargent wondered if he mightn't gain even something by a little rest.   Then came to him the thought of the fair woman and of all he was running for and of what would follow if he should fail.   There came, too, an undercurrent of something of the athlete's pride and he thought of the contempt in which he himself had always held any one who is designated in the language of the race-courses, and even of college athletics, as "a quitter."

He struggled forward at a reasonable speed.   For the first half mile it was level and then the man found that he was going down-hill at a slope greater than he had yet encountered, and knew that the down-hill course he must now take would be more killing than even the up-hill struggle.   For the first time he dropped from toe running to what racers call the flat-foot, that is, dropping from the spring of the toe to the more resisting flat of the entire sole.   Then came the inevitable which must always come somewhere in a ten mile race of a man across rough country.   Sargent may have been more or less wise in the things he had done in the first half of his body and mind distressing race.   It may have been that he was wise or unwise in walking into the creek and, after what he did, getting the cool comfort from head to heel which came from the creek's waters.   But almost any woman servant can wring out a stocking or anything else better than any man can—and this includes Cæsar and George Washington, and any one else one can think of—and so this strong man, this keen man, this brown man who had handled other men for years, this man who was exerting himself for the one woman as every good man ought to do, felt that in the matter of wringing out his stockings he hadn't accomplished all the ends which might possibly be desired, and there came across his forehead the perspiration which was the result of what began with being an annoyance and was reaching the dignity of being a torture. The stockings clung clammily, there was an abrasion between them and the linings of his shoes and he knew and feared, from experience, before he felt what was coming, that the now tender skin of the soles of his feet was, by this shifting abrasion, being scraped away to rawness. His shoes slipped backward and forward beneath his feet in a little way, but sufficient, with all the wetting and the heating of the running, to cut away that good hard callous which comes alike upon the soles of the greatest statesman, philosopher or poet, or of the most delicate woman who ever trod the earth, though violets might scarcely bend beneath her step. It is exceedingly hard, this particular sort of pain, upon a man, for no man, big and strong though he be, bears these sorts of the more commonplace agonies as well as the weakest woman; but he straightened out upon his toes again and so saved a little of the suffering. He weaved a little as he ran and worried over the time lost.

Then came a time when physical and mental stress were nearly alike. This was, though Sargent knew very little of it, so far as definite knowledge of distances went, somewhere about the beginning of the eighth mile of his long run; there was still a slope downward and he drew in his breath and tried to feel what was in his muscles again and exerted what energy he had in covering ground until the rise began. He knew now that whatever his opponent might be doing, either one of them could not be at a running gait save for a portion of the time, though the Indian might trot. There was a half mile of this good work with lungs and mouth and feet all in tolerably good condition, until he faced a steep uprising hill again. The very sight of the hill seemed to affect the mental condition of the man. The headache came back. The feet, under the rasping of the wetted, half dried stockings, were but raw things on their soles. Everything bore upon him, and he was beginning to give out. There must come a time when any man who ever lived and fought or ran, whether for fame or money or a woman, must feel himself beginning to give out. Still, though his physical machinery was weakening, the mental powers of the man were in good working order. He staggered up the hill and wished he could "kick" himself for being such a weakling. He used bad language to himself. He wondered why he hadn't kept himself in better trim—though there was no particular reason why he should have done so—and, in a general way, made little of the person he was. He thought of how much better bursts of speed he had made in college days over even rougher ground, and became even more enraged at himself and used more bad language, from the stomach—if language may originate there.

Then came a level stretch again and the foolish fellow's mind cleared and he began again to know what he was doing. He had sense enough, even after all that tapping of his physical resources and its effect upon his mind, to remember that his forces should be conserved and, even when he again came upon the level, attempted no great burst of speed. He ran steadily, evenly, but within limits, for all there was in him as long as the level lasted. Then came to him the queer feeling which comes to runners of long distances. He felt as if his arms and his feet were dropping off. There was something the matter with the joints. The muscles around where they worked seemed too flexile and flaccid and his limbs departing from his body. There was something the matter, too, with the muscles of the top of the spinal column, for his head lopped forward as he ran. And still he maintained his speed.

Suddenly, the man emerged upon the crest of a hill from which were slopes far down into a pleasant valley where nestled a little northern town, with its two church spires and its somewhat preposterous court house dome, the court house being in the center of what was known as the "City Square," and surrounded by a stiff board fence about seven feet in height, the sole entrance to this square being upon the eastern side, opening thus from what was recognized as the main thoroughfare, because assuredly the best boots and the best whisky could be bought along that single block. Here, in open sight, was the goal of the running man. It was there before his eyes and he was run-ning down-hill again, and this time as he ran down-ward there was very little imagination about it when he thought to himself that there were no soles upon his feet. With the attrition of all this varying striding, his feet were skinned, and but for the excitement upon him, he would have been suffering one of the various forms of torture such as were devised in mediæval times. But he scarcely knew it. He saw the town in the distance and he had an object. Take a strong man and some excitement and some water and a woman to win, and what that man may or may not do depends upon accidents—and the man. As he ran, Sargent knew that the bottom of his feet were raw, that the stockings he wore were now sticking to them and now pulling away, and again came to him the feeling that his arms and legs were unconnected with the rest of his body. Another odd feeling came to him. His head was like a furnace, and he imagined foolish things. He imagined the road suddenly lifting itself up at a hard angle in front of him, and then, too, he had great difficulty in avoiding stumps and trees which existed nowhere in the vicinity. It seemed all right in a way, even the passage through these varying things, but there came suddenly a gulp in the throat of the man as he ran and a sort of quiver through him, and he was scared. He was scared, not for himself, that is as to whether he were dying or not, but whether or not he could be a "quitter." As he stumbled down the pathway, for it was little more than stumbling now, he came upon a spring and had at least sense enough, or if not sense, instinct left to throw himself beside it and bathe his head and hands. Then came sudden reasoning power again and comprehensiveness of all surroundings. Tottering somewhat, he resumed his course and came out upon the open. The little town lay before him to the east. He glanced around and across and there, to the south, he saw, as he emerged from the woods, the Indian, John Halfday, who had issued from the forest at the same moment and who stood looking at him, poised and astonished. There they stood, the white man and the Indian, at the two corners of an equilateral triangle. At the other corner stood the court house, with the opening of its high board fence on the Indian's side.

The two men, the white and the red, looking at each other across the valley, knew what each must try to do. The amount of time lost then would have to be considered by the finest of stop-watches. They simply hurled themselves down their respective hills together, each thinking and thinking "mighty hard" in his own way.

It is very doubtful if, since the world began, a man ever really knew when he had "given out," as we would call it. Sargent had thought that he had given out at three or four places during the tremendous run, and, assuredly, he thought he was exhausted when he reached the crest of the round ridge surrounding the little town. But it never occurred to this man who threw himself down the hill that he was exhausted at all; it never occurred to him that he had been running for some distance on this particular day. And here comes in an odd thing. It may be to his credit or to his discredit, but as he ran he forgot that he was running for a woman or for right or for anything in particular. There but uprose in him in this last great strait and strain of his exertion of all that was in him the one feeling, which the Berserker knew, which the Anglo-Saxons know and have in them to-day, the feeling simply that the other fellow must be beaten. And this was all that Sargent thought, and even that he thought but vaguely, as he burst down the hill toward that brown board fence.

Good running did that Indian as well, and he knew the town and knew what he had to do. There was just what might be called a streak of Indian from the forest clear down to where the court house square was, and each yard's advance of his opponent was noticed by Sargent in his run. And now, after all distress, his mind suddenly seemed clarified. He gauged relative paces. He knew that the Indian entering at the east gate and the only gate at the Court House Square must reach the Recorder's office before he could, by keen running, straight away. Were it not for the high board fence he had a chance. Oh, for a vaulting pole! But wherever in a town of northern Michigan are vaulting poles lacking? The pike poles of the lumberman and the loggers lie all about, and upon one of these the eyes of the fortunate runner alighted. He seized upon it, and the uplifting leap as he cleared that great board fence was the last great effort of his long race. He fell in a heap among some clover, fell in a heap and scrambled up clumsily with bumble-bees about him, and little more than stumbled through the court house door and into the Recorder's office.

"This for record—" he almost croaked. "Look at the clock!"'

There was what seemed but a shadow in the hallway, and John Halfday leaped in. He looked about, said nothing, and then with a grunt laid a paper on the nearest desk and walked out again.

CHAPTER XXX.

ROSE IN BLOOM.

"And the world went very well then." Slowly the belated summer fared northward; the tender leaves of the maples, shaped as if patterned by the fantastic hand of some artist of the exotic East, were approaching their climax of beauty; the beech leaves were unrolled, and as their early red tints vanished there came to them a color so delicate, so refined and ideal, that looking at the sky through the branches they lived upon, the heart of the forest lover was exalted, so potent was their story of vigorous young life.

"To call those trees green, and the sky behind them blue," said Barbara, as she stood with Sargent wondering over the beauty of a grove of beeches outlined against the pure sky of morning, "is an evil misuse of words." And as Sargent assented, she continued: "In nothing is language so poverty-stricken as in its attempts at color description. The poets are driven to the flowers or birds—to nature—for words which give only a dim idea of what colors really are."

"And so we have 'daffodil skies' and 'violet eyes' and 'saffron dyes'," chimed in Sargent, but Barbara stopped him with an imperious wave of the hand.

"I hope you are not 'dropping into poetry,' or

trying to do so on your own account. If you are I warn you from the set of rhymes you are trespassing on! They belong to the Queen!"

"What Queen? I acknowledge but one, and what is mine is hers and what is hers is mine," the lover answered.

"Oh! but you are a true and loyal subject to this Queen!" insisted Barbara. "I have only to name her—Titania!"

"Of course," admitted Sargent, "and you are thinking of that reaching, imperfect perfection of a speech of hers, where at first the rhyme is to the eyes and not to the ears, and then there is a jar at the end of one line—a discord, to make the coming music sweeter."

"I am sure that is one of the things that has always stuck fast in your memory, as it has in mine!" cried Barbara, for in such discoveries of common tastes and delights the two always reveled. And they chanted together like two children the sometimes almost cloying sweetness of the Poet of all human passions as well as of the most unearthly fairy fancies:

> "Feed him with apricocks and dewberries,
> With purple grapes, green figs and mulberries,
> The honey-bags steal from the bumblebees;
> And for night tapers crop their waxen thighs,
> And light them at the fiery glowworm's eyes,
> To have my love to bed and to arise;
> And pluck the wings from painted butterflies
> To fan the moonbeams from his sleeping eyes,
> Nod to him, elves, and do him courtesies."

They strolled into the deeper woods, along the

creek, and, after a little silence, when the song was ended, Sargent returned to the attack Barbara had begun on words.

"They are almost good for nothing," he declared; "in any stress of feeling they are useless. In love—"

"Then why say anything?" interrupted the girl, who foresaw the coming homily and anticipated its conclusion by promptly getting ready to be kissed, and in this important transaction they agreed that there was no inadequacy or disappointment.

Then the two sat down by the stream under the trees and watched the water slipping over the brown stones in sunlight and shadow. From the hill rising near them, where lay the spring which fed the creek, they could hear the sighing of the pines; an undertone deeper than the rustling sound of the trees above their heads. It was a time of measureless content; of reverential happiness too deep for speech, and there was silence for a space between these two who usually had so much to say to each other.

At last from fullness of heart spoke one, and there came from the other reply so apt in tone, in feeling and thought and word, that to the keen comprehension of one who could understand, no earthly music could compare with such harmony.

They spoke of their coming life together, of what they hoped to do for each other and for the great, beautiful world which held them, and as they rose to turn their steps homeward, Sargent repeated to Barbara the words of the Odyssey: "For there is nothing mightier and nobler than when man and wife are of one heart and mind in a house, a grief to their foes, and to their friends great joy, but their own hearts know it best.''

As they reached the house the lovers paused by the door, and Sargent looked closely at the climbing rose vine which clambered over the rough logs on either side, sending out vigorous sprays tipped with buds. It was the beautiful Michigan Rose, whose pink, five-petaled blossoms, growing in great clusters, he had been waiting for longingly because of the promise of a certain Beautiful Lady who was never far from his thoughts. "It blossoms late in this 'northe countree,' '' he complained, while Barbara showed the true rose color in her loving face. "But it must blossom!" he declared, triumphantly.

A few mornings later Judge Sloan looked up as Sargent's shadow darkened the open doorway where the morning sun shone in. The young man was coming in from the garden, looking for Barbara, who was not yet downstairs.

"Why do you look so buoyant?" asked the elder man, smiling as he noted the sparkling eyes and springing aspect of his guest. Sargent had in his hand a blossoming spray of half-opened roses. They were pink, five petaled, and growing upon a long, thickly leaved stem. He held it up for the Judge to see.

"The Rose is in bloom," he said,

THE END.